THE STERLING GOSPEL

ATTICUS MULLON

Printed in the United States of America
Print ISBN: 978-1-956019-10-0
eBook ISBN: 978-1-956019-11-7

Library of Congress Control Number: 2021923761

Published by DartFrog Plus, the hybrid publishing imprint of DartFrog Books.

Publisher Information:
DartFrog Books
4697 Main Street
Manchester, VT 05255
www.DartFrogBooks.com

Join the discussion of this book on Bookclubz. Bookclubz is an online management
tool for book clubs, available now for Android and iOS and via Bookclubz.com.

To Tallie, Ava, Lyle, and June.

Since to write of our communion would be to ruin, I offer only this;
I will tell you, with my eyes in view of yours, what you mean to me.

—Atticus

MARCH 12, 2085

I had watched the man for days. I knew what time he arrived in the morning and what time he left. I had watched him itch his ass and yell at his employees. I had watched him wash his Mercedes two times, an absurd number considering the short time I had tailed him. Despite the intensity of my preparation, I could feel the creases of my palms filling with sweat.

"God, get over it, Amir!" I whispered to myself.

I was angry because my nervous discomfort was not in anticipation of the timing and stealth needed to perform the theft. I knew I could pull it off. Instead, I was paralyzed with some ridiculous sense of morality. In the quiet reprieve of my mind, I tried to counter with a more accurate ethical assessment. Two criteria stood out: I knew he was a son of a bitch, and I knew we needed the money. Having quieted this internal dissonance, I straightened my legs and stood from my uncomfortable position behind a nearby dumpster.

The man's name was Albert Mustep, and he owned a local jewelry store. As is often the case with small-time success, he enjoyed articulating the wealth he had accumulated on every facet of his being. His shoes were shined, and his clothes were distinctly from money. However, it was his watch that was of interest to me. I had noticed it simply in passing on the street and quickly knew it was worth some time.

I walked slowly and deliberately to my preordained position, a concealed corner near the back door of his shop. Alongside me stood an equally stealthy partner: my skinny and rather pathetic hound named Bear. I knelt and stroked his head, whispering a few last-minute assurances in his ear. I heard the door to the shop open and quickly stood, prepared to initiate the plan.

Using a small mirror to peer around the corner, I measured his location. When the small, portly man was no more the five feet from the corner, I nudged Bear into the open. Having performed this routine many times, Bear needed no further prompting. He immediately began to snarl and, displaying some impressive acting skills, even raised his hair on end to give the convincing impression of an attacking mad dog. The man immediately yelped in surprise and placed his back against the wall with arms in the air.

"Good dog. Easy," he muttered, trying to tame the snarling beast before him with a quiet reserve that impressed me, considering his overall appearance of a sniveling kiss-ass.

Meanwhile, of more consequence to me was his left arm. During the unexpected encounter, he had unknowingly placed his arm, and more importantly, his watch, against the wall just around the corner from me. As I saw the item come into view, I outstretched my dingy fingers and smoothly released the clasp. The man was adrenaline-fueled and noticed nothing as his entire focus remained on the threat before him. The watch slipped off into my outstretched hand. Holding it by its bulky, ridiculously gaudy face, I began to run down the alley and turned a corner toward home. A couple of minutes later, Bear sauntered up beside me, clearly happy with his performance.

As I rounded the corner to emerge a few blocks away from the apartment, I slowed to a walk. Finally given the chance, I inspected the watch. Its face was massive, larger than I would think was comfortable, and surrounding the beveled glass surface lay a row of small diamonds. It was definitely a good score and would put a dent in the growing bills. As I turned the worn-out handle to enter our flat, I slipped the watch into my back pocket.

"Mum? You home?" My voice died in the small space.

"In here!" she retorted from the direction of the kitchen. I walked through the small living room and jovially popped up before my mother. "Ah! You scared me! How was work?"

"Good. Good day at work," I muttered.

She was under the impression that I still worked at the valve plant, and I had no plan to disappoint her with the stained reality. As she continued to cook, I slowly inspected her appearance. She had always been slender, but after my father's passing, what once was held with an elegant poise was now feebly crooked over the counter. Before her lay a meager bowl of brothy soup, which was not at first glance a recognizable variety.

"What do you have there?" I inquired, peering over her shoulder.

"Ah, this is a new specialty of the house," she mused with forced optimism. "It consists of all the produce sporting that beautiful green patina that represents very nearly spoiling."

I pursed my lips and drew in a breath as if viewing a rare treat. Within, my mind started to churn. How had we gotten to this point? I was all we had, and I was obviously falling short. Theoretically, my intermittent grabs could be far more frequent. However, by some obvious shortcoming that passed as careful planning, each event took too much time. Just as this line of thought began to spiral into depressing depths, I felt a sharp edge on the watch dig into my hip. I was hopeful that the grab would offer a moment of reprieve from wretched poverty and was eager to get rid of it.

"I am going to hop the Vac to the city tomorrow," I pronounced as I settled into a structurally unsound chair at the kitchen table, its composition shifting from the intended square to an acutely stressed fold.

"Oh, that will be fun! You should take your brother! He would love to see the Portal again!"

"Well, I'm not sure—"

"Please, Amir. He needs something to take his mind off . . ." Her voice trailed off as she tactfully turned on an ancient blender. This discussion was obviously over.

I would actually relish bringing Hasim to the city. He was all I had besides Mum, and such acts of normalcy were few and far between. But in this case, I was traveling to hock the watch. I always worked hard to insulate him from this part of my life. I turned and again watched Mum. Her back was to me, and her head was awkwardly still. I could tell she was in another place, perhaps thinking of our circumstances. I silently slinked to place my arms around her in an embrace that didn't need speech.

"I will bring him," I whispered in her ear as I separated my clasped fingers and moved to the back door.

I walked out the off-kilter screen door and gazed at the muddled common space shared by several surrounding flats. There, as always, was Hasim, his knobby knees visibly pronouncing the posture of a small boy engrossed in narrative. I took a silent first step toward him in an attempt to surprise him, but he heard the audible friction of a small gravel piece and turned his head. He cracked an ornery, toothy grin. He slid his hands under the aged binding of the book in his lap and quickly closed the volume with a notable thud. Hasim was clever, and not just for a poor kid from Hillshire. I was perhaps not a good measure, but he ran circles around my understanding of the subjects. He set the book down near where the wall met the ground and gently toed an old soccer ball to my noisy foot. We silently passed the ball and exchanged questions about the other's day. Just as my fabricated recollections from the workday were getting dangerously elaborate, we heard a quiet pronouncement from Mum.

"Boys, time for prayer," she rang from the kitchen.

This was one of Mum's oddities. Having been raised in a traditional Palestinian home, she was held to a strict Muslim faith. However, as she transitioned to adulthood, she "boldly considered the story of Christ." This was the way she put it, often focusing more on the exhilaration of familial disobedience rather than her new faith. I thought the phrase sounded like some canned bullshit from a TV preacher, but it was her story, not mine. Ultimately, she was unable to completely abandon the regimented teachings of her upbringing and instead combined the two into a rare form of disciplined Christianity. Accordingly, we were expected to join five times a day in prayerful connection to Jesus Christ. We trudged from our outdoor escape and back into the depressing flat. Walking past the kitchen, we entered our—what could be titled eclectic—living area. There, our mother was resting her knees on a small patch of dingy carpet. Although lacking the swirling threads and proper orientation, these prayer rugs were another odd, derived tradition of my mother's combined faiths.

I softly dropped to my mat and waited for Mum's strict, yet entirely fabricated, standard prayer to Christ. As my lips operated on ingrained muscle memory, my mind wandered. The truth was I found little use for contemplation of Christ's morality, let alone His deity. Studying and communing with such a system would only complicate matters in order to provide my mother with the only help I knew how. I had my own analysis of ethics, which was far simpler and allowed for my vocation: consider only the end result. I feed Hasim. I feed Mum. The only moral consideration relevant to my situation were these pure dependents. As my lips continued uttering mother's required supplication, I glanced in her direction. Her eyes were shut tight, and her forehead was gently resting against the carpet. If you were to examine these scraps of fabric, they would physically articulate the difference between our hearts. My mat bore little sign of use—a couple of slight depressions where bent knees occasionally sat unmoving and uninspired. Her mat was tattered. It had two small holes radiating wear, spots where her knees, so animated in moments of worship, had contacted the floor below. The fore of the mat bore more sign of penitence. Where my mat bore a distinct front boundary, hers trailed off into airy threads extending forth from a jagged line. This was where her forehead stopped. She would undoubtedly contort herself as low as possible before her god. She had already passed through the rug, and now as I sat silently watching, I noticed a worn spot on the floor below. I pondered if my mother's head would one day disappear beneath the floor, when she snapped me back to attention.

"Amir!"

"Sorry, Mum," I sputtered, beginning again to feebly partake in the ritual.

As if walking a familiar route, the remaining prayer passed quickly. As Mum exhorted the final verse, Hasim and I quickly rose from our prone position, eager to move to an activity in which we could be honest. However, as Mum led the way to the kitchen and ladled her newly trademarked soup into three small bowls, we realized that more charades were in order.

"Mmm . . . this has a good flavor, Mum," Hasim managed to mutter as he subtly veered his eyes to peer at me.

I turned my head to preclude Mum's view and silently grimaced. In truth, it was a very sad state of affairs, but as if a couple of desperate comrades, we bonded over our suffering. I turned back to Mum and made my offering to the effort.

"Yes, Mum, really good." Not exactly a review to remember, but anything more would have seemed disingenuous.

As we slowly spooned down the foul composition, I considered tomorrow's trip. We would be traveling to nearby Boston to hock the watch. Although our suburban community of Hillshire was of notable size, I never sold my grabs within the community of origin. Instead, I thought it safer to disperse goods in a wide variety of distant seedy shops. Considering Hasim was to travel with me, I tried to think of which mercantile was in the safest area. Additionally, I was expected to bring Hasim to his favorite marvel of the urban-built environment: the Portal. The Portal was an amazingly complex tensile bridge completed in 2054; I knew the year from constant unprovoked lessons from Hasim. Personally, I found the decadence of the city's architecture to be infuriating. Rising as a manifestation of corporate wealth, the towering structures offered a message divergent from the one purported following my father's death.

Having been killed by a form of cancer very likely linked to research performed while employed by Envirotech, our family was offered no assistance, no compensation, and only a few impersonal notes of condolence. As in the case of most employers, Envirotech had long ago abandoned the idea of retirement funds, health insurance, and other employee investment. With the continued advancement of health sciences leading to longer life spans, the human population had grown rapidly. In the wake of these trends, cooperate employers had finally found arguable reason to abandon the supposedly unsustainable health and wellness components of compensation. And yet, each time I traveled to the city, it was clear that these justifications were hollow propagations designed to maintain outlandish profits at the top.

As dinner drew to an anticlimactic end, I pronounced that I was going to our shared bedroom for an early bed in anticipation of tomorrow's journey. Hasim furrowed his brow, disappointed at my supposed prudence. He saw right through the excuse. That's one aspect of being poor that was often overlooked. Our limited funds didn't allow for much more than the bare minimum utility bill. Accordingly, as the sun dropped below the sharp horizon, we too often retired to early rest. As was the case with those ancient pilgrims, or so I would imagine, our opportunity for communion with one another was largely restricted to those hours graced with light.

I entered our living space and tugged on the worn corner of a pull-out mattress concealed beneath the lone sofa. It slid out with ease, having long ago cleared any obstacles that remained. I pulled it into my spot, which was generally the same arrangement used in prayers, and flopped into position. I could hear Hasim speaking to Mother in the dim kitchen. I could vaguely discern his voice excitedly reporting a series of facts likely regarding some modern marvel. His naïve ramblings quickly gave me a reprieve from existence as I dropped off to sleep.

———————

The next morning, I woke early and began to prepare for our travels. Equipped only with an ancient rucksack sporting a single unhinged zipper, I loaded foreseeable necessities. I scoured the refrigerator to find tucked away a banana and an orange that had escaped—certainly not due to freshness—last night's broth. Additionally, I stuffed away a small, tattered blanket in case Hasim wanted to rest on the

Vac ride and a rusty pocketknife that had belonged to my father; his initials, MHS, were carved into the dark wood handle. I then placed the watch deep into the base of the bag in a position that seemed secure. It was tempting to simply close the clasp around my own skinny wrist, but such an ornate addition to the general appearance of an underfed twenty-seven-year-old street kid would draw immediate attention. As I noticed Hasim stirring, I gently informed him of my completed preparations.

"We are packed, so once you get up, we can head out and leave a note for Mum."

He needed no further prompting. He quickly stowed his thin mattress and slipped on a pair of shoes that had once been my father's, then mine, and now belonged to Hasim. We scribbled a succinct garbled message to greet Mum upon waking and quietly emerged onto the darkened street. As we began to walk, Hasim wasted no time informing me of facts about potential urban sites.

"Did you know that the Meinard Tower uses a twenty-four-ton layered steel counterbalance to resist lateral movement due to wind?"

Tempted to say, "Why would anyone possibly know that?" I instead indulged him with a rare appeal for more obscure facts. As if delivered a captive audience, he regaled me to the very moment we approached the Vac gate, at which point I sharply interjected. "We need to figure out which line to take and what time it will be there."

Unfazed, he launched into another series. "Vac is an abbreviation for sealed vacuum conveyance capsule, a transportation development that had drastically reduced travel times starting in the early 2030s. Each hardened, rigid capsule holds approximately twenty passengers and can reach speeds up to five hundred miles per hour."

"Okay, okay, just shut up for a minute," I retorted. I scanned a matrix composed of rows of departure locations crossed with columns of destinations. Within each intersection was written a series of transfers in order to accommodate the specific route. I grabbed a chained pen, suspended for just this purpose, and scribbled the sequence on my palm. I turned back to Hasim. "Our first Cap will be here in one hour. We can sit here and wait or we can explore a bit."

"Explore," he curtly retorted, evidently sore at having been told to shut up.

We walked back from the gate and emerged at the mouth of a now bustling market street. Hasim announced that he would like to tour the market, realistically a nice way of saying, "Observe new objects unobtainable with our current funds." I didn't mind, as I could conversely peruse the passersby for lightly used objects obtainable with no funds. As we walked, Bear followed close in tow, his wild hair audibly creating static as it contacted merchants' fabric tablecloths.

As Bear and I purposefully strode down the centerline of the double-loaded aisle, Hasim darted back and forth to closely observe every glistening attraction possible. With only the intermittent interruption of his shoes finding enough traction to pivot, I observed many potential grabs: an old man with a large leather billfold sticking from his rear pocket, a smartly dressed businesswoman with a fur scarf, and a tantalizingly ambiguous briefcase held by a pompous suit. However, as I gazed back at Hasim running from one booth to another with unencumbered wonder, I realized none of these operations would be appropriate for the outing.

My eyes followed his darting movement. The preservation of this naivety was worth any cost. As my eyes struggled to keep up, suddenly, they instinctually stopped. They had been captured by an equally focused set of orbs staring directly at mine. It was Albert Mustep, the watch's rightful owner. Before I had time to fully consider the reality of the situation, he lowered his gaze to Bear then slowly back to me. He knew.

I immediately broke his gaze and located Hasim. He was deep in discussion with an annoyed merchant as I scooped him into my crooked arm, for once overjoyed at his malnourished slight. I took off back toward the entrance to the Vac and really began to pump my legs as Hasim attempted to yell through my focus. As we entered the convergence of boarding passengers that were to enter the arriving Cap, I slowed to blend in. I wasn't sure if this was the right arrival for our route, but it was undoubtedly less risky than staying. Still toting Hasim as one would a heavy duffel, I scanned the faces around us and saw only strangers focused on securing a spot upon arrival. Having concluded we were likely safe, I gently rotated Hasim and placed him on the ground.

"What the hell was that about?" he screeched at me through gritted teeth. I had rarely heard my brother use profanity, and it was clear he was really pissed and confused.

"I saw someone I didn't want to talk to," I retorted, having long ago discovered that the shortest lies were the most effective.

I rocked myself onto the throbbing tips of my toes to see over the crowd. We were getting close to entering the Vac Capsule. With each step, our proximity to one another was reduced, the entire group operating on some palpable but mysterious swarm logic. Finally, Hasim and I were a mere two rows of passengers from the thick threshold forming the door of the Capsule. We strode confidently forward, happy to be rid of the marketplace when my right foot was suddenly unable to return to the concrete floor. I stared in disbelief at my unruly appendage, as would a captain being faced with mutiny. However, as this instantaneous reaction dissolved into a measured inventory, I turned to address the actual force at work: a stout, bearded officer whose fingers were securely closed around my old rucksack. I quickly tried to slip out of the arm straps, but as my arms contorted in coordination with my back, he caught my wrist and pinned it to my back.

"Hasim! Hasim!" I cried out into the mass of people, which was rapidly parting to form a bubble of fascination around the scene.

Just as I finally met the dark, almond-shaped eyes of my brother, the door to the vessel he had just entered snapped closed, and the entire container surged forward into the darkened tubular expanse.

"Stop! Stop! Please, I will come with you, but my kid brother was on that Capsule!" I shouted at the officer as my voice cracked as I held back tears.

For the first time, the officer paused his forced guidance through the crowd to address my claim. He grabbed a radio secured to his hip and spoke quickly into the perforated receiver.

"Dispatch, connect me to Vac control."

The radio let out a long breath of static as he released the button. Soon enough, a voice retorted from the black box, reporting that he was being patched through.

Once connected, the officer addressed the Vac control center. "This is Officer Nick Grenwal. I am trying to locate and detain an unaccompanied minor whose status is unknown aboard Cap #265." He turned to me sharply. "Describe your brother," he barked, holding the radio close to my mouth.

"He is nine years old. He's . . . about four . . . foot eight inches. He is of Middle Eastern descent and is . . . wearing . . . blue jeans with a green shirt," I sputtered through intermittent bouts of tearful breaths.

The officer withdrew the radio and waited for a response. Meanwhile, he secured my arms to one another using a glorified zip tie, and we again began to walk. I withdrew all senses but my ears. I lowered my head, and through some engrained brainwashing of my mother's, began to beg any power that is to bring news of Hasim. I knew he wasn't likely to be spontaneously murdered in the next few minutes, but even so, I was panicking. Hasim could regurgitate so many facts, but he knew nothing about the real world. Just as I began to imagine the genesis of terrible endings that could face him, the radio sputtered back to life.

"Officer Grenwal, we have located and apprehended the minor in question. We will coordinate with dispatch to organize his transport home."

He thanked the distanced help and gazed at me. We were now completely out of the crowd, and he placed my back against a concrete wall.

"Thank you," I expelled through quivering lips. "He's just a kid."

He did not address my comment. Instead, he knelt and began to search my bag. After taking a few moments to consider the rusty pocketknife, he removed the watch and quickly attached an adhesive tag around the band. He looked at me and began to mechanically recite the facts.

"You are under arrest for possession of stolen property. You have the . . ." His voice seemingly trailed off as I withdrew to my own thoughts.

How had I been so careless? I should never have let Hasim and Bear come along. It occurred to me that some in my position would be responding internally as intended: regretting the immoral act of theft itself. However, as I sat and for a moment attempted this convention, I found no remorse. I had to steal that watch. I had to steal all of it. I didn't feel any pity for the portly man who, for a short time, couldn't express his superiority with a gaudy trinket. I felt pity for my mother and my brother. Widowed and fatherless, they now stood little chance of any form of living that one might call comfortable.

I was snapped back to reality as I was jerked away from the wall and led away from the terminal. We emerged onto the ever-lively market street, and the officer silently raised his arm into my field of vision to point out his cruiser. As we weaved in and out of the crowd, I remembered Bear. I turned my head as far as possible to find Bear following close in tow as if nothing had happened. He would be fine; he had found his way home many times after separation. As we covered the last few feet before the idle car, a man emerged from a concealed corner.

"You got him! You got the dirty varmint and his filthy theatrical director!" Albert exclaimed as he stared directly at me with an apparent sense of righteousness.

"Yes," the officer said flatly. There was an undertone in his voice that seemed to dismiss the man's hyperbolic assessment of our character. "He will be arraigned according to procedure. You will be allowed to claim your property following any necessary investigation."

Despite Grenwal's rigidity and apparent lack of organic character, I was beginning to like him. As if the anti-character to Albert, he had complete power to embarrass me, and furthermore, to hurt me.

Instead, even I had to admit the whole experience was starting to feel routine. I found a bit of solace in the clear sequential undertaking.

The drive felt quick, not even allowing time to prepare for what was to come next. Grenwal pulled me slowly out of the back seat, and we moved in tandem to a lonely door at the rear of a large brick expanse. I relaxed my neck, letting my focus blur on the ground below. Meanwhile, Grenwal underwent a series of security measures to gain access to the door. Finally, a prolonged buzz sprang forth to wordlessly articulate our admittance. After leading me down a tight corridor, Grenwal deposited me in a chair, one in a long row, and gestured to a tall, lean officer standing obscenely erect behind a nearby counter.

"He will take down your information and bag up your stuff from here." He paused and, for the first time, looked into my eyes, letting his occupational formality seemingly dissolve as his voice grew so soft even I could barely make it out by the time he was finished speaking. "We all have choices to make. Some are not so easy. What you did was wrong, but I would guess that to not have done it would have been wrong too. Sorry to be part of such a tough day for you, kid."

With this final pronouncement, he turned and left me. Left me, I couldn't help but imagine, to characters without his unlikely sensitivity.

Eventually, the tall man, whose build was so unusually elongated as to negate any intimidation, approached and told me to stand in front of his station. He took a step back and inspected my appearance. Apparently having determined that I was of no notable threat, he clipped the temporary hand binding and ordered me to undress in the adjacent room and put on what was supposedly a prison jumpsuit but appeared to be little more than a heap of orange cloth sitting in the middle of the concrete floor. As instructed, I emerged a few moments later, dawning the one-piece garment. Without looking up from his station, the guard beckoned to a seat just next to his own. Reluctantly, I settled into the position and awaited whatever step was next. Eventually, he swiveled in place, clutching a shining instrument that was obviously surgical. At its glinting presence, I recoiled, and he started laughing.

"Relax. Just have to get a blood sample." He chuckled, apparently very entertained at the thought of innocence.

Eager to present a more macho persona, I placed my arm in front of him with a resounding thud. Looking down, I realized the presence of such a scrawny appendage was in no way impressive, and the guard seemed to agree as he forcibly pulled taut a portion of skin and drew a vial of blood. Once he was satisfied that the instrument was full, he deposited it into another apparatus with a metallic click. He turned back to his station and began typing information into the interface. After some time, as if I were his wife who had finally determined her outfit suitable for dinner, he grabbed my upper arm, and we shuffled along an adjacent corridor whose white walls eventually gave way to the iconic jailer's partition of steel bars.

"You're in here," he scoffed, shoving me through an open barred gate.

I swiveled my head instinctually in search of any cohorts, who I couldn't help but imagine to be of a more serious nature than me. But, as my eyes rebounded fruitlessly in each corner, I realized there were no other occupants.

"You're in solitary. Don't ask me why. Small-time snatcher from the street like you. Got the order from above, though; must have somebody that knows ya." He wasted no time after his rudimentary analysis, immediately striding in long leaps away from the cell.

Again, I scanned my surroundings, the steel bars intermittently precluding my vision. Nothing. For a moment, I felt uneasy, considering the absence of even guards, but eventually, I noticed a small dark lens that was undoubtedly monitoring my activities. Somehow comforted by the oversight, I sat on a narrow bench along the back wall. At first, solitary confinement seemed a gift, but as the stark silence left me with only my thoughts, it was clear that it was a curse. How had this happened? How was this the best I was able to do? My father had been smart. Before his death, our house felt so perfect, so insulated from any problems that plagued other less fortunate people. Now, with my ass beginning to lose feeling against some filthy prison bench, I was faced with the reality. We were now the pitiful ones. Without Father's guidance, I had silently careened our vessel into wanting. There was no easy end to this internal analysis, considering the lack of some threatening tattooed brute, which, at this point, would come as a welcome distraction. Instead, subject only to my own abuses, I drifted with open eyes to some form of purgatory awaiting any interjection.

Sometime later—the exact duration of which was now indiscernible—I was snapped to reality by the cell door being unlocked.

"You're up, kid."

It was the same uniformed beanstalk as before, sporting the same articulate vocabulary. He again steered me down another blank hallway, an action of obedience that I realized could rapidly become almost comforting, and we eventually emerged into a large open area. There, in a series of worn chairs, sat a multitude of delinquent clones made alike by their identical orange garments. At the head of the room sat a small, robed man whose voice intermittently rang out in the unadorned room.

"Five months and a $5,000 fine," he pronounced, staring blankly at a hunched, weathered man standing before him. "Next."

Now having an understanding of the unsettling, simplified nature of the process, I peered down my row to estimate how long I was to sit. Five more judgments were to be pronounced before my own, and now, as I waited through each, I realized I was actually eager to accelerate this process. More accurately, to accelerate whatever process would lead to even temporary communication with Mum and Hasim.

"Two years and $15,000," the judge continued. "Eighteen months and $8,000."

The pattern was becoming overwhelmingly clear. Each degenerate, the vast majority of which were there for theft, was to offer a piece of time and a piece of treasure. The amounts of these components were fairly predictable after only a few cases, and as the bailiff approached to gather me, I had estimated that I would face three years in prison and a fine of $10,000. The bailiff bent and collected me again by the upper arm, a favorite in the anatomy of control. I was deposited squarely in the almost palpable breadth of the judge's gaze. He looked at my file, supposedly studying each component.

"Amir Saleh. The evidence has been found of sufficient valor to warrant conviction of Larceny in excess of $50,000." My mind raced to recalculate my sentence. $50,000! How was that stupid watch worth such an obscene amount? This would undoubtedly lengthen my sentence. "Traditionally, a theft in this amount would warrant a ten-year prison sentence and a sizable fine." Any sense of optimism was evaporated. "However, due to the fervent intervention of a respected member of this community, you are being released to house arrest under the supervision of said entity. You will be transferred to his custody following this proceeding."

Audible grunts of surprise rippled through the silent horde. I, too, was struggling to understand the wordy pronouncement. The bailiff stepped forward and assumed the familiar arm hold. Still reeling from the judge's strange soliloquy, my steps lagged behind the bailiff's movement.

"Your Honor, where am I going?" I managed to stammer, temporarily halting the forced procession.

"Into the custody of an ardent and respected community agent of justice. You are being delivered a gift, young man. Make the most of it."

Although the explanation offered little more certainty than before, I nodded at the judge out of formality and turned to travel close in the shadow of the bailiff. As if reversing and accelerating my entrance, I was quickly led to a room to change. I dropped the jumpsuit and pulled on my tattered pants, which still bore the familiar scent of my mother's curry. I could never have imagined such a mundane scent would bring such comfort. Having changed and again assumed my original, and now far more appreciated, dingy street clothes, I emerged to a large waiting area presumably near the exit to the facility. As I pivoted in place, trying to figure out what was to happen next, a figure strode toward me, visible only in my periphery. Before I could turn, they were upon me, and there was no chance to react before a hand gripped my shoulder hard and thrust me toward the door.

MARCH 14, 2085

I sat silently in my latest confine and quickly realized the car would offer little information about my location or the identity of my mysterious driver. There was an opaque divider between the driver's seat and my own rear compartment. The windows were tinted to such a degree that I was able to only see my reflection. As my eyes shifted from trying to look through the pane to staring at the darkly shrouded version of myself, I discovered I looked worn. The creases that permeate one's face, typically only notable by subtle shadows, were now caked with dirt. My cheeks were marred with tiny scratches. But the most telling feature by far was my eyes. My mother told me almost every day that my large brown eyes were one of her favorite vestiges of my father. Now, instead of being defined by beauty, the orbs were obscured by puffy lids above and below. Again finding myself envious of the distraction that I might have found in a chatty cellmate, I thought of Mum and Hasim. I wondered what they were doing and if they had any idea of my fate. As my eyes started to well, considering our separation, the car's movement slowed.

With gasoline engines long ago outlawed, the electric motor offered no clue to the finality of our position. *Thud.* I heard the front door close. Imagining a violent extraction, I braced myself in the center seat, squarely able to address either door. A few moments later, I heard voices outside, and the right door's latch audibly clicked open. The daylit sliver at the top of the door grew as it was slowly opened, powered by some unseen operator. Unable to resist, I edged forward to peer out of the darkened interior. Expecting some brutalist alternative to prison, I drew a sharp breath when I instead was faced with a sprawling estate perched in the midst of rolling hills. My eyes darted to adjust to multiple scales. First, I scanned the home's massive façade, a rich mixture of brick and stone, obviously from an era before machines. Then my focus drifted past the boundary of the roof peaks to rest on the blue above. I had for so long breathed the tarnished air of human development that the striking clarity here was arresting. Finally, I forced my eyes to the human scale and observed two figures standing at the estate's front doors.

Bearing his weight on a peculiar-looking cane, intermittently glinting due to an apparent metal composition, stood a bent man who I would estimate to be in his eighties. His wrinkled white cheeks were contorted to an intensely focused smile from ear to ear. He looked as if a long-awaited companion had arrived, and he could not contain his elation. To his right stood a much younger woman. She had long brown hair that framed a more reserved face. She, too, seemed intently focused on my movements, but she bore an expression one might expect in such a situation. Her eyes were as large as mine on a typical day, and she stood with an alarmingly rigid posture. Having determined that, at first inspection, these characters were of little threat, I began to stride across the drive toward the door. With every step in the fine gravel, I could feel their intense, unrelenting gazes.

"Amiirr!" the old man sang, again as if greeting a long-lost companion. "We are so excited to have you. Please follow me, and we can all sit down for a time."

Without more explanation, he turned his back and disappeared into the darkened house. The younger woman waited patiently, implying through her unmoving stature that I was second in this three-person order. I lurched awkwardly forward as not to make her wait unnecessarily before turning to follow. I subverted my eyes as I passed her, not eager to make contact until more confident of my situation. I followed the dimly lit silhouette of the old man as he traversed a series of turns to emerge in a large warm parlor. A fire crackled in the corner, and for the first time, obscured the intermittent clicks of the man's cane on the floor. He lifted his free hand to gesture to an open seat. I sat and watched as they occupied two velvet chairs opposite of my own. He slowly leaned his space-aged cane against a polished wood side table as his female companion continued to stare at me. Every attempt to look past her at the intensely burning fire was subverted as it seemed all light reaching my position was filtered through her long, straight hair. Accordingly, I was basked in a warm amber glow emanating from around her unrelenting gaze.

"How are you feeling? Did they hurt you at all? Anything broken or damaged?" the man spit forth in an oddly abrupt way.

"No, I think I am fine, thank you," I responded, unable to reciprocate his informal tone.

"I am sure you are confused. Firstly, let me assure you that your brother made it safely back home. He was transported with care back to your mother, and I made sure both of them were told that you were safe," he purported with an evident air of self-praise. However, regardless of his intentions, he seemed to be telling the truth, and this was welcome news.

"My name," he continued, "is William Sterling, and this is my daughter Abigail. We are all aware of the circumstances that led to your presence here today, but I am certain you have deeper questions regarding the nature of our . . . program," he said, the cadence of his words faltering before the final word. "I am afraid that considering the waning hours of our current day and the undoubtedly traumatic experiences you have undergone, these queries should wait for morning light. This evening, I will simply leave you to your room to wash up, eat of our humble storehouse, and of course, call your beloved mother."

I sat silently as the quiet became apparent. I realized my eyes were bearing straight ahead into space as I considered his cursory explanation. The spoken words themselves elicited little alarm, but the tacit undertone was suffocating. My congenial captor obviously had little experience in crafting a believable message. Such unprovoked salvation was more than unlikely; it was unbelievable. Instead, my mind raced, considering alternative motives for my cushy detainment. I measured the old man and his daughter in my peripheral vision, not wanting to actually move my eyes for fear of having to return to our paused dialogue. Even in the blurred extremities of my perception, I could feel their unrelenting observation. Perhaps I was here to take part in some form of medical testing. Of even more plausibility, I found myself fearing I was there to satisfy some perverted fantasy of the old man. Why else would I be provided such accommodations and crafted secrecy?

"The only rule I must insist upon is a certain discretion in your calls to your mother," he pronounced with overstressed clarity. "Please feel free to use the phone in your room to assure her of your well-being and treatment, but the specifics of this residence and our identities," he gestured to himself and his stoic cohort, "these must remain concealed. At least for the time being. I assure you this is not the way I would have it. It is a requirement of the judicial system." He allowed the corners of his pale lips to curl slightly, satisfied with the simple brevity of this transparent lie.

"I suppose," I struggled to say as if my vocal cords had atrophied in my long silence. "Thank you," I finished, temporarily adopting his strategy of abruptness.

I slowly allowed my eyes to shift in line with his to gather one last scrap of information for later assessment. The orbs, which so often gave one's intentions away, were of little aid. They offered no confirmation of either contempt or lust. Rather, an intense focus devoid of emotion was at hand. I gently nodded my head to further articulate my gratitude, first at the older Sterling, and then to his stoic daughter. As I shifted my gaze to her younger, brighter pupils, I was further confounded. Here I was met with dissonance. She stared at me as if glaring at blank space but shining through the forced soberness was an undeniable warmth. Her eyes' deep brown glow comforted me as if humanity had failed to be fully disguised.

"I assure you no thanks are necessary," he reported. "Abigail, would you show Amir to his room?"

She nodded in response, still not gracing the space with any pronouncement. I was beginning to wonder if she was a mute. She stood with the same purposeful rigidity as before and began to walk from the parlor. Not eager to be left alone with her father, I pitched myself forward to follow closely. As we walked, I breathed in the foreign smell of the vast halls. Each plane of my surroundings was adorned with trappings consistent with what I would imagine of an old rich pervert. Above a deeply stained wainscot hung a series of portraits. Each was without a name, but all were young and of striking similarity to me. Their skin was brown, and their eyes were large. In an odd twist, they all wore strange tunics like something from ancient times. Twelve in all, the photos added to the growing evidence that I was here for some unsavory requirement. The sound of her heels slowed as we approached an oversized wooden door.

"Here you are." Her long-anticipated voice caught me off-guard. As compared to her father's, her voice was undeniably gentle, lacking the same forced focus. I waited for a moment to see if she would offer more exhibitions, but she just stood at the precipice to the room.

"Thank you, Abigail," I addressed her directly, trying to make some human connection that I imagined might save me from her father's intentions. Finally, I turned and crossed the threshold into the room. As I turned to shut the door, I stared one last time at her eyes. "What does he want with me?" I said softly.

"Good night." Her voice died quickly as she turned and strode away.

I turned and retreated to the lavish room. The bed was a sea compared to my pull-out pad, and the furnishings were of undeniable beauty. However, staring at the carefully stitched fabrics, I desperately missed the tattered corners of my home. Spotting the aforementioned phone, I dialed the number for home. The phone scarcely rang before my mother's voice cut through my fog.

"Amir!? Is it you!? They said you would call. Please be you." She spoke so fast the words blurred together.

The line's soft static took over for a moment as I collected myself to sound calm.

"Yes, Mum, it's me." As if my voice had physically affronted her, she audibly sobbed.

"Are . . . you . . . okay?" she forced between sharp breaths. "Are you hurt? Where are you?"

"Mum, don't worry. I am completely fine. They took me to jail, but instead of prison, they trucked me to some old guy's hou—" I paused as an audible static overtook the connection.

As the fuzz cleared, her voice sounded desperate, "Amir!? Amir!?"

"Mum, Mum, I'm here. Can you hear me now?" I hurriedly reported, not eager to contribute to more anxiety.

"Yes," she answered, "I can hear you now. Where are you? You had just said they took you to jail when the phone cut out."

"I am at some weird old dude's house," I carefully pronounced. Even so, once again, as I spoke, I heard the line faltering. I continued to speak over the light fuzz. "Don't worry, Mum. I am completely fine. They say I am being given the opportunity to be in some kind of program instead of prison. I don't know much at this point, but I will call as much as I am allowed." I paused to consider my next words. *Sorry Mum, for endangering Hasim. Sorry for lying to you for years. Sorry for failing you both.* Seeing a pattern emerging in my options, I simply pronounced, "I am sorry, Mum. I am so sorry."

She drew in a sharp breath and sobbed.

"Why?" she sputtered. "Why should you be sorry for growing up with nothing? I know you were just trying to help. I am sorry, Amir. I am sorry that this is your world. I miss you. Hasim misses you." As she continued, my own emotions finally spilled forth as short, breathy sobs. "Amir. There is only one way to keep going: pray. I know you don't care. I know you think I'm stupid to look to a God that has given us so little. But please, for me, promise me you will try. At least to cling to hope."

"Okay, Mum. I will. I prom—" Before I could finish my insincere guarantee, this only form of communication clicked to an unprompted end. "Mum!? Mum, are you there!?" I nearly shouted.

Suddenly, static gave way to a robotic address. "This concludes your daily permitted offsite communication. Please return the receiver to the linked docking station."

I stared at the handset, irate at the unexpected termination until I was startled to attention by a soft rapping at the door. I turned around just in time to see the door creak closed, a small plate of food sitting in its wake.

I picked up the plate, gingerly gripping the fine china, and examined the offerings. Smeared in a thin layer lay a yellow mash of curry atop a bed of rice. I audibly chuckled to myself at the overtly racist selection. However, as I grasped a spotless fork, the sight and smell seemed oddly familiar. I knew this curry. Not this type of curry, this exact preparation. A few times in the past years, I had accumulated a bit of excess cash and brought Hasim to experience my favorite treat: yellow curry at Masimam in Midtown. Recollections of the creamy potato-laden dish were some of my only carefully stowed memories, a rare blip in my impoverished routine. Now, as the same fragrant concoction lay before me, it brought more questions than comfort. How did they know about this private comfort? However, as if on cue, a resounding grumble sprang forth from my abdomen. Accepting my body's convincing case against over-analysis, I scooped a heaping bite onto my fork and dug in. I immediately forgot any qualms I had regarding the dish and decided this was by far the most acceptable form of creepy enticement.

I inhaled the remaining kernels and sauce and, having deposited my dish near the door, turned to evaluate my quarters. The room was large, probably in excess of our entire flat, and occupied with the same gaudy furniture as the parlor. Opposite the door, a large window dominated the wall's length. I approached the polished pane and looked to the expansive grounds below. There, the grassy hills lay in dark sleep. In the moon's bright glow, I was mostly aware of the land's overall form, as little more than shadow and light were perceivable. As I examined the gentle curve of one vast expanse, a more focused light glinted momentarily. I trained my eyes to the spot now exhibiting only darkness. After a short while, the point again unexpectedly illuminated. This time, as my eyes began to water from lack of intermission, there was made clear the outline of a man. The succinct interval of illumination was not enough to reveal the man's appearance or operation, instead providing only a stark outline etched against the manicured backdrop. In addition to the ruffled organic boundary consistent with a heavily clothed figure, there extended the surreal outline of a machined barrel: a gun. A guard. A home, this was not.

I sighed, turning away from the now fogged glass. Any hope I had regarding the sincerity of my hosts had been extinguished with the stark image of the guard. With little left to investigate, given my limited access, I lay in exhaustion on the massive bed. Having actually made no preparation for nightfall, I lay in awkward light, instead allowing my mind to drift far enough to extinguish the bright. Hasim. Mum. I imagined them lying in our simple flat. My tattered mat lying unused under the couch. These anguished images carried me away from the light and into the dark.

I awoke, or rather was awoken, via a cutting buzz that occupied the room. My eyelids slowly parted to reveal my still brightly lit room. I sat and turned to find the source of the noise but was instead assaulted by an additional voice.

"Amir, please report to the parlor when you prepared," Abigail's distinctive voice rang through the door.

Realizing I was still fully dressed in my filthy clothes, I searched the room to discover provisions. Hanging in the sizeable closet was a casual yet obviously tailored sweat suit. I donned the entirely gray clothes, discovering that they fit my build precisely. Ignoring the mounting set of unnerving coincidences, I opened my door and peered down the long hall. Nothing. No Abigail, no guards, and no metallic cane. I strode down the hall past the twelve portraits and struggled to remember the route to the parlor. Just as I decided I was completely lost amongst the vast halls and endless wall hangings, I heard the distinct crackle of burning embers. I followed the sound and eventually strode into the cavernous space of yesterevening's conversation. There Sterling sat, alone and unmoving, in the same chair as before. It was as if he had never left the room following my departure. I looked around, struggling to dislodge the unsettling feeling of déjà vu. I sat slowly in my presumed velvet seat and turned to face the beaming old man.

"Amir," he sang into the air. As the pronouncement rang through the halls, he shifted his face from an expression of uncandid infatuation to one of seriousness. "Today is the beginning. The genesis of a new endeavor. From this point on, I am going to be very honest with you regarding the goal of your stay with us. I am certain that you have many questions, the most pertinent of which is . . . what in the bloody hell are you doing here?"

I nodded in agreement, reluctant to provide an additional voice to the monologue.

"I am afraid the answer to this question is a bit complicated, but I will do my best to provide brevity. The background of our current situation begins earlier this century. I was a much younger and assuredly better-looking computer scientist." He gestured to his bald head, emphasizing the previous grandeur of his now lackluster appearance. "My life changed dramatically after I developed a very early computer coding language that is still utilized today. As my work was quickly adapted and utilized throughout the world, I went from a young man who grew up in fiscal straights not so unlike your own to a very rich one. It was also during this time that I met Sophia, Abigail's mother. Oh, Amir, she was a singular beauty, as I am sure you could derive from Abby." He paused, and in a rare moment of palpable sincerity, he gently smiled. "I loved Sophia the moment I met her. She stubbornly took some convincing, but eventually, we were wed and had Abby."

My mind began to wander as I watched his lips move ever onward. Although I had only known Sterling for a short while, his rant was on the boring verge of a grandfather reciting the same old story. What on earth could this possibly have to do with me? Having now missed several ramblings more, I forced my ears back to service and attempted to manufacture interest.

"To put it simply, we were very happy, Amir. Then she became ill. It happened extremely quickly. I watched in horror as her frame lightened and her skin paled. We sought expert after expert, but all gave a similar prognosis: six months. Six months to reconcile one-self to unknowable death. She responded by loving us even more, drawing every day to the ultimate length allowed by her pain. I, conversely, responded with anger. The difference," his words slowed and crescendoed, reaching some semblance of a point, "was faith. My wife, Amir, prayed each and every day. I clearly remember she spoke with her deity as if with a friend. She came before God with triumphs and sadness. Questions and answers. And in her end, she came away with hope. Hope that this was not a sad finality but yet another moment to trust a more potent love. I, meanwhile, railed against this idea. Reason would prevail that no such guardian would allow Sophia such pain. I, never having found faith, instead cursed the name of such an idea. In the end, neither faith nor reason halted her departure." He paused, again appearing convincingly emotional. His tired eyes pursed as he tried to damn the tears.

I couldn't help but feel a deep sense of empathy for the old man. My own father's "departure" was remarkably similar. As if locked in some ridiculous two-person cult, my mother and father prayed with impossible vigor during his slow advance, pleading for life, or at the very least, peace. However, as I now realized was a common condition of humanity, the outcome was unmoved by such correspondence.

"Amir, I have since searched for God. I have studied His many names. I have combed through thousands of accounts from all cul-tures." He suddenly turned his head deliberately toward my own. "I have not found Him." He dramatically let the statement reverberate as if having delivered some unknown wisdom. "And yet, I saw it. The hope. Regardless of my own skepticism, this hope was as real as any tangible medicine. It was unable to save her from death, but it deliv-ered her from despair."

He stood up and approached a nearby rolling bar adorned with tonics, accompanied as always with the metallic click of his cane. I watched as he slowly uncorked a deep amber decanter and allotted a healthy dose. The sluggishness of his hands killed me. The slowness of his account was killing me. I had achieved the limit of respectful silence.

"Sir, with all due respect—" I paused to consider my finish. "What in the hell does this have to do with me?" I asked, having decided to err on the side of rudeness. I watched intently to see if I had angered him. Instead, he turned from the drink cart, silently chuckling.

"Very good question. Very good question indeed." He considered the glint of his newly concocted aid. "It was with the preservation of this hope in mind that I first considered the making of a new God, or perhaps an old one. It occurred to me that the singular event that subsequently created the greatest faithful elixir of hope was the life and death of Jesus Christ. Do you know very much about Jesus, Amir?" He posed the question, suddenly sounding akin to some deranged evangelist.

"Yes. My parents, well, my mother, observes her own concocted regiment surrounding Him," I said, subtly trying to hint at my own skepticism.

"And you? What about you, Amir? What do you believe about this person?"

"I believe He was probably just that, a person. I have no idea how the stories were eventually recorded, but I have seen no evidence that He has ever been involved in my mother's life. And if He has not intervened for her, then He is not present for anyone." As the words spilled forth, I immediately regretted my candidness. What if this was some form of religious test, and now my lack of faith was revealed? Perhaps seeing some contortion of my face, Sterling addressed me again.

"Don't worry, Amir. I promise you are among fellow skeptics. I, too, deny the deity of Christ. However, I could not deny His effect. It was with this in mind that I considered an alternative hypothesis. I realized that the trajectory of technology would very quickly accommodate the miracles of Christ. Simply through technology, a person would likely appear to walk on water, heal the blind, feed multitudes, and so on. Essentially, given the opportunity, we could recreate the life of Christ today with technology. So . . . was Christ more likely the incarnate son of an invisible God or simply a man utilizing an array of concealed technologies in order to deliver hope?"

"But that was over two thousand years ago!" I interjected, realizing I had somewhere along the way become engrossed in the old man's crackpot theory. "You think some dude used sticks and stones to fool all of those hordes of people? What tech did they have?"

"This," he pondered, "was the last tool to consider—the ability to send a man back. Not one of their own, besides in appearance, but a modern man toting a concealed arsenal of future developments. Relying on a good performance, and the ancient trust in the divine, those ancients could be fooled, and more importantly, inspired." At the pronouncement of his final words, I realized what a ridiculous turn our conversation had taken and decided to insist upon an explanation once and for all.

I looked up to stare carefully into the old man's eyes.

"I'm serious. I know I am 'detained.' I know I am at your service or whatever, and I appreciate the story hour. But what does any of this have to do with me?"

He sputtered on as if he hadn't heard my protest.

"At first, I shrugged off the thought of such a fabrication, attributed to the musings of a dejected atheist. However, the idea festered and grew into an all-consuming undertaking. I realized that I was poised to deliver on such a hoax, and ever since, I have prepared to do just that. I have covertly scoured scientific discoveries to acquire and hide away all of the pieces to such a complex puzzle. As soon as some much-needed component was discovered or developed, I worked to attain the first edition and conceal any intellectual trail leading to its existence. We are to preserve hope not just for the past but for the future. No one must have a concurrent knowledge of the technologies utilized for fear that some wise soul would arrive at the very same conclusion. Truthfully, it was quite easy. Concealed drone

technology accommodated many physical impossibilities, such as
walking on fluids. Newly developed bioremediating ointments could
account for healing the blind with some mud. But until very recently,
we lacked the key: a means to get back."

He showed no signs of stopping this insane rant, and I was alarmed
at his use of the word "we."

"What does this have to do with me?" I practically shouted to halt
his momentous account.

"Amir. Don't you see? The man sent back. The man to administer
the greatest cure in history. The man is *you*."

MARCH 15, 2085

stared blankly at Sterling; my eyes rapidly reduced to merely holding the old man at bay while my mind reeled. My station was now clear. I was an entertainment, perhaps not in the classic sense, but an entertainment, nonetheless. I was to entertain Sterling's wild imagination. The ravings of, as he himself so accurately verbalized, a dejected atheist. His story was admittedly engrossing, but now, as he injected me into the revisionist narrative, an unease welled. Perhaps the old man had acquired some tech toys with which to experiment, but the penultimate feature, a time machine, was surely unobtainable. However, as I once again allowed my eyes to transmit Sterling's intense gaze, his conviction was evident.

With a particularly loud crack, the fire momentarily snapped my focus as could only a force unfettered by man. I stared at the ever-ambitious tongues, each licking higher than the last, contained in a beautifully ornate altar. As I was temporarily detained by the mantle's detail, the decision at hand was made clear. This. A palace. Carved. Crafted. Comfortable. Or prison. Poured. Formed. Hardened. I was happy to play dress-up, preparing for a journey to not. I was reminded of an image of astronauts wading through water-filled pools, preparing for the weightlessness of space. The accompanying text had noted that most were performing in earnest, never to actually ascend to the black. These were in fact the fortunate, I mused. Faced, as was I, with duty instead of danger.

"So, you believe that the accounts of Jesus Christ," I paused reflexively, "were in fact describing me. Sent back and equipped with technologies in order to manufacture God?" I carefully repeated his premise, if only to let the absurdity stand austere and resolute.

Apparently possessing a perception not yet exercised, Sterling spoke softly. "In order to manufacture hope," he corrected. "I know,

Amir. I know it sounds absurd. But consider the alternative: an omniscient, omnipresent being distilled to the form of a man and sent not only to save via some cosmic victory over death itself, but also to make known the nature of God. Then this figure, so concerned as to die with us and for us, has never again used His considerable power to communicate in the slightest. Such a being redefines absurdity. I speak of a scenario supported by real technologies." His voice rose, revealing an ardent passion. Perhaps noting my furrowed brow, he rose and muttered to himself. "Smart. Requiring proof. Just another reason you're the man for the job." He beckoned me to follow in a direction not yet ventured.

He led at a pace representing the limit of movement with a cane. His feet shuffled forward and back with vigor ahead of my own, the cane occasionally contacting a hard material along the ornate floor. He turned left, then right, then left to arrive at a large door. I had become rapidly accustomed to the design vocabulary of the estate. Carefully profiled edges. Polished brass protrusions. Even the crystal chandeliers now seemed mundane. But the door standing guard before me contrived awe anew. The surface was not notable due to the implementation of traditional craft, but rather due to a mysterious material. Shimmering flecks were laced within a palpable luminescent grid. I attempted to focus on the surface but was met with the familiar feeling of a struggling camera. As if grasping for the proper aperture, my eyes could achieve no clarity in the depth of the array. The only reason I was certain the plane represented a door was the presence of a molded metallic protrusion somewhat resembling a handle. Before having the opportunity to ask about the peculiar boundary, Sterling grasped the apparent handle and pivoted the face inward. Expecting to find the conditions hereafter different in some way, I was surprised to return to familiar and now unremarkable carved wainscots.

"Forgive the gaudy entrance," Sterling addressed the dissonance. "The fiber inlay is necessary to mask the distortion's ripple."

Having no idea of what he spoke, I tried to forget the door. Its apparent advanced materiality made me less confident in my analysis of Sterling as raving mad, a perception I was not eager to abandon. Finally, after passing a great many identical wooden doors, he abruptly halted and pressed into the nearest face. I followed close behind and emerged in a cavernous, and now dissimilar, volume. The only material visible here was concrete. Concrete, and as I inspected the length of the space, a perceivable drop to air at the far end. Sterling shuffled forward to disappear around a corner almost imperceptible due to the monotone nature of the walls. As I rounded the corner, Sterling met my eyes with a smile. He gestured to a vast array of small black boxes on the floor before me. Each cube was approximately two feet from the next, and the rows repeated countless times.

"Amir, what do you find most unbelievable about my theory?" he inquired, staring hard as I examined the array.

"I think the time travel part," I said with evident sarcasm. "That bit seemed hard to believe. That I was meeting the first person in history to time travel, and our encounter was due to an alternative punishment after stealing a watch. Yeah, I think that part seemed strange." I almost laughed as the words reverberated in the hardened shell.

"Precisely. In order to accelerate acceptance of this most unlikely truth, I have devised a demonstration. Before you lay over ten thousand boxes. Each box contains a small but notably valuable trinket. Examples include a gold-plated spoon, a finely crafted pocketknife, a hand-sewn leather satchel, or any other imaginable item. You are to select and unwrap a box. We will then send this item back via the induced distortion to a specific location and time." He again slowly stretched an arm out over the array to induce a selection.

As instructed, and now again convinced I was following the mad ravings of a lunatic, I proceeded along one of the rows. Attempting some imagined randomness, I eventually turned right and knelt next to the nearest box. Upon contact, I realized the black surface was merely cardboard, a disappointing mundanity considering the setting. I strode back to face Sterling, my newly acquired box cradled in my palm.

"Just go ahead and open it?" I asked once I was in earshot.

"Please," he gently retorted.

I tugged at the securing cardboard flange and reached within as if to dramatically withdraw the contents. As my hand emerged, the object glinted gold between my fingers. My grasp relented to provide an unobstructed view, and I drew a sharp breath in. The form emerging was not novel within my mental catalog. Instead, the now visible gold flask was the focus of a very personal recollection. Some years ago, I had bounded up the chipped stairs of our flat to find such a flask sitting perfectly upright at my door. Staring at the item now, the specific detailing drifted back to focus. A silver chain connected the threaded lid to the body. Five small gems adorned the length of the chain, somehow embedded in certain links. It was, as Sterling had claimed, a distinct object: obviously one of a kind. Now, as I inspected the body, I noted an inscription that was nearly forgotten. *Believe. So they may believe.* Those years ago, I had scarcely read the line before selling the flask to pay bills. However, it had always emerged as a peculiar blip of fortune in an otherwise unlucky existence.

"How did you do it?" I shouted, turning to anger to avoid belief. "You've been following me for years? Now you loaded ten thousand flasks into these boxes just to trick me?" I continued to bellow.

I surged forward to the boxes and started rifling through the array at full speed. Yet, as I recklessly revealed the contents, I found no two alike. Plated silverware, a strange pocket watch, a fine wallet. The only visible commonality was the inscription. I looked up at Sterling to find him beaming.

"I presume the selected item is of some significance to you?" he smartly asked.

"This was at my flat. This is not possible. Maybe they made a bunch of these even though it looks unique! It looks just like it, but I know this is a trick."

"Even if several of those flasks were in existence, the likelihood of selecting such an object years later from such an array is unthinkably small. No, Amir, I am afraid it is the very same flask that appeared . . ." He paused, considering his next words, "eight years ago? I believe that's the date currently entered. Now, come this way, and I will show you the means by which this occurs."

He started toward the far reaches of our volume, where the floor faded to air. I watched Sterling slowly cut the distance but remained stagnant. I once again inspected the flask, dragging my fingers across the inscription, hoping to expose some simple explanation. Instead, the words only invaded deeper, further destabilizing my skepticism. *Believe. So they may believe.* Believe what? Believe that this was real. Believe that I was Jesus. Believe. So that they may believe.

Having been detained by my thoughts, I realized that I could no longer hear the intermittent clicking of Sterling's cane. I looked up from the flask and located him at the precipice of floor and air. His head hung downward, appearing to stare at something yet imperceptible from my vantage. I hastened my movements to catch up and quickly found myself within arm's length of his crooked back. At this proximity, I could hear a continuous sound consistent with that of swirling wind. Slowly approaching the now clear concrete edge, I carefully peered below. Void extended in sharp contrast to the pure form of concrete. Slowly shuffling toward the boundary, even more depth became visible. Finally, as my stomach turned in a familiar biological alarm to height, I could see the end below. As if replacing the light at the end of a long mesmerizing tunnel, the concrete walls gave way to what can most simply be called a blur. Perhaps most akin to the perception of heat waves rising from a fire, the base of the drop seemed to manipulate the very air above. I drew my eyelids tight together to negate any simple lack of focus that might be causing the disturbance, but the mirage remained unaltered. The color was palpable, although not exactly known, in the swirling mass. After staring into the abyss for an elongated span, I forcefully snapped my gaze back to Sterling.

"This is the key." He calmly stared straight at me, evidently comfortable with the strange mass below. "This is how we send something back." He gestured at the flask, now barely perched within my loosened fingers. "This is how we send you back."

He pivoted his frame to again take in the blur.

"The phenomenon before you is best termed a distortion." He pronounced the final word with a palpable arrogance, obviously confident in the over-stressed profoundness of his own words.

"A distortion of what?" I flatly retorted, attempting to sound unimpressed.

"Of gravity, to be most accurate. But more importantly for our circumstances, a distortion of time." He again let the words resonate for effect. "Three years ago, researchers in Greenland discovered a small sample of an ancient meteor. This cosmic rock, if you will, they estimate intercepted with our earth roughly five million years ago. These facts alone are unremarkable, as our earth has been joined with a great number of space objects in its lifespan. However, no object has possessed the defining characteristic of this object: density. Extreme density. Its materiality remains a mystery, but in quantitative terms, it weighs six tons per cubic centimeter. This is far and away the greatest density ever observed, or even theorized, and it is from this immeasurable mass that we are able to distort the gravitational waves that bind our universe." He paused to take a few audible breaths, his age for a moment evident.

"Shortly after their discovery, an interdisciplinary effort was made to evaluate this new mass for potential technological uses. And, to my long-awaited pleasure, the distortion shortly followed. By placing this mass in the centroid of a rapidly revolving encasement, the two micro-gravitational forces offset and attempt to separate the very gravitational fibers which are invisibly binding the dimensions around us. The obscenely massive stone creates a powerful micro-gravitational force drawing particles toward its core. Conversely, its now-revolving distanced shell creates a powerful tendency outward traditionally titled centrifugal force. The space between these two opposing gravitational pulls is temporarily voided of any such forces, thus allowing the unseen dimensions of time and space to upheave their typical shackles and perform new, and far less typical acts." His words slowed as he finished the wordy explanation.

I stood, staring at a blur. Holding a long-forgotten memory. I stood and worried. This was becoming too real. Too big.

"Now, hand me the trinket if you please, and I will place it in the distortion. We can send it back to guarantee the look of concerned belief I now see invading your glib exterior."

I raised my hand to bring the flask into view, its small gold casing now seeming to represent far more than a simple bauble. I slowly extended my hand into the range of Sterling's grasp. As had been the case in my initial capture, it felt as if my arm was in a coordinated mutiny against any prudent will. This couldn't be real. Yet. Yet even my body ached to entertain the idea. To believe. Perhaps not in the story of a rewritten past, but at least in the fascinating possibility before me. However, before such internal dissonance had a chance to halt the action, the deed was done. The flask slipped quietly from my grasp to his. A simple action, but in staring into Sterling's unrelenting eyes, it was clear that far more had been conceded.

He turned and strode along the boundary of the void to a previously unnoticed monolithic protrusion from the floor. Again unable to control the urge to better understand the old man's plot, I quickened my step to follow. As we approached the form, I could see a glow emanating from the object's face. Slowly, the dim, blurry glow became discernable as a screen coordinating some mysterious set of controls. Sterling addressed the interface and began to command with confidence the complex directives. After one discernable swipe of his finger, a metal plate audibly emerged from the void wall. Sterling carefully knelt at the point of emergence and placed the flask gingerly upon the platform. Clearly placing the entirety of his frail frame on the shining cane, he levered up to again face the screen. After several more robotic taps and swipes, the plate, and more importantly the flask, protruded ever farther out above the swirling blur. Finally, the linear movement halted, the gold shell glinting in the light. Mesmerized by the series of actions, I gaped at the perched ornament. However, after several moments of no further movement, I turned to examine Sterling's position. He, too, was staring at the mechanized sequence. Considering the sudden interruption in the sophisticated operation, I was for a moment afforded some doubt in the convincing outfit. However, just as the non-action began to construct some level of comfort, a descending glint snapped me back to attention. I turned back just in time to see the flask released from its post by some previously unseen mechanism. It fell. Its descent seemed to last longer than the distance would require. Maybe this was something to do with the gravity stuff described by Sterling, or perhaps simply the effect of my unwavering attention. Finally, it contacted the boundary of the distortion and promptly vanished.

"Now. Your past has been fulfilled by your future. What you witnessed was a timed release into the vacated region of gravitational restriction. The object was given the opportunity to enter unrestricted dimensional space and provided a destination in terms of space and time. Namely, your stoop. Eight years ago. I hope that one day you will forgive such an intrusion into your story. But it was a necessary involvement to promise belief." He carefully examined my expression. "Amir." He spoke my name with palpable sincerity. "Are you with me?"

As was now becoming a theme of existence, I withdrew to my thoughts, relying only upon my eyes to keep Sterling at bay. Suppose it was real. The unexplainable anomaly before me really did send back the flask to fabricate an experience of faith spanning years. This would mean that the shriveling old man before me intended to send me back. To drop me into the abyss. And then, assuming the machine didn't kill me, expected me to assume the role of Jesus. Jesus. The same Jesus whose story, if I properly remembered, had a less than happy ending. Jesus Christ.

"I am certain I have only spawned more inquiries but let us retire for lunch at the moment. Something sweet adds eloquence to every answer," he mused, his lofty diction becoming exhausting.

I forced my now stiff legs to follow back within range of the ever-crackling fire. As we entered, Abigail came into view, already seated at a round table set for lunch. A beautiful array of foods was arranged in the center, coordinated by color. Such an arrangement of riches would have garnered amazement only days ago. But now, considering the nature of our most recent excursion, I was numb to such a mundane display. I sat, unsure of how to best carry my churning thoughts, settling on normalcy.

"Could you pass the butter?" I asked, settling into the charade of a tea party. Abigail gracefully extended the silver dish to me as Sterling constructed his own plate.

"Amir, what would you like to know first regarding your involvement in the operation?" He looked up before biting into a carefully speared bite. I sat silently, considering my response before finally determining a hierarchy of inquiry.

"Two." I swallowed reflexively. "Two things I want to know. Why should I agree to be involved in such an outrageous plot? And—" I swallowed again, feeling an unrelenting weight to my next words, "doesn't Christ die at the end of this story?"

"Perfectly reasonable questions." He paused for a prolonged draw on the amber elixir before him. "And here are the perfectly reasonable answers. Firstly, in response to why you should choose to be a part of this plan."

He turned and snapped his fingers in the direction of the nearest wall. Light immediately flooded the pale surface, and after a few moments of adjustment, an image was clear. As my eyes matched the focus, I instinctually stood. It was Mum. And Hasim. They were getting out of a van.

"What the hell is this? I swear if anything—"

Sterling cut me off. "Amir, Amir! Please continue to watch. I assure you no one is to be harmed. In fact, quite the contrary."

I turned back to the screen and surveyed, intent for the first time on believing the old man. Mum's crooked frame wobbled up a manicured path. As she approached, the frame widened to reveal a carefully crafted residence, its scale and detail of obvious value. She stopped to examine the façade, reminding me of my own arrival at Sterling's home. Hasim bounded to and fro, observing each facet of the exterior with a quick touch and careful nod.

"Where are they?" I asked gently, my anger giving way to genuine interest.

"Their new home," Sterling pronounced. "What you see is their new home. They have been informed that you have been selected for a covert government operation based upon aptitude, and this residence is the considerable compensation. They—" He paused, obviously considering his next words. "And you. You all will never want again." At his final word, he broke into a toothy grin.

I stared again at the screen then back to Sterling. I could discern little regarding his sincerity based upon the unsettling expression and accordingly turned to Abigail. Here, too, lay a smile, but one defined only by a gentle upturn. This was palpable compassion, and upon further inspection, her unblinking eyes led me to a forced belief. This was, as Sterling had asserted, a reasonable answer. Such a marked change in the trajectory of our story was worth almost any sacrifice. Almost.

"And what of my second inquiry. Do I have to die for this new home?" I asked with focused energy, now consumed by the idea of deliverance from our circumstances.

Sterling didn't move. His position remained unaltered, and for a moment, it seemed he was about to finally define the price of this operation. After this notable pause, he finally shifted in his seat and addressed me again.

"It wouldn't be much of a home if you did." He pondered. "I always considered this a requirement of the endeavor: the preservation of the dutiful soldier. The answer," he stood to stoke the nearby fire, his voice diminishing as he turned away, "turned out to be more challenging than anticipated. However, as in the case of the distortion, my expectation regarding the trajectory of technology within my lifetime was proved accurate. In this case, the development has come through a combination of many advancements in humanistic robotics. I slowly acquired and hid each component away until before me stood a fully functioning anatomically accurate android indistinguishable from the human body. This robot is to be outfitted to match your characteristics in order to take your place in the final hour."

He paused as a particularly loud crackle erupted from the hearth. I took the opportunity to interject.

"If this thing is so convincing, why doesn't it just go back and fool everyone for the entirety of the story?" I posed, hoping that somehow I had happened on the simple alternative yet unconsidered by Sterling's wicked genius.

"I wish it could. I really do, Amir. However, although the android is convincing enough in small doses, over the course of prolonged testing, it has always failed. Sometimes it was compromised by its adaptive conversational software, unable to keep up with organic human conversation patterns. In other instances, its physical infrastructure succumbed to the anticipated elements: dust, moisture, and light aged its components and led to dramatic breakdowns. No, this machine is perfect for a short dramatic appearance, but the entirety of Jesus's ministry, one lasting years and undoubtedly composed of hundreds of unpredictable interactions, necessitates a human. It even seems the act of switching you and the android is written into history. I believe that Jesus's pursuit of isolated prayer in the Garden of Gethsemane was simply a planned opportunity to make the change. As if an actor exiting stage left to make a quick exchange with the stunt double, this momentary exit allows us to instead implant the android. I couldn't have written it better myself. Which, in some branch of time . . . I did." He halted in speech, allowing this last premise to resonate.

My mind reeled, trying to understand the implication of his final words. Could it be that there was in fact perceivable evidence of such a plot written in the Bible itself? I didn't know the stories well enough to take an inventory of other such possibilities, but even the premise captivated my interest. However, before I could feebly try to recount my limited biblical knowledge, Sterling interjected.

"Now. Amir. Are you ready?" His eyes glared in stark unmoving contrast as his pursed lips deliberately pronounced each word.

I stared back with an energy bordering on contempt. Ready. Ready for what? Ready to accept this scheme? Ready to travel back in time? Ready to assume my role in a hoax that would leave me temporarily stranded in time? Ultimately, I responded as simply as possible.

"Ready for what? Mr. Sterling, this whole thing . . . this whole story has been . . . captivating. But . . ."

"Yes . . . But what, Amir?" he eagerly prodded.

"But . . . how are you so sure? I admit, it seems you have the elements to perform such a hoax, but what if you're wrong? What if the premise you have proposed is wrong, in fact an unnecessary construction in the face of a real visit from God? I'll admit I don't believe in the divine visit, but it seems unlikely that just because we have all that is required, this is the obvious alternative." I stopped, feeling somewhat satisfied that I had finally articulated the essential disquiet regarding his proposition.

"Ah, but it is not a jump. Not at all. Given the two potentials, which is more likely? That we applied the very real and palpable technologies that I have just demonstrated, devices built on principles that we know to be true, in order to guarantee the propagation of hope and moral character? Or . . . or that a person defied every physical law known to govern the world around us because his human body was housing the undefined energy of a formless power called God? A God never to be experienced in the same repeatable way again?"

His hands reflexively punctuated the statement to emphasize the obvious conclusion desired. I matched his passionate display with an unwavering glare of skepticism. He sighed deeply and averted his eyes, muttering what appeared to be expletives under his breath. This was the first time I had sensed that the progression of conversation was not according to plan, not perfectly aligned to Sterling's intent. He abruptly stood and strode to a small wooden box sitting atop a nearby dresser.

"I didn't want to do this, Amir. I may be the first person to propose the manipulation of time, but even I acknowledge that it is unclear how the transfer of information from past to present may manipulate what will be reinjected again into past." His words seemed almost nonsensical due to the ridiculous subject. "However, it is clear now that convincing others of my belief is even harder than an evangelist convincing strangers of their ridiculous God. Accordingly, I have a solution. You, Amir, will assume the role of Jesus. The character you have learned about was you. And these," he said as he slowly withdrew a stack of weathered papers from the box, "will prove it to you."

As he slowly shuffled back to his seat, I focused solely on the clutched documents. The paper had at first seemed conventional, but now I noticed that with each teetering step, the fibrous planes glinted in the light.

"It will be impossible to send all of the technologies and necessary supplies back at once. In addition, some elements are time-sensitive. For instance, the story of Christ feeding the throngs with fish and loaves. In order to perform this seeming impossibility, I will send back a massive supply of fish and bread to be distributed using some practiced sleight of hand. These letters . . ." he stopped to gather an aged breath, "are to ensure that I send the provisions back to the exact time and place required. These are communications which were written by you . . . two thousand years ago. As will be instructed in your training, each letter contains a summary of the day's events, a schedule of necessary provisions, and a personal insight that confirms your identity. It is the last component that is in question today. It is necessary to inject such a requirement to counteract the essential disbelief I am now encountering."

With his final word, he stretched out a wrinkled hand to present a single page from the mass. I stared for an elongated moment then allowed my hand to reluctantly grasp the strange sheet. Its texture was unlike any paper I had ever known, a glistening grid of fibers that almost irritated my skin. I slowly brought the page within my field of vision and considered the script.

Sterling,

Today: it was another of routine. We spent time walking the boundary of town discussing teachings as applied to passers-by's lives. I described ideas of selflessness as demonstrated by the golden rule. Peter again stood out with an eagerness as described in the text. At times, he seems to take the teachings, which we simply fabricated in some wrinkle of time, and construct a far more convincing cult language. As if easing the load of my acting, he effortlessly amplifies any perceivable passion I can muster, and renders instead a convincing religious experience. The other disciples are quick to follow suit and feed on the energy he presents. I do not perceive that any of today's events are to make it into the recollections within the Gospel record, but as I am quickly realizing, those stories of the text are needles in a haystack of interactions.

Tomorrow: in the coming days, there are to be interactions along the Red Sea, only hours east of our position. Considering the biblical events I have already experienced, it seems likely that this is to be the moment of reality for the described feeding of thousands. I will work in the days to come to better understand the populations at hand and identify coordinates for the drop.

Yesterday: I remember a time before my father's death. This was so long ago, at least in my own progression of time, that the image is now grainy in my mental storehouse. Yet, his voice cuts through. Each night, he would read me to sleep. As he spun each tale, his small round glasses would slowly slip from their intended perch. As the frames lowered, I knew the story at hand was drawing to a close, and when he was finally forced to address their precarious position, I knew we were to part ways for the night with a gentle hug.

-Amir

As I finished the final lines, my fingers lost grasp of the document, my body diverting all energy to the crisis of reality now at hand. I had been shaken by the undeniable technologies presented, but the memory I now beheld, written in my own hand, left me no room. No room to retreat. No room to question. No room to "play along with Sterling." And, most depressingly, no room to choose. I had already chosen. The fact that I was reading such a letter was confirmation of my future actions. I stared incredulously at the crackling fire and considered this new undeniable reality. I knew at some point I would have to address Sterling's piercing view and finally confirm his proposal. I recounted the most important criteria within my own moral code, which now suddenly gained credibility. Mum and Hasim would be taken care of. I would not have to die. I would be back . . . eventually. Mum and Hasim would be taken care of. Finally, with these simple ideas anchoring my resolve, I turned to face him.

"Okay. I will do it. I will be their hope."

MARCH 15, 2085

Sterling smiled. This time the smile was unnerving, clearly not rooted in the supposed pursuit of hope but rather in Sterling's selfish pride. Again, I turned to the silent Abigail to gather a more traditional response. She, too, beamed but seemed to be more intently studying my own face than embracing the offered confirmation of their long-hatched plot.

"Amir. You are a hero. You are a soldier. An antidote in the form of a man, and the audience before you, despite our necessarily small numbers, will never forget your bravery." His praise was so laden with cliché its worth seemed diluted. "As it seems we are finishing lunch, let us retire and consider a grander view of the mountainous task ahead. Take one last drink and follow me."

He awkwardly gestured to the practically full glass at the head of my plate. I thoughtlessly took a long drink as I stood, awkwardly prepared to follow, already accustomed to Sterling's endless directions.

He strode with newfound vigor ahead of me to another novel space. This newest room was stark in contrast to our past environments. Each wall was adorned with neither art nor ornament but was instead laid bare in apparent contrast. In the center of the floor stood the only prior occupants: three rudimentary chairs lying in wait.

"Please sit, Amir." Sterling gestured with his cane to the center chair.

Again, slipping into a comfortable routine of submission, I bent into the crook of the intended seat. As I lowered, I perceived a waft of sweet air, its scent affected by the evident movement of Abigail's streaming hair as she sat to the right. Sterling remained upright as if demonstrating some reversed version of conventions, the oldest and feeblest to render seats to the young. As I considered the strange arrangement, the lights dimmed without perceivable direction, and the wall behind Sterling was suddenly basked in the gentle glow of projected imagery. Apparently satisfied with the setup, Sterling launched into a classic rant.

"An astronaut, preparing to travel past Earth's orbit, trains for approximately eight years. Eight years in preparation for a matter of months separated only by a few hundred miles from the home they know. You, Amir, are twenty-seven. Jesus's recorded ministry started at age twenty-nine. This leaves approximately two years to prepare for a mission spanning years in a place separated from every reality you have ever known not just by distance, but also time. Accordingly, your rise will be far more meteoric in nature. Your training, I am afraid, will be defined by fourteen-hour days with few exceptions. Each day will be composed of two parts. The first six hours and forty-five minutes will be spent with me, getting familiar with the technologies necessary to perform our endeavor. Considering the time gap between us, you will need to be more than a user of these devices, but instead an expert. An experienced support staff should you encounter an issue. I will train you on the use of each device, and how to successfully address any issues which could arise. The latter half of the day, resumed after a thirty-minute lunch, will be spent with Abigail. She will instruct you in all of the necessary cultural aspects defining the era to be occupied. These include the language—Aramaic—dining customs, biblical history, theological practices, etc. Admittedly, we could elect to take longer developing these skills, thus sending you back at a later age. We are, after all, only beholden to our own imagined timeline. However, any altering of the timeline we currently see recorded in the Bible would lead to rippling changes in the entirety of history to follow. As I am interested in preserving the goodness in this version of history, and not in creating an alternative one, I would want to keep your age as recorded."

Sterling stopped for a long while and breathed heavy, his exuberance obviously outlasting his conditioning. As he caught up on much-needed oxygen, a new consideration occurred to me.

"How do you intend to simply inject a person? If I suddenly appear at age twenty-nine, how are these supposed local cohorts going to corroborate my past? You know . . ." I stopped for a moment, suddenly feeling somewhat dizzy. "You know, like the whole virgin birth thing? How will that story be recounted if I appear at twenty-nine with no connection to Mary, Joseph, or anyone?" I finished my inquiry just in time as my vision felt undeniably out of sorts. My seat audibly whined as I involuntarily teetered.

"Amir, it is as if you are reading my notes. As I can see that you are now experiencing its effects, let me reveal the answer to this question. You have heard it said that the sense of smell is closely linked with the memory center of the brain, called the hippocampus. This is true, but in fact the visual input centers constantly input far more information to these regions and accordingly are provided a more robust connection. During lunch, you ingested a calculated dose of dialectant, a chemical recently developed to dilate your eyes to such a degree that a bolus of information coded as light can be accommodated."

I stared blankly at Sterling, taking little away from the complex explanation other than the fact that he had drugged me. My anger was displaced by the now palpable sense that the room around me was too bright, despite the lights being dimmed. In no surrounding form was found the detail usually noted, but I could perceive movement as Sterling's cane clacked across the room. As I watched the blurred outcroppings that represented his appendages adjust some set of controls, the lights at last subsided and gave way to a dim but more focused reality. Sterling simply stood, his form somehow appearing poised for a yet undefined climax to my condition. I swiveled my neck and took in Abigail's profile. The small distance between our seats accommodated an unprecedented view of her face. Even considering my altered vision, I couldn't help but overtly study the gentle profile of her face. Just as I began to forget my induced state, a deafening crack occupied the space. I instinctually turned to its source, seemingly toward the front wall. As my eyes strained to discern any disturbance in the planar surface, the entire face suddenly burst into light.

White-hot blindness overtook. I reeled as reality seemingly evaporated into pure light. Any sense of form left my conscious perception, and now even the anchoring of consciousness itself seemed tenuous. The only perceivable input was the feeling of falling. I was certain that I had fallen, not only out of my chair, but somehow much further when the light began to fade. Slowly, I felt the familiar sensation of being and again perceived the shadows that construct the world of form and void. The effect continued to dissipate until I found myself simply staring, with perfectly conventional senses, at an irritatingly grinning Sterling.

"What the hell was that!? I was blinded by that . . . that . . ." I struggled to articulate the consuming light.

"That," he addressed, "was a memory." His words rang in my ears as a newfound headache resided.

"What? What memory. Please, for the sake of my sanity, forgo the dramatic reveals and just tell me what happened," I pressed.

He chuckled to himself, his shoulders visibly rising and falling.

"Okay, okay, Amir. I apologize for the theatrics." He seemed to genuinely acknowledge his overdone performances. "What just occurred was the insertion of a memory by mass light input through the optic nerve. I am curious, how long do you think the event occupied your vision?" he inquired.

I considered the already fading memory of the light and tried to guess at a time.

"Maybe thirty seconds?" I said, feeling as if the event had been more disorienting than lengthy. Sterling again flashed an unnerving smirk.

"The input, in fact, lasted nearly an hour. During this time, a memory, in the form of visual frames, was rapidly replayed at calculated wavelengths to continually transfer directly to the hippocampus. A traditional motion picture plays at approximately sixty frames per second, representing a great deal of transmitted data. The hour-long memory contained 240 frames per second. The accelerated nature of this input, coupled with the forced dilation of your eyes and neural connections, led to the direct insertion of a memory indistinguishable from one of natural creation."

An hour! I struggled to grapple with the apparent hijacking of my experience of reality and time. The now clear manipulation of my body. The undeniable rape of my senses.

"A memory of what?" I logically inquired, despite my growing rage.

"What was played was a memory of my wife—Abigail's mother—Sophia. My interest in the miracle drug that is hope was spurned by her faith in Christ. I could find no better demonstration than to engrain the same recollections of hopeful demise that have so motivated my efforts to your own traveling memory bank. Do you remember, Amir? Do you remember her olive skin, so similar to Abigail's, jaundiced and marred? Do you remember her frame, once poised in elegance, now reduced to little more than a heap of bones? And yet. And yet, she was happy. Grateful even. She spoke to me, Amir. Do you remember what she said?"

With every word Sterling pronounced, the images flooded in. A small, shrunken figure shivering in a darkened hospital room. A gentle smile emerging in the morning light. I could so clearly remember her touch as she deposited her hand in mine and stroked Abigail's sleeping head nestled at her waist. Her gaze stalled as our eyes met, and she whispered in a voice so gentle it was barely audible.

"She said . . . she said . . ." I fought back tears induced by the realness of the injected experience. "She said that it was all part of love. The beginning and the end. Part of his love."

Sterling's grin was now gone. I could sense he was satisfied with the answer and the demonstration's success, but now a tear forged a path down his wrinkled cheek. He wiped it away with his free hand and visibly gathered his resolve. Abigail suddenly stood, apparently unable to overcome her emotions as well as her father could, and exited the small room. Sterling watched over her exit, then turned back to face me.

"This is how we are to place you, a fully formed, fully functioning savior, in their midst and simultaneously create the myth of virgin birth and conception. The exact particulars will be discussed in your training exercises, but essentially you will covertly insert the dialectant solution into the village's water source. All relevant parties will ingest the chemical and be rendered temporarily susceptible to such memory injection. Once the community is blanketed in the darkness of night, a sonic event will guarantee mass attention in the northern sky. Finally, after a small pause to allow them to focus upon the unidentified noise, we will begin the insertion."

"You mean begin blinding them. Begin raping their senses. Begin screwing up their heads!" I practically shouted.

"Now, Amir. Don't go getting high and mighty on me now! One rule that must be observed to ensure the success of this endeavor is a healthy distinction between knowledge and belief. You will be required to memorize the teachings of Jesus Christ. However, you must not allow this knowledge to cripple our actions due to some contrived morality. All of the parables and rules are of our own construction at the beginning of this time loop, and therefore only useful as tools to combat the despair that so plagues our human condition. We are to be the only humans privileged to know the true purpose of these instructions. They are tools of utility, not inherent validity. I am curious, Amir, are you familiar with utilitarianism?"

Eager to insert some evidence of my own intellect into the growing record of Sterling's, I hurriedly recalled the multitude of Hasim's lessons in search of the inquired term. However, as my silence transitioned from thoughtful consideration to awkward denial, Sterling interjected. In dealings with a person of a more familiar character, I would have been confident that this interruption was to save me from embarrassment, but as his voice cut in, such a nicety felt unlikely.

"Utilitarianism is a system of morals. Just as religion seeks to establish moral criteria to evaluate decisions, so, too, does utilitarianism. In the case of religion, the metric is a series of rules to be considered inherently valid because of their superior source. This principle has proved to be extremely potent in the propagation of societal cohesion. However, that which pulls at the puppet ought not pull at the puppeteer. As overtly denoted, the guiding principle of utilitarianism is utility rather than morality. We are to consider any notable crossroads only based upon possible results for the entire population. The greatest good for the greatest number. I'm curious, Amir, by what moral system have you lived?"

I paused to consider both the question and the implication of Sterling's own moral guidance. The apparent calculation process at hand guaranteed neither loyalty nor honesty. If he was willing to manipulate thousands of people to benefit billions, I shuddered to consider the infinitesimal value given to my own life. However, as I finally addressed his question, I realized my own calculations were not so different.

"I suppose I adhere to a form of utilitarianism," I admitted reluctantly, "with one notable distinction: I consider all junctions not from the perspective of billions but from just two. My Mum. My Hasim." As I pronounced their names, my emotional core stalled, momentarily stunned as I focused on their absence.

"Why do you think this is?" Sterling daftly inquired. "These two people are no more human than any other. They are not endowed with any characteristics or abilities not found in another. Yet, this tendency to consider only these tribal adjacencies is the overwhelming alternative to religion. Why do you believe this is, Amir?"

Sterling shifted gently as he finished his probe, his constant energy unable to endure the prolonged dialogue now at hand. Although this was perhaps his most existential mystery yet posed, I felt I had a perfectly reasonable explanation to present.

"Because they are me. What you are viewing as a special case of extreme empathy is perhaps better explained as extended selfishness. All people admittedly house similar characteristics and perspectives. However, I have not been granted to view the lives of all peoples, only these two. I have seen every step. Every fall. Every experience and endowment. And now, in the case of only these two,

I understand their perspective. I feel their pain and rejoice in their victories. Although their views are gathered through another aperture, I am no less bonded. No less enslaved. No less selfish to act upon these inputs."

I finished my analysis with a tinge of regret. As if an impressionable youth corrupted, I felt that I had succumbed to Sterling's reductions. I had taken his tempting bait to academically reduce the unknowable loveliness of life into condescending appraisals. As the folds of my face trended morosely downward, his pointed markedly up.

"Amir, you are no mere actor. You are a philosopher. An articulate reductionist. I am certain that in the beginnings of our current time loop, you had much to do with the creation of our contrived morality. I could not have better explained it myself." He practically sang the words, perhaps happy to discover an aptitude useful to our goal. "I would urge you to cling to your shrunken version of utilitarianism. The task at hand will be, at times, grueling. Motivation by considering the faceless masses will lack potency. Instead, I say cling to your two loves whose faces are so worn in your memory as to become your own. They, in addition to being granted faith along with the masses, are to be individually rewarded for your efforts. Let this focused progress drive your labors."

He stopped to purposefully capture my meandering gaze. I took the opportunity to examine his unwavering pupils. However, as if a physical manifestation of the system just described, I only sensed distance. A distance created. A distance required.

"Now, having addressed what I predicted to be the last major hurdle in the effort, let us this afternoon consider the overall structure of your training." As he introduced the topic of discussion as if at some forced seminar, Abigail slipped quietly again through the door. Her eyes, typically defined by clarity, were now fogged by the tearful departure. She assumed her previous position in my periphery as Sterling began again.

"There are thirty-four miracles recorded in the New Testament. These seeming impossibilities can be classified into five types: physical feats, knowledge of unknowable obscurities, curing of ailments, sovereignty over external objects, and finally, authority over death itself. To perform these distinct demonstrations, we will utilize seventy-two separate technological components. These tools range from complicated mechanizations to healing ointments. Each will require in-depth knowledge and a practiced hand to properly implement. We have approximately two years before the opportune moment of insertion. Considering these two pertinent factors, time allowed and components to learn, you will be trained on one component per week." He paused to shift his weight more squarely upon the loosely grasped handle of his cane. As he adjusted, I considered the proposed math.

"Two years is a hundred and four weeks. At one technology per week, that still leaves thirty-two weeks remaining. What am I to do in these weeks?" I posed, hoping that there was some scheduled reprieve from the daunting task.

Sterling nodded to Abigail. I slightly pivoted to view any notable reaction. She silently aimed a small controller of sorts at the wall beyond Sterling, initiating a much-needed visual aid. I turned back to face Sterling and the newly illuminated surface. Still recovering from my forced blinding, I squinted to make out the defining features of the image projected. It was a schedule, and before I could begin to determine the answer to my question, Sterling accompanied the image with his never-ending instruction.

"The reason there are extra months, as you so accurately noted, is to allow for intermittent theatrical run-throughs. The final week of each month will be spent performing a complete performance of the newly mastered components. The components will be added sequentially according to the order of appearance in the text. Therefore, this final week of every month will fulfill a practiced portion of the growing messianic performance required. The final month before your departure will be a comprehensive performance combining all of these weeks into one convincing charade." He articulated the schedule as one might a plan for a simple day out, overtly in denial of the complexity disguised by brevity.

"One month," I countered. "One month to practice a performance spanning years? How am I supposed to memorize the sequence if I have never actually performed the long-form entirety?" Droplets of saliva aspirated as I passionately punctuated my reservations.

"To memorize," he carefully commanded my attention, "is not to be. Most of your interactions do not appear within the Bible. We have no transcript with which to polish some scripted dialogue. Instead, we have four separate accounts of notable experiences. We will only practice the physical actions and sleights of hand required to account for the written miracles. The rest, the everyday dialogue and human experiences that make up life," his voice rose, prestressing his coming words, "will rely upon your cultural training with Abigail."

He raised one sagging shoulder to my right. Abigail turned to me to address her role in the ever-growing operation.

"Father will equip you with external tools to allow momentary feats of impossibility. I will equip you with internal knowledge to allow prolonged relations. Each week, just as you expand your technical library, so too will you add the language and cultural knowledge necessary to create not a convincing parlor trick but a beloved friend." She pursed her lips in an awkward pause. "Amir, do you know how long it takes to learn a language? Not just to ask for the bathroom or some other nicety but to learn how to love in another language. You are to be with these people for thousands of hours. To love them. To inspire love within them. All with words. How long do you think it would take to learn that?" She finished her repeated inquiry and sat noticeably still, convincingly interested in my response.

"Longer than two years?" I sarcastically answered with a question of my own.

"A lifetime. It takes life to speak the unspeakable. Unfortunately, we do not have a lifetime, but we do have the ability, as you have just experienced, to accelerate this process. Using light enco—"

I cut her off as I started to recognize the newfound vocabulary.

"No way. No way am I doing that light bullshit again!" I profaned at the idea of being again subjected to the blinding takeover. "That cannot be good for you, and I am not going to be the guinea pig to find out." Abigail's smooth skin contorted into a look of empathy, but before she could address my comment with some reasonable tenderness, Sterling interjected.

"Amir, people all over the world subject their bodies and minds to far worse to support their loved ones. Are yours not worth this sacrifice? No, we all know you will do it. Because you already have, as evidenced in the text, and because you love them. Your precious mother and Hasim. If you want the house and the money, this is it. You have to," he proclaimed with an arrogant note of finality.

I felt a twinge of hatred as Sterling stared ahead blankly, seem-ingly unapologetic for using my only loves as pawns. Abigail, perhaps sensing the palpable tension, again attempted her own more empa-thetic response.

"I know, Amir. I know it hurts to not even control one's own per-ception. But I assure you it is not dangerous. You will not die. I have undergone all the sessions necessary for your own development. I can teach you not only because of a traditional education process but also because of the light. I have stored a lifetime of memories. Memories of joy. Memories of pain. Memories of every manifestation of life reframed in an ancient way. We will still need to exercise these stores of knowledge, but it is the only way to prepare for what is required: an inspiring articulation of hope." She again stopped and observed me in a manner so converse to Sterling's. Her eyes shone with bright care.

I had to admit, being able to identify no obvious deformities or defects, I was comforted by her firsthand knowledge. I found myself nodding a silent reflexive agreement. Seeing that empathy had gar-nered my consent, Sterling hobbled toward me and leaned awk-wardly low on his cane.

"Let me see your eyes, Amir. Almost done for the day. Let's see if you are ready to accept the lights again." He gestured to the room's still dimmed conditions.

I reluctantly turned my head from Abigail's direction to face Sterling's wrinkled façade. As he met my gaze, I felt as if a mad man on the street. I channeled all the will I could to the surface of my eyes. I wanted Sterling to know his exercises in forced control were not met with simple obedience. Rage prevailed in the ocular exchange.

"You are good," he said, pivoting from my seething view as quickly as possible. "Abigail, please show Amir back to his room. Amir," the clicks of his cane ceased in silent focus, "get some sleep. Tomorrow, we begin."

I watched as he turned and left, careful not to again meet my gaze, then turned to find Abigail already silently waiting to lead me, the ever-present vassal. Before I was finished rising from my seat, she was turning to lead. The unhuman efficiency of every transition was becoming tiresome as I longed even for the never-ending barrage of facts from Hasim. Even just the momentary consideration of my distant loves began to infect my thoughts. Soon, my steps were the result of mindless mechanics rather than careful consideration as I tried to picture each face with perfect accuracy. My forced recollections only paused as Abigail's steps audibly slowed at the approach of my door. She stood a silent guard to my implied retirement. Just before I pivoted to close the door, I turned to address her.

"Last night, my phone was acting up. Is there some adjustment that can be made or step to be taken?"

"Hmm . . ." she mused unconvincingly, "I will ask Sterling, but I'm sure it's working properly. Good night," she finished, her rehearsed answer as convincing as a parent addressing a young child's uncomfortable question.

Before I could press further, she gently grasped the door and swung it closed. Just as the door precluded her from view, I quickly grasped the handle on my side as the wood face contacted the frame. In an act practiced during rebellious teenage nights, I stretched to simultaneously grasp a nearby closet handle. Just as she finally pulled the entry door shut, I loudly clicked the alternate handle while carefully preventing the first from fully latching. The result, I knew from experience, was a convincing illusion of locking. A convincing illusion of detainment. A convincing illusion of control.

I stood in the awkward stretched position until her steps faded down the long hall. I slowly opened the entry door just enough to prevent the mechanism from springing to lock and allowed my arms to relax. I was not certain of what opportunity this minor freedom would allow, but despite his supposed honesty, Sterling's lust warranted investigation. However, before I made any effort in clandestine observation, I needed to call Mum. I strode to the supposedly immutable phone and dialed the number that now represented my most coveted connection. Before I had time to prepare any rehearsed recollections, Mum's voice eagerly cut through.

"Amir? Are you there, Amir?" Her voice was less shaken than the night before, but no less hurried to confirm my presence.

"Yes, Mum! Yes, I am here!" I pushed my voice to sound upbeat.

"Amir, are you okay? Oh, Amir. You won't believe what has happened, Amir. They gave us a house. A brand-new house!" Every word was laden with mixed emotional stress. "But then I was thinking why. What is going on, Amir? What are you doing? They said you are part of some program, and this is the compensation. So, then I was thinking . . . I was thinking . . ." she stammered as the words slowed in anticipation of the worst.

"It's okay, Mum. Really. I am perfectly fine." I paused to listen to her anxious human presence translated through the mechanical connection. "Is it nice?"

"Is what nice?" she retorted, revealing her priorities.

"The house! Is the house nice?" As I pronounced my question again, I realized the irony of our dialogue. I, so focused upon their newfound circumstances, had forgotten my own. She, so concerned with my unknown conditions, had forgotten about the gift.

"It is amazing. It is, Amir. It even has a library for your brother. But Amir . . . don't lie to me. What is going on? I told them there must be a mistake. That I just wanted to go by the normal process. Just get you out and nothing weird. But they said this was the procedure. What is going on, Amir?" Now a palpable fear entered her voice as she vocalized the wealth and scale now injected into our lives.

"It's complicated, Mum. Probably can't say much. Just know I am okay. I will be required to travel for a . . ." The phone shuddered in carefully timed static. It was clear that we were not the only parties listening. I began again, this time conforming to the implied rules. "I can't really say, Mum. But I am perfectly fine," I reassured her. "Mum, before the line cuts us off . . . I love you." Silence overtook for a time, and I worried the phone had again interjected.

"I love you too, Amir." She was crying, and the words were little more than enunciated sobs. I dwelled for a moment upon her sentiment before carefully inserting a final statement crafted for our silent third party.

"Mum, I want to talk more, but I am really tired and need to get to bed. I will call tomorrow." She conceded, and we each offered a quick goodnight before ending our short connection.

I sat still for a time, considering the brief transport back to the familiar. Mum's worry. My dodging. Finally, I turned to address the door. A sliver of light defined the right edge and represented possibility. I had no intention of mounting an elaborate escape, only of observing my constructed captors without the forced formality of consent.

The door slightly creaked as it swung, a first in my recollection and confirmation that the world itself was conspiring against me. However, as I turned my attention to the grand hall, I was met with no resistance. No hulking guard or hunched Sterling. Only the decadent trappings that lay in silent wait of observation. My feet elevated and thrust as only a practiced thief's might, gingerly giving no clues to my movement. As I rounded the first turn, I realized I had no idea where I was going. Sterling had never revealed his place of origin and retreat. Attempting sound logic, I stood at the first junction and strained for any palpable sound. As silence began to deafen, I heard a slight metallic click to the right. At the mercy of my newfound guide, I proceeded with little confidence in my method. Many careful steps—and quite a while—later, I approached another convergence of halls. Finally, another audible click, this time closer, oriented me to the left.

After two more turns, I was within earshot of Sterling's movements. His cane was now depicting every step with unstrained clarity. Waiting until the sounds grew progressively softer, I peered around the precluding corner. As indicated by the sounds, Sterling was indeed in the hallway and proceeding slowly away in the dim corridor. As he rounded the next corner, I silently sprang to pursue. While he was audibly detained in the next hall, I hurried to gain ground in my own. When I again carefully observed from my position, Sterling was hunched at the mechanism of one of the many identical doors, simple machines whose purpose was never more evident than in Sterling's manor of mission. Simple pieces of wood. Harvested and immobilized to boundary the known from the not. Now that I knew my purpose here, each face stared at me in the long halls. Each face laughed at me in passing. Each face knew more than I. However, as the lock audibly acted, it was clear this particular face would relent.

As the door swung inward, Sterling paused. It was a deliberate halt that was recognizably human in nature. He was listening.

My breath caught and matched the pause, awkwardly confined without warning. Hold it. Hold it. My physical requirement ached, unconvinced of the imperative at hand. Finally, just as my chest began to heave for lack of breath, Sterling shrugged and moved into the space. I finally reinitiated intake and out and followed suit. Cradling the stained door frame in my spindly hand, I carefully took in the room.

Even from my peripheral existence, the space emitted a scent akin to a dusty library. Ancient scrolls lined the walls, carefully stowed in a complex grid of organization. Sterling paid the documents no mind. Instead, he strode directly to the room's center and hunched over a glinting glass case. From my vantage point, I could make out only a general shape: an oblong chunk. Neither crafted nor hewn, its form was clearly natural. It was either rock or wood but not an object that would normally warrant such inspection. Yet Sterling was arrested in its presence. He held his shining cane close, not even allowing the meandering tip to distract from the subject at hand. I could see his lips silently articulating some self-beheld truth as he peered through the glass. After what felt like minutes, he finally allowed his cane to fall again, an ambulatory partner at work. I turned and hurried to get ahead, rapidly covering the ground back to my room. The familiar exhilaration of escape reminded me of the sequence from not long ago, and as I rounded the last turn, I instinctively turned to check for Bear's scruffy grin. The lack of any companion deflated the sentiment as I secured my own bedroom door. Confined again to my silent dorm, I drifted to sleep, the mysterious chunk clouding the sinew of any potential dream.

MARCH 16, 2085

The alarm sounded, again signaling the coming dawn. I lay dormant for a moment, wrapped in bedclothes, imagining any reality alternate to my current. Any reality at least cloaked in the mundane, aided by the experiences of others. Instead, as I pulled the soft fabric layers away, I was forced to acknowledge the same environment as the night before. Each step toward the closet already felt routine, as if an inspection of the carpet fibers would reveal that I had taken the same deliberate steps yesterday. However, as the closet door creaked open, the idea of routine was spoiled. Instead of the fitted bottoms and top of yesterday, an ancient-looking tunic hung limp within. The weave was loose and unregulated, not the work of machines. Every edge added to the effect, allowing each strand to extend well beyond any implied bound. For a moment, I considered not donning the ridiculous garment. Under some semblance of normality, I might call for my hosts, inquiring of the intentions of the odd garment. But now, considering the nature of my detainment, it seemed not worth the effort. This was undoubtedly part of Sterling's plan.

With the garment, which extended from shoulder to knee, drooped over my frame, I traveled the familiar walk to the parlor. Within the walls, the fire crackled, an endless articulation of warmth. Sterling sat, face precluded by some ancient manuscript. He made no effort to lower the document despite my audible arrival. Not eager to accelerate any contact, I accepted the invitation of silence and approached the breakfast array. However, as I slumped into one of the massive velvet seats and bit into the tasty treat, Sterling loudly folded his document. Within seconds, he was upon me, and despite his aged frame, he managed to impart impatience with intimidating clarity.

"I see you found your new tunic," he proclaimed while he waited. I nodded, all the while chewing. "It is in these types of details that we will forge success. You will learn to move as one of them. Learn what positions cause the garment to bind. How the cloth behaves in every condition. How to avoid rips and tears. How to live in this ancient reality."

I again silently nodded, feeling the explanation warranted no response.

"I'll be done in a moment," I sputtered through bites. He stood without moving and watched me finish.

"Ready?" he asked, turning before I had time to answer.

I threw aside my soiled dishes and practically ran after. He led with confidence through many intersections, finally arriving at a novel door and paused to actuate the lock. I was reminded of my covert operations of the night before and wondered what this newest door would reveal. After a small click, the paneled surface gave way to permit our entry. Without turning to confer, Sterling stepped inside, beckoning me to follow. I urged my steps to reinitiate, not eager to face my newest unknown.

The open door gave way to another expansive void. However, the volume was rendered unremarkable as the creaking wood floors gave way to earth. Apparently devoid of any foundation, it seemed the manor had allowed the natural floor to temporarily prevail. Desert-style vegetation peppered sandy earth. Loose tufts of grass emerged, naturally random in placement. I looked up to determine what form of light was at work. The ceiling presented a high dome, broken only at its convergence by a circular oculus allowing light to intensely stream forth from freedom.

"This is your light, Amir," he said, turning his gaze upward. "This is your dirt. Your green." He nodded to the plants at my feet. "Every facet has been carefully coordinated to simulate the environmental conditions to be faced. The humidity, the species, the soil composition. All remarkably like those you will encounter. Even the air has been thinned to simulate the altitude of your travels."

As I again pivoted to take in the expanse, the ridiculousness hit me.

"Why didn't we just go there!? Just because we are in the future, surely the environment is similar. Why didn't we just train on the sites?"

"Good question," he acknowledged, likely only to emphasize the impressiveness of his imminent explanation. "We couldn't risk it. We couldn't risk the observation of some quick-witted student of logic. If we can imagine our plan, so can others. And although I have gone to great lengths to hide away any common knowledge of the technology, our movements and exercises must be performed in secret, known only to us three." He paused, considering whether I appeared convinced. "Even the orifice above—" he again gazed upward toward the gaping hole "—is obscured. The light you see is reflected. Redirected with a series of mirrors to preclude any incidental observation from above." This newest truth was somehow depleting, as if even my newfound connection with the sun had been stripped, again left only with my captors. "Now, Amir, do you notice anything out of place in the landscape around you?"

He pivoted left and right to indicate the intended breadth of examination. I played along, subtly rolling my eyes at yet another obviously scripted dialogue. However, as I grasped to find some vegetation that looked obviously foreign or a component that seemed out of place, I was unable to muster an answer. Sterling looked on as I continued to pan the landscape and finally interjected after no response was rendered. His cane kicked up dust as he approached an unremarkable patch of vegetation. However, as his legs alternated in sequence, the grass and sprigs began to look strange. The deep green color that had defined the leaves started to shimmer and shift, an effect akin to some distorted digital image. The composition continued to devolve until any trace of the patch of landscape was gone. In its wake lay a massive hole, probably twenty feet across and eight feet deep. The boundary of the void was manufactured, indicative of some mechanization rather than any simple spade. As my eyes traced the clean dirt floor within the void, a subtle grid was noticeable atop the hole in plane with the ground. I adjusted to consider this newfound element, kneeling to examine its composition. Extending my arm as if to swipe into the depth of the hole, I instead contacted a velvety surface denoted by the shimmering grid.

"It is a biomimicry concealment layer," Sterling spoke over my shoulder. "The image is derived from an aerial photograph taken prior to the hole's creation. Any vegetation or ground cover is then projected from below onto this incredibly rigid layer to render the void completely invisible." Upon punctuating his final word, the hole again became indiscernible, apparently rendered invisible as described. "Walk upon it, Amir. I promise no one will ever find such stations, giving us ample room to stage provisions as they are required." I stepped gingerly within the area of deception, expecting to perceive some minor deflection in the material. Instead, the surface remained unmoving, giving no clues to the void below. "Upon emerging from the distortion, four components will quickly follow: a concealed drone to capture the aerial image, a computerized excavation tool, a collapsed version of the surface before you, and the ultra-high-resolution projector to receive and reproduce the photograph."

I considered the oddity of his statement. I was convinced of the premise of the plan, but hearing the details articulated bordered on absurd.

"What happens first?" I asked flatly, eager to replace the dramatic presentation with mundane training.

"To begin, you will locate a large, flat zone suitable for such a depression. Your general location is to be a secluded scape near Nazareth. It has been selected for its notable isolation, which leaves little chance of bystanders noticing anything odd or out of place. However, you will need to consider the topography to avoid flooding. The surrounding land should slope away from the selected region as the biomimicry layer is only watertight when assuming controlled runoff, not standing water conditions."

I turned back to the zone to examine the criteria in physical reality. Sure enough, the zone in question appeared to be a notable high spot in the landscape surrounding.

"Once you have selected the proper site, you will initiate the mechanized excavation tool." He paused to turn and gather up some object from behind a nearby shrub. As he turned, a small metallic apparatus was clear under his arm. Simple in form, it appeared to be little more than an elliptical mass with a few wheels and exposed cogs. "This device will extract the required soil."

I stared at the small object, then back at the scale of the hole.

"How long does it take—a year!?" Sarcasm rang through my voice as I addressed the ridiculous juxtaposition.

"Although it appears small, this robotic tool developed at MIT utilizes a powerful vaporization core. Coupled with a rapid drive train and automated dimensional programming, it will make quick work of even the largest dig." Sterling paused, perhaps noting my blank expression brought forth by too many technical terms. "Basically, Amir," he said, turning the small mass over to expose a glinting lens, "this little guy uses a powerful laser to vaporize any substrate. Its path is preprogrammed, meaning once you select a site, just initiate the program using this button." He pointed to a small white protrusion representing a glorified "on" switch.

"Okay, I think I've got it." I sarcastically proclaimed, "Turn it on. Is that it?"

I was encouraged that perhaps my training would not be as vigorous as previously advertised. However, as I turned my attention from my own silent musings back to Sterling's unbreakable gaze, he was not amused.

"Although this machine may seem a small component within our overall sequence, your lessons today surrounding its operation will be indicative of the detailed nature of our preparation. You now know how this contraption is intended to work. However, as you shall see, it will undoubtedly encounter intermittent issues. Often one of the tiny lenses that work to amplify the laser will become dirty or misaligned. Or perhaps the device's speed will not be a good match for the substrate, in which case you will need to adjust internal drives to accommodate slower movement. There are several malfunctions that will be discussed. If any occurred without proper training, it would represent a significant setback to our plan." He paused for effect. "Now, to begin, please select the nearest suitable site condition and initiate excavation."

I considered my surrounding topography. Because of the elevated nature of our stance, the immediate ground was notably lower. However, as I pivoted to consider all directions, I noted another high spot about fifty feet away. Silently, I grabbed the digger from Sterling and made my way to the spot. With feet firmly planted atop the mass of ground, I gently set the smooth ellipse flat on the ground. Uncertain of the nature of the device's start-up, I reached from a distance to depress the button. Just as my finger finally elicited an audible click, the small contraption surged into motion. Immediately, I felt foolish for having doubted the object's effectiveness. With great haste, the small mechanism completed a concentric series of rectangles, noticeably carving the ground with every pass. Within a couple of minutes, it had already created a rectangular depression a foot deep. Just as the tiny workhorse seemed unstoppable, the progress seemingly slowed. With each pass, I noted less headway made; despite the continued lateral path, the machine descended less and less. Before I could address Sterling to verify the observation, the machine suddenly halted.

"And here we are, Amir! Our first opportunity for instruction. We will need to investigate the likely causes of fault and determine a solution. Please grasp the excavator with the initiation button facing dow—" As Sterling launched into a canned DIY fix-it speech, I began to realize the monotony of the proposed mission. If these sessions of troubleshooting were indicative of my training, this was to be a long series of years.

Sure enough, as the day progressed, Sterling explained, in the most boring manner possible, the inner workings of the excavator. I learned how to reveal its innards and fix any number of potential issues. At the conclusion of our morning session, we had successfully created ten large depressed base camps, and my hands were aching from the sharp cogs and gears that had pinched and pulled at my skin during repairs.

"Tomorrow, we will practice deploying the drone to capture an aerial image of the landscape prior to excavation." He gestured to a nearby container apparently housing this second contraption. "But now it is time to transition to culture and language. Let's go meet Abby in the parlor so you can begin your lessons." He turned before finishing his final words, as if revealing a lack of interest in any potential response I might muster.

I exhaled and followed suit, tired of being reminded of my powerless position but glad at the idea of leaving Sterling for the afternoon. After a mesmerizing procession of clicks from the ever-present cane, we emerged to find Abigail waiting near the popping flames of the fireplace.

"Grab something for lunch and follow Abby." Sterling wasted no time exiting the room, his posture seeming to suggest certain tiredness after the morning's operations.

I strode to the table of lunch items identically prepared each day. Having grabbed a series of items, I gestured to Abby that I was ready to follow to my next session. She accepted the silent proclamation and immediately began to travel toward one of the parlor's many outlets. I hastened my step, not eager to be lost amongst the endless halls. However, as we traveled the corridors, I realized the path was familiar. Indeed, as she opened the door to reveal a stark white room, the déjà vu was confirmed.

"No way! The first day, I am supposed to deal with that light thing again!?" I exclaimed, making no effort to disguise my dismay.

"I am sorry, Amir. I really am. To be honest . . ." Her conciliatory speech halted as though considering what to reveal. "To be honest, the first six months of our sessions will consist of ocular insertions. I'm afraid it's the only realistic way to absorb the necessary information in such a short time. After these sessions, we will begin to exercise these memories and lessons." She walked toward the lone table as she spoke and grasped some small object from atop the surface. "Now, one improvement upon your previous experience with the insertion will be trust. Instead of slipping the dilation compound into your water or food, we will ask you to simply swallow this pill each day."

She revealed the small object she had stowed: a chalky white pill. I scoffed at the assertion that any freedom was being afforded me but grabbed the pill to accelerate the inevitable. I gulped down some water along with the chalky tablet, which tasted awful upon contacting my tongue.

"How long until my eyes are ready?" I asked, remembering the effect of extreme dilation.

"Around ten minutes. For now, please sit down, and I will explain today's subject." She pointed to the lonely chair, not having acquired any companions since yesterday's visit.

Having had little time to sit during my time with Sterling, I allowed myself to slump into the rigid chair and began to silently observe Abigail's body language. Her posture was typically rigid, the position of someone with forced discipline. However, other aspects of her appearance refused to be conquered by restraint. Her hair shimmered in any light, and as she walked to and fro, I noticed some sliver of colorful socks hidden beneath her serious black slacks.

"Must have been nice, growing up with all of this," I awkwardly announced, referring to the grandeur of the estate.

She seemed to chuckle in response. "What do you mean? The wealth? The trinkets? The money?" Her voice descended in tone as she progressed. "Or do you mean the scheduled existence? The endless lessons? The loneliness?" I averted my eyes as she continued, now feeling like quite an asshole. "I assure you, Father's conclusion regarding the reality of faith has not made life easy. The story is fake, but the sacrifice is real. We have all sacrificed our lives. Perhaps not in death, but indeed in life."

"Sorry, I didn't mean . . ."

"It's okay, Amir. I get it. Sterling and I have had far more time to consider the ramifications of the fabricated reality. Far more time to realign our motives, and most of all, more time to become accustomed to the absence of Mother. The feeling of anger you feel at having been ripped from normal life and thrust to duty will wane."

As she continued, I considered the irony of our parallel losses: her loss of a mother and mine of a father. Each had obviously upheaved our worlds, but now as she described her own prisons, I was surprisingly aware of the beauty I had missed. After Father, we were poor, but we were still free. Still bound in a love one might classify as suburban. Abby conversely was afforded all luxuries but was thrust to the oddest of existences with a father driven by theory.

"I have often struggled with the reality. At times, I hate it. No God. No momentary contact with something more powerful, more pure. Instead, we are left again to rely upon our own intellect to manufacture what is needed. Yet we, too, the few involved in the great hoax, need the idea of God just as much but are forever spoiled by the truth." With every word, my eyes began to feel the effects of the dilation drug, rendering me in a trance considering both the poetic admissions and the overwhelming lights above. "My only advice is not to abandon the idea of God completely. The story describes an entity sacrificing. One for all. A small group of people driven to alleviate suffering. We are these ideas embodied, Amir. I have learned to find God within our own actions. There is purity within. Admittedly, any pure intentions share close quarters with hubristic musings, but I urge you, for the sake of sanity, to cling to your own actions for a reflection of clarity." As she concluded, I realized my mouth was hanging agape, my mind having become so engrossed in the articulation and sensory overload as to lose focus on the simplest of controls.

"Now, you should be about ready to begin the ocular insertion. Are you experiencing sensitivity?" I slowly turned to the lights above but was unable to pry my eyelids apart, considering the blinding strips.

"I am ready," I assured her.

"Today, you will begin learning basic culture and language skills. Some information will be in the format of instructional sessions, and others will be firsthand memories of life in ancient times. These memories are obviously not authentic, not gathered from ancient peoples, but are from accurate documentaries from the past two hundred years. Language lessons will begin with common root terms. Mastering these components would usually take weeks. At the end of today's sessions, you will have stored the same information." She walked across the room as the lights dimmed in anticipation of the awful warping of reality. "Eventually, we will begin to exercise these stored skills in concert, but it will be some time before there are enough components to be considered in tandem."

She was now entirely out of view, and as silence prevailed, I started to dread what was to come next. However, in accordance with an inescapable buy-in to the effort at hand, I forced my eyes to the point that was to explode. However, as moments spent in focused antici- pation tend to leave one, I was quickly wondering why it was taking so long to begin. Without fail, just as I relaxed, abandoning any sense of preparation, the room again gave way to all-consuming light. This time, presumably due to a longer session of immersion, I felt com- pletely disconnected from consciousness. The sequential experience of moments gave way to a blank field of view. The horizon outstretched far before me, beckoning me to completely abandon any physical circumstances. I swam in the light. It enveloped and consumed any thought of self and recollection of form. As I became accustomed to the static realm, I felt the first tinge of pain. I did not remember this from my previous forced immersion, but now, as I struggled to fight the prison, all senses were burning as if on fire. Every facet of percep- tion was dedicated to pain. I expressed my discomfort, perhaps not in some human articulation but on a more primordial level. Indeed, the energy channeled toward alleviating my suffering was not aided by words but instead a dissonance in the very fabric of my environment. Despite all my infectious will, the burning only grew. Just as I was sure my being would relent and cease the struggle of existence, the light waned. The pain was quick to leave, but I could sense a deep imprint. Finally, I made out a form. Light streamed past the dim silhouette, creating a fuzzy halo around the boundary. It was Abigail, her features becoming more defined by the moment.

"Wh . . . Whatth . . . Whatth . . ." Pronunciation escaped me as I yelled out in frustration, "What the hell! It killed me. I swear to God that thing killed me. Maybe even worse. It was . . ." I swallowed, looking for more words but finding nothing compelling. "Worse than death. What was that? That didn't happen the first time."

Abigail looked deeply into my eyes. Even in my dazed condition, I could make out tears welling in her own. She looked concerned, but even more than that, she looked empathetic, as if she knew exactly of what I spoke. She was sad for herself and me. Sad for us.

"I'm sorry, Amir. The first session was much shorter: only an hour. You just experienced seven hours straight of immersion. It is not dangerous, but somewhere around hour three, the sheathing on your optic nerve becomes so overheated that it fails to insulate the surrounding matter from the signals. The result is a powerful sense of pain. This is only in your head, Amir. It has no physical ramifications. As soon as the input is stopped, you will experience no pain and no lasting effects. It's all in your head."

"The hell it is," I muttered, examining my appendages, looking for some evidence of the agony. Nothing was marred. Nothing corroborated my experience, instead only confirming Abigail's claim. "Even if it's just a nerve thing, it has to be bad for you. I can't do that again. There must be another way to prepare," I asserted, trying to appeal to any sense of empathy that might override protocol.

"There is no other way, Amir. We have searched. Father tried and tried to achieve a painless immersion for my sake, but it cannot be done." She stood still as she spoke, her words unwavering and poignant.

I withdrew, realizing there was no discussion to be had. She had backup. Forceful backup in the form of hired guns. Not yet utilized but ever-present stood guards with shining instruments of force. Should I refuse, I was certain they would arrive, silent and strong, prepared to force compliance. However, upon closing my eyes within cradled hands, it was not these hulking figures which appeared. It was Mum and Hasim. Their shining eyes and gaunt frames motivated more than force ever could. I didn't want to give Sterling any reason to void his deal.

"Do you remember?" Abigail's voice intruded into my pitiful introspection. "You have some new memories. Do you remember anything of Aramaic language? Anything of their way of life?"

As she enunciated the words, images flooded forth. Dust swirled around tired feet. Groups gathered at worn tables. And strange syllables, hundreds, each with a distinct meaning. Some of these new-found terms were easy to understand and translate. But others left me grasping for an idea yet to be articulated in modern words. Some experience perhaps forgotten by the languages I knew.

"I do. I remember the dust and the people. Talking and eating. Washing before eating, and there was a method. Not just to wash, but for everything." I raised my left hand as I continued, "We couldn't use this hand to eat. Only the right. And the food was different. Simple looking." I stopped talking and considered more of the vocabulary encountered. Despite the suffering endured, the volume was miraculous. I was no bookworm like Hasim and had not learned this much in my entire life.

"That is good, Amir. You have reacted well to the process. Not all neural systems can properly store the information at such a rate. Your brain seems to have no issues with keeping up." She smiled, and for a moment, I felt a rare warmth, as if back with Mum. "Let's retire for the night. I am sure you are exhausted."

She was right. As I stood, my legs ached from being stationary so long, and my head was splitting, presumably from the unnatural hijacking of my brain. Even my lesson with Sterling had an impact as my fingers protested every intermittent grasp, swollen from the morning of mechanical maintenance. I followed Abigail down the endless gaudy tunnels and to my familiar door. She stationed herself to the left, waiting to ensure my successful detainment. I strode willingly inside as she silently closed the door behind me. I collapsed atop the looming bed, exhaustion overcoming any aches and pains as my internal conversation lost all order and descended to darkness.

AUGUST 24, 2085

My eyes parted moments before the buzz sounded. Despite the intrusive sound, I lay still in the oversized bed. After months of routine, my biological clock required no such sound, no such reminder that the day was to inevitably follow. However, despite countless appeals to Sterling, he always provided the same scripted response, "This alarm is not for today. It's not for tomorrow. The abrupt buzz is intended to ingrain this schedule in your very being. Our endeavor will require time each day before the prying eyes of your followers. With a light step, you will rise early and, concealed in darkness, make preparations. If your eyes are betraying any selfish desire to sleep, the exercise is working."

Now, as I lay still in the dark, I imagined what tasks a day in the world's past, my future, would demand. The first day of training had presented a certain energy of anticipation as he demonstrated how to dig the massive hole that would serve as our center of operations. I was mesmerized as he rendered the depression completely invisible by placing a mysterious expandable screen atop the hole. The sheet-like object gathered visual data of the surrounding ground cover and derived a convincing digital camouflage. However, despite the exciting nature of this first endeavor, the days and weeks that had followed were defined by simple repetitive exercises: exercises in sleight of hand, the mixing of ointments, and reconnaissance to identify key village members from a distance. The afternoons with Abby provided no reprieve from the endless days. Instead, my body was laid fallow, unmoving as the blinding light placed thousands of hours of language and culture into my subconscious.

Today was to be different. According to the schedule, of which Sterling constantly reminded me, today would begin the practical exercise of my lessons. I was unsure what this meant, but the minor disruption in routine at least provided motivation to pry myself from beneath the bedclothes. I slowly stood and moved to the window. The rolling grounds below were still blanketed in darkness. Occasionally, a flicker of light gave away the position of some patrolling mercenary. It was a dissonance that had been slow to quiet. Finally provided freedom from the physical sanctions of wanting but newly shackled with boundaries of opulence.

I forced myself to turn away from the window, condensation and anger welling as I had studied my surroundings. I turned to the closet door and reached to grasp the rough cotton gown stowed daily in my absence. The garment was heavy and bore no marks of the modern age. No crafted buttons. No hemmed boundaries. Instead, the weave was course and loose, each fiber extending slightly beyond any hint of a defined boundary. Despite its out-of-place appearance, Sterling insisted I perform all training in accurate attire. "You must move as one of them. Kneel as one of them. Have the intuitive mechanics to avoid catching the garment on your surroundings. Details will define."

This sentiment had become an irritating credo of the old man. "Details will define. Details will define." Its ramifications were countless. My feet were housed not in comfortable tennis shoes of the modern era but in roughhewn leather thongs. I strode down the hall to meet in the study, the estate's ever-beating heart. Sterling was already seated, poring over some aged documents. He did not acknowledge my arrival; such a nicety was long ago wisped into the many days of routine. I strode past his hunched frame to address the daily breakfast array. After plucking a banana and some cereal, I sat to eat, the sound of Sterling's pages providing the backdrop to my meal. After a few minutes, he placed the weathered pages on a nearby table and finally turned to me.

"Ready?" he exclaimed as simply as a father might to a waiting child. I looked up from my breakfast and nodded in the affirmative. In truth, I could still feel the morsels settling within, but I had learned not to mention such trivialities.

He turned and strode from the room, cane leading him, him leading me. We traversed the never-ending halls, which I now knew gave access to room after room of preparations. Left, right, right . . . In the previous weeks, we had primarily occupied a stark-white lab filled with ointments and vials, concoctions we had practiced administering until my hands and wrists were tired from the careful timing to conceal their introduction. But now, as we passed our typical exit, I realized we were to enter a new space. Sterling stopped at another door, identical in every facet to the previous one but undoubtedly housing some new circumstance. He carefully pressured the knob and drew the face slowly inward to reveal our latest training ground.

As I stepped into the opening, the scale was disorienting. The walls rose far beyond the typical height and were coated in rigid white plastic. The floor plane extended forward from our position but disappeared some fifty feet later. In place of the hardened surface, there churned fluid waves. A small sea frothed and foamed as peaks rapidly formed and dissipated in quick succession. Before I could express surprise at the unusual indoor circumstance, Sterling strode toward the heaving mass. His ambulation was purposeful as one leg extended beyond another, finally arriving directly at the precipice of the pool. To my surprise, his cane suddenly dropped from his grasp, loudly contacting the floor. Mesmerized by the strange occurrence, I found myself walking forward to offer aid, apparently having developed some misplaced sentiment for the old man. However, as I approached, he stepped away, out over the ever-moving surface. The sight was arresting. I stared incredulously as the foot contacted the water below, but as sequential instances of movement collected to form palpable effect, belief was suspended. His downward momentum was halted, and as he raised the other leg to stride forward, the result was undeniable. Sterling was walking on water.

I stared hard at the interface between fluid and solid, between wave and sole, looking for some obvious illusion. There were no perceivable oddities. The water was clear, allowing an uninhibited view of the depth below. There was no platform. No deformities or out-of-place effects. And again, conventional circumstances were found above: no cables or cords. No harnesses or booms. Only a man, barely able to walk on dry land, standing atop the waves.

"Well. What do you think, Amir? Do you find it convincing, compelling? Is it clear why we, in some long-forgotten initiation of the time loop, included this charade in our repertoire?" Sterling inquired, now having pivoted on the surface to face me from his impossible perch. "I have to admit, though it is perhaps the most overt of gestures, it has a certain potency," he turned in place and paced across the mild tumbling. "As you shall see, the actor must keep a sense of reality because this sensation does make one *feel* like a God."

I grasped for words, not eager to admit that Sterling had again managed to invoke awe. I was unable to muster a retort worthy of uttering. Instead, I decided to stow my obvious amazement and get on with the business at hand. "How are you doing it?" I flatly asked, not taking my eyes off Sterling for fear that he might suddenly descend below the surface. He commanded his feet back to solid ground, finally stationing himself above his obsolete cane.

"To walk on water," he pronounced, "was thought to be beyond the limits of man. And in fact, it is. I am sorry to say, Amir," he paused to gingerly bend to reclaim his ambulatory aid, "you will need to become more than a man."

He suddenly turned toward a door yet unexplored on the far wall. I followed, anxious at Sterling's cryptic words. The space revealed was intimate in scale, housing only a large, reclined chair of sorts. Its frame was tightly upholstered in supple leather, and several metallic knobs protruded from its different facets. Despite the warm hue of hide, the overall form was so human, so molded, it was ominously surgical. The walls hung bare with few exceptions, basked in bright light emanating from a series of orbital lights, seemingly trained on our position.

"Amir, I must now admit that there are a couple of," he paused, considering his next word carefully, "improvements that must be made to accommodate our endeavor."

"Improvements like your so-called culture lessons!?" I exclaimed, now starting to sweat at the thought of more manipulation, exercises cloaked in purpose but clad in pain. Sterling stared hard at me, only further revealing a driven, aged lunatic.

"Yes, Amir. I will not mislead you, as I believe we are past that now. You will undergo pain. You must." He turned to face a simple illuminated box hanging on the white wall. "This is a subdermal image of my upper body. Do you notice anything odd?" I barely heard his last words, as my mind had stalled at the overt admission of upcoming torture. If at war in some long-forgotten outpost, I would not be legally subjected to such treatment, but here in the luxurious trappings of the old man, there was no such reprieve.

Upon stepping forward to examine the document, I panned my eyes back and forth from low to high, searching for some oddity in the white of Sterling's skeleton.

"The shoulders. These tiny features in the tops of your shoulders!" I exclaimed, now examining Sterling's real shoulders to see if I could spot the small vertical nodes.

"Precisely! Those two darkened masses are magnets, Amir. Each only one-quarter inch in diameter, they are easily anchored into the structural mass of the scapula." He pointed to the tops of his own bones. "These small but extremely powerful posts enable me to invisibly link to a silent companion." He looked up just in time to reveal a sudden blurring of the air above. As I watched, some twenty feet in the air, a small, suspended aircraft materialized in the sky above. "It is equipped with the same environmental mimicry as the basecamp screen, utilizing panoramic cameras and pixelated surfaces to create invisibility." I stared at the newly realized companion in disbelief. "But the most important part of this hovering apparatus is the linked magnetic cores. These are essentially three-dimensional tethers. Once locked into quantum memory with those imbedded in my skeleton, the two points are bound in constant relationship until released." Perhaps seeing that I was still confused, Sterling somehow beckoned the silent drone closer to his position. "For instance, using my neural insert, I was able to call the drone closer. And once I initiate the quantum lock," he paused for an almost inaudible click, "my position in relation to the drone's cannot change."

With this, the drone suddenly started to rise, effortlessly taking Sterling along for the ride.

"So what am I doing today? Learning to fix that thing?" I grumbled toward the now-floating figure.

"You will eventually, but today, we must insert the magnetic poles into your skeletal structure. This will, unfortunately, be painful, but using a small-bore insertion bit will leave no lasting effects."

I looked back and forth from Sterling, hovering a couple of feet from the ground, and the surgical chair, which was now obviously intended to restrain me during this procedure. "Will I be awake?" I shouted, angry that I was simply being informed of the required operation as if it was some business seminar or mandatory inconvenience.

"No, of course not. You will be anesthetized for quite some time to accommodate not just this but two other components as well."

"What!?" I exclaimed, now practically crying at the utter lack of sovereignty over my own condition.

"I am afraid so. We will also be inserting a neural insert, allowing telepathic communication with all necessary technologies, as well as a membranous insert into your sputum. The latter will attempt to deter the propagation of germs native to ancient times. Your body will have no developed immunity to these microorganisms, and considering the intimate nature of the recorded ministry, you would be highly susceptible to deadly infection. To combat this, we will insert a membranous boundary tuned only to allow healthy bacteria growth. Since the sputum is the first step in many disease processes, this membrane has been proven to significantly reduce risk of infection."

As he finished his explanation, the drone silently lowered his frail figure until feet contacted ground. Another small click apparently noted disconnection with the overhead workhorse, and Sterling strode forward to the surgery station, now aided only by the rudimentary cane. His wrinkled fingers emerged from folded stow to manipulate a series of knobs and adjustments. He spent some time preparing the suite, satisfied with our discussion of the interventions, despite providing little assurances of risk or detail. As the controls clicked and rotated, I withdrew from the disturbing reality of having been reduced to something akin to a lab rat.

Actually, my own thoughts provided little reprieve. The personal memories and endowed patterns had been muddled by the months of forced additions. Now, as I entered this most sacred realm of self, my familiar conversation was continuously interrupted. My guttural fury at Sterling's forced surgeries was immediately diluted with ancient traditions of selflessness and silence. I struggled with the dissonance between contemporary experience and ancient code. I couldn't help but consider the sense of duty felt by King David. The courage displayed by Rahab. Most confusing was the interruption of the Christ story itself. Sterling had proven the fabrication, the trickery performed. But now, as I was reduced to contemplation, he showed up. The accounts, the parables, they all weighed upon my judgment. The Christian story had been imprinted as a tool but had inescapably manifested, even if minutely, as a faith. At times, I even found myself whispering hushed appeals to the nameless "Father," a communication I knew to be one-sided, of benefit only due to the verbalization of some previously undescribed emotion. Now, as Sterling prepared to hijack my body yet again, I felt like just a shell. Whereas I used to be a vessel seamlessly bound to the experiences which formed, I had been shucked, innards replaced with those of another. Confused at what had become of my mental refuge, I returned to the scene at hand.

"It's time." Sterling extended a shaky arm to the prepared seat.

I stepped one foot after the other as my lips involuntarily whispered, "Father, please watch over me in this trial." The end of each word was truncated, begun with vigor, and ended in disbelief. However divided, I did walk. I strode to the seat and faced my shaky, aged surgeon, supposedly so concerned with the faceless as to ignore the very man before him. Canvas straps dug at the skin on my arms. Stirrups gathered and immobilized my feet. I was finally as constrained as I had felt for months. Sterling then crept back into view from some position to my rear. He moved slowly, carefully cradling some vial of fluid. He stopped to face me and extended the clear fluid to my lips.

"Drink this, Amir. Do this to go to sleep."

I sipped on the glass rim, its gentle bevel giving way to the small flow. I pinched my lips to keep any more prayers from spilling forth as I descended into obscurity.

———————

I awoke violently. My arms fought their bounds, and each leg attempted release. "Aghhh!" I cried out, finding no suitable word in English or Aramaic.

"Amir! Amir! It's okay! Relax your arms. That's it, relax. You are here with me, Amir. A violent adjustment period is not uncommon for young men."

Sterling stood at a distance, apparently trying to avoid the striking distance of my shaking head. My eyes squinted hard to draw the scene into focus. However, as the image finally found clarity, the pain also became known. The tops of my shoulders were on fire, angered to the point of failure. I swiveled my head to the limit of each direction, trying to pinpoint the epicenter of pain. Try as I might, the region was located just out of my field of vision, able to be perceived and mapped only via the intense pain. But as I closed my eyes, overcome by the intensity, other discomforts yelled in the darkness. My throat was gummy. The sensation was suffocating, as if the typical round, cross hollow had collapsed and fused. Left in its wake a gummy, closed amalgam.

Even more concerning was the addition of yet another voice within my consciousness. Every thought seemed to be accompanied by an unspoken binary option. The sensation was too undefined to be articulated, but I could feel some sort of sieve through which thought was streamed. I couldn't quite discern what I was to think or do to engage this presence, but it was undeniably there.

"You are probably already feeling the neural link, Amir. Don't worry; you won't even notice it in a couple of hours. Simply put, it is a means to effortlessly communicate with the other actors in our play. For instance, beckoning the drone to walk on water can be achieved with a simple thought. The only requirement is framing the thought in a certain format. Begin any communication intended for a machine with the word 'command.' This will access the localized network emanating from camp. You will then contemplate the desired effect in clear and concise terms. For instance, if I was calling the drone to my position, I might think, *Command. Move concealed drone to my position and link magnetic tethers.* That's it, Amir. No remotes to hide in your tunic that might give you away. No voice commands that would seem out of place. We will practice these commands in the coming weeks, but the software is fairly intuitive and does not require trepidation."

He finished, lips curled, looking quite pleased with himself, as if I should be happy to have such an intrusive object placed in my brain. *Can he hear my thoughts?* I wondered in the very realm in question. Just for good measure, I conveyed a quick message.

Command. Drop Sterling in the water. Nothing. Sterling continued about his business. No drone sprang forth to take the old man away. It didn't seem that Sterling could hear my thoughts, but it also didn't seem to work.

"Are you trying the command prompt?" Sterling turned to face me.

"You're using it. I knew it. You're using it to get in my head!"

"No, Amir. I simply predicted that you would likely be thinking some less than benevolent thoughts about me at the moment." He met my eyes for the first time in a long time. "I am sorry, Amir. As Abigail empathizes with the pain of your culture lessons, I empathize with the pain of these surgeries. The ache in your shoulders. The splitting headache. I am sorry it requires this." He broke the gaze almost as soon as he had finished as if this were all the emotion he could muster. "You won't be able to move your arms much for a couple of days. Accordingly, we will spend time practicing command prompts, and I believe Abigail will begin conversational exercises to practice using your rapidly acquired knowledge."

Sterling shakily unclasped the now useless straps to release me from my confines. I stepped forward, aching shoulders, splitting headache, and constricted throat: a tool practically broken in preparation for use. I wished I had Sterling's cane as we walked. The idea of an aid to support my tired frame seemed prudent as we traversed the endless halls. And indeed, as we entered the familiar study, my appearance was apparently as pathetic as my self-perception.

"Amir! Are you okay!?" Abigail exclaimed the second I came into view.

I staggered forward to one of the enormous chairs without responding. She approached and examined my condition. I watched her carefully through squinted eyes. Even after all these long months, I was still covertly studying both captors, trying to catalog moments of deception, honesty, and everything between.

"Father told me today was your surgical day. I remember how hard this was on Father." Her hand moved ever so slightly in my direction as if to touch my shoulder, but she halted the movement before it was apparent. "At least we will have an easier session today. We will just be talking, trying to test those language skills imparted. Honestly, we will be mostly talking for the next few weeks."

I tried to express satisfaction with the change of course from the blinding light, but as I attempted a small smile, my face contorted in pain. This time, Abigail did not restrain herself from aid. She gently cradled my arm in both hands and helped me from my seat. Equally as consuming as the pain was this long-forgotten connection with another. It had been months since Mum's last embrace. Months since Hasim tugged on my hand. Now, as Abby's hand warmed my arm, I was overcome with long-forgotten warmth.

"Abigail!" Sterling's voice suddenly cut through the atmosphere.

At the sound, her hand quickly separated from my arm, taking the momentary comfort with it. I looked to see Sterling glaring intensely at his daughter, unhappy with our interaction. I looked to her face, so close to mine as to be slightly distorted. *Please. Please stand up to him. Please help me.* Her head lowered, and as her chin gently contacted her chest in the ultimate symbol of defeat, my hope was lost.

In silent, awkward succession, Abigail led me to our latest quarters: a space much different than the stark, white room where I was typically subjected to the light. This new space was consistent with the house's general appearance. Each face was clad in rich wood, and every corner housed some gaudy trinket. In the center of the space sat only two chairs. There were perhaps five feet between the seats, and they were positioned to render each user regarding the other. Abby strode ahead to the nearest seat and cleared some cushions out in preparation for my ginger arrival. As I approached the seat, she extended a hand to help me down, apparently galvanized against Sterling's rules once out of his sight. I gladly accepted the gesture and descended into the plush seat.

"Thank you." I stared up at her.

"No," she responded in Aramaic. I stared, confused, worried that I had misunderstood her kindness. "In this room, we only speak Aramaic, Amir. Now . . . try again."

Her words clicked, initiating some sequence long ago input. I thought. The words sprang forth without reference, obviously inserted in our sessions. I focused hard, trying to access the palpable library that had claimed so much of my storage space.

"*Baseema,*" I pronounced, thinking the sentiment in English as I spoke. *Thank you.* She nodded approval at the spoken words. I paused again, trying to find the right Aramaic. "*Why do you help me?*"

"*Because I want to. Because no one can be freed from their own will, even if it is against the rules. My will compels me to care, even when my father's does not.*"

"*I am glad of your will. I am alone in my commission.*"

"Do you still call your mother? Your brother? Do you not find comfort in their voices? I envy you and them. Their love is without mission, not muddied by assignment."

"I do call them, but I am allowed to share so little. They can't know of my pain, of the sacrifice."

"Would you tell them if you could?"

I paused the rhythm of the dialogue to consider her inquiry.

"No. You're right. I couldn't sour their reward with the price. One day soon, I will be back again. In the house that I have earned, to watch my mother pray to the savior I have created. I am not sure how I will feel, but it is at least the future instead of the past." I reached and took a swig of water as she watched me. "Is your mind ever fooled by the inputs of faith? The people praying, the generations of God? Do you ever find your lips silently whispering Father?"

She smiled so slightly I thought I imagined it, and as she began her answer, her voice was so hushed I could barely hear her.

"It's, as you said, a 'trick.' Nothing more. You have a knowledge of the entire Bible. Every story of relying on the faceless God, and these stories, as any other, manifest in action. Do not worry about this effect, Amir. It is not a deficit of stupidity, for we all know the truth. The silent whisperings are a reflex conferred by a lifetime of memories."

"Do you whisper?" I asked again. She looked to the door before turning and leaning close. As her presence invaded mine, I could smell her sweet fragrance.

"Yes. But do not mention this to Father. He did not undergo these lessons, and the reflex of prayer angers him. We are creating God. Not the other way around."

Her answer was poetically heretical despite its truth. Regardless of having been authentically interested in her answer, I was now more concerned with her proximity, as I again momentarily felt the aura of human connection. I soaked in the feeling as she retreated to her formal position. The remainder of our afternoon was spent locked in correspondence. Her Aramaic was distinctly more fluid than my own robotic version, but with every answer, I felt the shackles of formality loosen, my mental storehouse brought forward and sprung from its bounds. The hours went quickly and revealed much about Abigail. She spoke of losing her mother and her unending resolve for her father's covert operation. I spoke mostly of Mum and Hasim. Describing, without much elegance, the nature of each which rendered them so potent in my heart.

The daylit hours gave way to evening moments until finally, the conversation had to end. In an estate containing a time machine, I was confident the exchange had distorted time more so than ever would be again. The day, I felt, had been so manipulated it was hardly recognizable, the morning lasting days and the afternoon lasting minutes. I had almost forgotten any physical infirmities until I tried to emerge from my afternoon perch. The pain rushed back all at once, urging a quick retirement no matter the desire to continue. Still, as we approached my nightly prison, I had the sudden urge to again do some covert observation. And so, as Abigail pivoted the door face inward, I performed the clever trick. Knowing the cadence of the operation so well, it should have been easy, but as I reached back to grab the other handle, I whimpered in pain. The considerable distress almost convinced me to stay in, but as often happens with humans, I was unreasonably compelled to action.

This time, I was bolder in each step. I didn't wait for Abigail's steps to die around the corner but instead carefully timed my own cadence to match. She followed a familiar path to eventually address a seated Sterling in the study. Without Abby's intermittent paces to conceal my own, I was forced to stop some distance around the corner. As their interaction began, I could scarcely make out the words from my position.

"How was your interpersonal linguistics training?" Sterling inquired, of course reducing the organic conversation to something sterile and planned.

"It went quite well, actually. The optical insertions have taken well. His Aramaic is still a bit rigid, but quite proficient, and . . ." Her voice suddenly died off as if she wanted to revoke the final word.

"And? What?" Sterling's condescension was evident, regardless of proximity.

"And he is quite stimulating." I leaned in closer to the wall. "I just mean he is charismatic. Well suited for the job."

"Do not get attached to him, Abigail. I know the training requires considerable investment, but we must stay focused."

"He'll be back. After the assignment, he'll be back. So it's okay for us to care for him!"

Her voice was now strained, expressing confusion. However, despite her sentiment ending in an inquiry, the silence stretched on. This was not unusual as Sterling often read during conversation, showing no concern for etiquette. Just as I was convinced they had sensed my bated breath around the corner, Sterling responded.

"Yes . . . he will be back, but he might be changed, Abigail. Affected by the strange reality. And besides, this is not our purpose. We must preserve hope. To stay focused and ensure proper training. To ensure success. Don't forget how long we have prepared, how many hours you sat with the light to learn. He is just another person, Abby. I am probably slightly to blame, considering your lack of socialization, but please trust me in this. He is just another person."

Sterling's brutal reduction scalded. Even though his insolence was always evident, I was not prepared for such an overt characterization. Or perhaps not prepared for the truth. As I heard feet shuffling, I realized I didn't have time for introspective analysis in my current position. I strained to establish a directionality to the movement. With each percussion, it was clear they weren't moving toward me but toward the outlet to their rooms. I listened to the fading sounds until I was left standing alone and aching amongst the vast halls. Distinctly lonely and wishing I had stayed in my room. However, once back in my room, it was not the cold words of Sterling that echoed in the darkness. Instead, Abigail's ardent appeals provided a hopeful resonance. A light amongst this existence that was distinctly dark.

JANUARY 29, 2087

I didn't notice the buzz as I donned my tunic. The timed sound intended to regulate my daily preparation served as an apt measure of my progression. And as the rough fabric slipped past worn callouses, I was reminded of the stories of captives, so long entangled with the lives of their captors as to embrace the new existence. I was ready. The objective, which had initially seemed a coerced manipulation, had unavoidably become a priority. Aramaic was no longer an unsolicited mental distraction, but rather a beloved library with which to express ideas foreign to the modern world. The neural link, at first providing only a splitting headache, was now a silent partner, as intuitive and potent as a long-held companion. Despite the months left of preparation, the validity of Sterling's premise was no longer uncertain. I was Jesus Christ. I had to be, as it was far more reasonable than the divine alternative.

I approached Sterling in his typical state: entrapped in the pages of some dusty manuscript. The book's mass was so outsized relative to his own as to suggest a drowning child. He scanned the pages for a while longer before heaving the manuscript to a side table. He provided only a quick glance to acknowledge my arrival, having long ago abandoned the need for superficial gestures. And indeed, my reciprocal manners now bore little reverence to conduct. I strode past his seat and examined the morning culinary offering. The beautiful smorgasbord that had initially graced the morning had been slowly replaced over the many months to simulate the likely breakfast of Christ: a single piece of bread and a piece of fruit. The bread bore little resemblance to the processed loaves of modernity. Instead, its crust was thick and practically impenetrable, giving way only upon a considerable effort to an air-entrained web. Even Sterling admitted the flavor was likely not accurate, as even with his considerable resources, he could not guarantee the validity of the starter bacteria. Still, as I tore and ripped at the mass, it played the role.

Eventually, I stood, jaw sore and feeling somewhat groggy, and followed the idly waiting Sterling to whatever preparation the day held. Lately, our exercises had zoomed out, examinations of individual components had given way to questions of large-scale coordination. And today, as we entered one of the many prepared quarters, there hung a series of rendered diagrams appearing to depict the night sky. I surged forward, eager to take in the images, if only for a moment, without Sterling's condescending narration. I had only read a few words before the dreaded voice cut in.

"You will need to measure time in a communicable way to ensure the proper delivery of goods. For instance, if you require fresh fish to be stowed to accommodate one of the mass feedings, I will need to identify the exact day and location required. Your neural link should be able to record the geospatial position. However, the day and time required have proved to be slightly more confounding. Initially, we intended to simply count the days following your insertion. However, additional research revealed that the ever-changing physical characteristics of the earth's orbit would lead to conflicting coordination using this method. Instead, it will be necessary to recognize certain celestial occurrences and patterns as a reference for time and position. This will allow you to accurately describe coordinated drops in your letters."

I considered his words in silence, finding myself imagining scrawling some requirement for provision. We had already practiced using the decay-resistant capsules to daily stow my correspondence. The device looked to be a thick tube, reinforced with heavy walls formed from some newfound material that Sterling had acquired. After each day, I placed a letter in the cylinder and pried at an attached lever to engage the considerable seal. Once full, the container, which held around fifty pages, was deposited deep into the ground using a self-boring tip. Finally, two thousand years later, Sterling would excavate the capsules and use my words to prepare and send back necessary provisions, and as I had already seen, convince my modern self of my ancient presence using messages written in my own hand. The coordination of this process was admittedly complex, and more so as I stared at the lunar diagrams.

"Honestly, Amir, this skill is not only to aid in your correspondence but your general survival. We will also study some historical accounts of events correlated to lunar occurrences. You will be able to predict certain earthquakes, governmental upheavals, and other happenings just based on the moon's patterns. Now, there are generally eight distinct lunar phases created by the earth precluding the sun's rays. The portion of the moon not visible at any moment is rendered so because the earth itself is blocking the corresponding photons from reaching the moon's surface. A new moon is . . ."

I lost focus as Sterling expounded on the celestial lesson. As is often the case with professional students, I had become astute at understanding when to listen. Sterling would gladly explain the theoretical basis of wiping one's ass, and this lecture was no different. My travel would undoubtedly require some practical knowledge of the subject but not the in-depth analysis provided. Instead, as he droned on, my mind wandered to consider the only subject worth such examination: Abigail. In the days since our first dialogue, I had learned so much about this only warm companion. She had described her father's progression from loving parent to driven director. Confided in me her dreams unrealized because of our sacrifice. I, in turn, had described every inch of our small flat, an environment once thought sad now held in deep reverence. To define the nature of our relationship was to miscarry—a life without chance. Instead, a silent pact was evident: enjoy the time given. Nothing more. Nothing less. She had given light, and I, in turn, reflected.

"Amir!" Sterling shouted harshly, "Are you listening!?"

My pupils contracted, being quickly transported back to reality.

"Yes, sorry." I glared back, realizing that Sterling was entirely across the room from his original position.

"This is a waxing gibbous. At this stage, the portion of lunar surface receiving sunlight is increasing night to night. Remember, to determine the lunar stage, you will need to have observed the previous night's moon. Accordingly, observe and note the moon's characteristics nightly. Now, let us examine some notable events in the region that have been correlated to lunar events."

The remainder of the morning was spent examining cryptic accounts of political upheaval, natural disasters, and religious dates that had been related to the moon's movement. I was to remember these correlations and utilize them to ensure safe travel strategies and interactions while staying with biblical accounts. At the beginning of my training, such a task would seem daunting. But now, having become proficient in so many previously unimaginable subjects, I was not concerned. Sterling, despite his personal deficits, had planned the lessons well. His schedule accounted not for a perpetually focused pupil but rather a realistically distracted human. Accordingly, there would be more sessions to practice the lunar exercises, more sessions to hone my understanding.

Finally, after hours of dates and history lessons, I was finished with Sterling's droll lecture and allowed to proceed to Abigail's company. We made our way swiftly to the now-worn pair of chairs. The cushion so frequently depressed as to leave stuffing protruding at certain stressed seams. As I examined my chair, I was distinctly reminded of the tattered edges of home. It was now apparent that such degradation was, in fact, a personal history of the best moments of life. If one was so inclined to remain in place, the company was likely riveting. Abigail's throne was slightly less worn but not for lack of intention. Her slight frame compressed the cushion far less, but I knew. Regardless of her inanimate record, she was equally engrossed.

"How was the morning?" she asked as I pensively allowed our eyes to meet.

"Unremarkable."

She lightly grinned, obviously enjoying the subtlety of understatement.

"Today we need to speak of . . . God." I flashed a puzzled countenance but listened. "He, despite His apparent absenteeism, is to be at the heart of nearly all interactions. He is enigmatic. Human yet void. One yet three. And He . . . is difficult to discuss. Your Aramaic has become potent, able to eloquently express your own condition, your own reality. But these realities are ego. Self-found and self-held. God is the opposite. You must be able to speak so powerfully of this faceless presence to convert. To drive to madness. To change the world."

Her words dislodged my glib stubbornness, which had persisted through the morning. Unlike remembering some arbitrary data, this task was a question of passion.

"What do you want to talk about? His form. Genesis says, 'He began without form, but was manifest in creation.' His knowledge? Proverbs says fear of Him is the beginning of wisdom."

"I want to talk about . . . how God has changed your life. When did you first encounter Him, Amir?"

I sat starkly still, unable to compose an answer before the silence grew awkward.

"The people you encounter may not know about electricity or evolution, computers, or even basic science, but they know about God. Not just the lessons about Him. They know Him. Regardless of His reality, He is real to them. When they speak of His impact, it will not be in verse but in memory. Not in lesson but in testimony. So, Amir. How has God changed your life?"

"What do you want me to do!? It's kind of hard to talk about God, after all we've done to create Him! I know the truth. God is nothing! I know the scriptures. What else do you want me to do!?" I exclaimed, slightly irritated for the first time in our conversations.

"I don't care what you do. Think of your mum and cry. Make up some sob story and imagine her in pain. Pinch yourself to cause tears. I don't care how you do it, but you must convince me because . . ."

"Because what!?"

"Because otherwise, I am afraid we will wake up in another reality! One where you failed. Some alternate course of time where Jesus was just another teacher, a moment, not a movement. A reality without hope. A reality where we never meet." Her voice wavered in finishing.

"What are you talking about!?" I practically shouted. "I've seen the letters. They were written in my own hand! I know I will succeed because I already did. Sterling showed me!"

"Well, he didn't tell you everything! Just because you know about the latest looped iteration doesn't mean the next one will be the same. If you went back and delivered a less than convincing performance, they may not believe. Jesus would cease to be an integral figure of faith, and a drastically different reality would be pursued." She was practically in tears now. "So. If you like the reality we are in, one where you, me, even your Mum and Hasim exist, you had better learn to speak of your Father convincingly." She stoically pointed above at the word 'Father', denoting a divine sense rather than a biological one.

My confidence was shattered. Like a rock climber left stranded on a face with no lifeline, I was acutely aware of the risk at hand. The challenge of traveling back in time to play the part of Jesus had seemed daunting, but I had been reassured by the most potent evidence conceivable: my own success. Not fully understanding the nature of time and reality, the letter Sterling shared, and the story of Jesus confirmed the inevitability of accomplishment. However, as I watched Abigail tearfully explain the true mechanics of reality, my confidence was replaced with fear.

"Okay. I'm sorry." I paused for a long while, searching for the perfect words. "My Father," I awkwardly glared upward, "is manifest in everything living out His will. The chirping bird, the swimming fish, and the struggling mother. Each is a piece of creation, governed and behaving only in the manner intended. And indeed, even when the creature, being of limited will as compared to His, falters, finding itself living in dissonance, He forgives. He is in them and with them. He is able to forgive because He has seen and understands each perspective as if it is His own."

Confidant that I had delivered the sort of message worthy of recording, I carefully studied the corner of her eyes where moisture continued to collect, trying to measure my success with the severity of her physical reaction.

"No," she stated, her voice still shaky. "That's not it. You have the Bible watermarked in your conscience, and it sounds like it! Don't you get it, Amir? Those quotes written in red—all the parables, all the speeches—that was just the easy stuff. Wordy and provocative, but these verses are not what they believed. They believed the passion. You don't trust in your mother's love because she says the words. Anyone can speak these syllables. You know she loves you because she cries when you hurt. Because when you look into her eyes, you can sense, in a way beyond words, empathy. These sensations are not to write about, but to experience."

She turned her head for a moment, heading off the looming tears. I sat stark still, formulating another answer to her test.

"My Father makes His presence known in the silent moments between words, the mome—"

"Too wordy! Not buying it!" Her impassioned words interrupted violently, now accompanied with weeping.

"I'm trying!" I shouted back instinctively, allowing the filter of politeness to dissolve. "It's pretty damn hard to speak of some crock god when I know the truth! What do you want me to say? Some bullshit about how He saved me when my dad died? When dad laid in bed wheezing, and none of us had food, and mom prayed and prayed, and He never came? That now, He has delivered me to the clutches of some crazy old man?" I paused to take in a much-needed breath and resolve myself to a more curated tone. "I don't have anything but words for God. Not even long-forgotten moments of a fuzzy feeling. Nothing but the lessons."

She stared for a long while, long enough that I wondered if she had decided not to speak again.

"Do you still find yourself silently mouthing prayers? I know they're just a side effect of your lessons, but it might be a place to start."

I so badly wanted to say yes, to offer some positive ending to this abysmal exercise. But, in fact, the murmurings had stopped. Over the months, as <u>I was increasingly confident faith was a hoax, I was</u> <u>relieved of even a subconscious idea of God</u>. Such communications were contingent upon a scrap of openness on some level, but now all that rose from within was blasphemy. <u>I was certain of my own deity,</u> <u>not of His. I had been trained. I was prepared to become Christ, and</u> <u>even my soul knew it.</u>

"No," I finally whispered.

She stood without turning and walked to the door. I sat without moving. The disheartening reality of our conversation had converse effects: she had bolted, compelled to movement, while I was frozen in place. Considering it was only early afternoon, I didn't fight my compulsion. Instead, I used the rare opportunity to sit in silence. I was not forced to stare into blinding light or tinker with machines. Instead, in the rare moments of solitude, I considered the current reality. Twenty-nine years old. Dead father. Separated from Mum and Hasim. Trapped in some slave-like duty. Maybe changing this reality for some alternate self wasn't so bad. Maybe I need not focus on this hiccup in training. <u>Maybe an alternate course would result in a life worth living</u>. However, as I considered my meager bank of memories, their faces forcibly rose to the top: <u>Mum, Hasim, and now Abby</u>. I loved them. Assuredly, an alternate course would create more people, but never these three. It was impossible that circumstances and inputs would align to form these people again, and as I sat now sunken deep into my plush seat, <u>I realized this entirely composed my reality</u>. Not our <u>wretched flat or my gaudy prison. Just these three people were every-</u> <u>thing, and I would do anything to preserve their existence.</u>

Night came and went, presumably punctuated by some lunar phase like the ones described by Sterling. I was unable to ascertain the exact fraction from my window's vantage, but it must have been fairly full, considering the illuminated hills below. As one often does after a traumatic family argument, I laid in bed, considering every word spoken. Regretting every word spoken. <u>I was not sure</u> what <u>Abigail was to me, but at the very least, she was all I had</u>. I counted the hours until sleep finally granted me reprieve, seemingly only minutes before the buzz sounded. However, in the morning, I awoke without reluctance. I now realized every moment of this carefully crafted regiment was imperative. Even Sterling himself was now realized to be an effective and highly driven teacher. I had no option but to embrace the program to save them from omission. Sterling was visibly surprised at my vigor, an intensity that had long ago deserted our lessons.

"How many nights, on average, is the moon shrouded in clouds each year there?" I asked, trying to prepare for any potential pitfalls.

For the first time, Sterling was slow to answer and exhibited confusion. "Truthfully, Amir, I am not sure. It's a good question, and I will find out after our session."

This exchange was indicative of the rest of the session, but soon enough, our time was over, and I was forced to transition to a space without black and white answers. As I entered our room of conversation, I could feel my skin beginning to perspire. My answers to Abigail's questions were just as crucial as Sterling's facts, and these impassioned appeals couldn't be memorized. However, as we settled into our typical seats, I looked for the first time that day to Abby's eyes, and I began to feel energy long forgotten.

"Amir, I'm sorr—"

"Stop." This time it was I who interjected. "You were right. I didn't know I could fail. I didn't know I could lose everything. Everyone." I overtly glared directly into her eyes, forgoing our typically cagey subtext. "I'll do whatever it takes. Memorize the facts and find some way to elicit the passion." She was taken aback by my newfound energy. She flicked her streaming brown hair to clear a path of vision. "The truth is, I can't talk about the Father. At least not honestly. I may have once been able to summon some semblance of spirituality, a discussion of inner beliefs bordering on authenticity. But not now, not after my father and yours. Every paternal figure I have known has proved the nonexistence of the divine. No, I have no ability to even conjure such unscripted thoughts of this being." I suddenly stopped speaking as my protective casing revolted at my next words. My voice was notably weakened when I began again, denoting a caution akin to a reluctant surveyor. "Actually, I'm afraid I can hardly speak of feeling at all. It's as if this emotional musculature has hardened and, in time, atrophied. Since Father left, I can hardly feel and definitely can't acknowledge if I do." My vocal mechanisms seized as I collected more air for the painful exercise. Every anatomic system was now becoming aware of the approaching exposure of my core.

"Amir, this still sounds bad. I'm still no—"

"Wait. I'm not finished." My interjection sounded more forceful than intended, but I continued as planned. "I can't speak of Him. But I can speak of *you*. *Him* is just a word placed as the fulcrum to any mechanism. It is assumed to be infallible, reserved to refer to a distant deity. In fact, these three letters can be redefined, reallocated to represent another." I purposefully aligned our eyes, all of which were slightly watering. "I love Him. He alone sees me. His presence keeps me from thinking at all, dulls the fear. His beauty." Abigail's cheeks flushed as slowly I continued. "His beauty is arresting, impossible to realize yet demanding attempt. I love Him. He saved me from myself. From the inescapable ruin of self-deliverance. I love Him. I can't be . . ." I paused to stop tears from descending. I was distinctly aware of these manifestations as they were so foreign. "I can't be away from Him. I know I will be separated from Him. Thrown far from His presence to serve my role, but this will be as death since . . . I love Him."

As I waited for her to speak, to revolt against my admissions and again shatter this ability to open, she did not. Instead, her eyes were larger than ever before, commanding continued engagement.

"I'm convinced," she whispered with a tone that turned my stomach. It was autonomic, an involuntary reaction to found love.

Then, in an exchange previously concerned with verbal pronouncements, her physical posture interrupted. The angle formed between seated leg and upright back was lessening. At first, the reduction was so slight as to ignore, but with each moment, the effect became undeniable. She was leaning toward me. And now my own anatomy was staging a mutiny. Against judgment and

forethought, my muscles loosened to allow long suspended movement. All at once, our formerly independent momentums converged
and stopped everything. Sterling. Jesus. The world. None of it mattered. It wasn't the right time, the right place. None of it mattered.
Suddenly, a feeling novel to my experience was consuming it all.
Burning every trace of daily life to oblivion. To stoke this fire was the
charge. To propagate more of this feeling was worth anything.

The embrace lasted moments cloaked in minutes. We finally
parted to examine, at close range, the other's reaction to the auda-
cious moment.

"I'm sorry," she whispered. "I'm so sorry, Amir. I know we can't,
but . . ."

"Why not? Why can't we? I'll be gone, yes. But I'll be back! We will
still be us. Please, Abby. Please don't take this. Don't you see? If you
care about the mission, don't take this. If you want to motivate me,
then kiss me again. If you want me to care about this reality, look at
me again. I can't do this without you. You placed the language within
me. You instilled the history in my memories. Now you have ensured
dedication beyond shallow bound."

She leaned again to convey a message, this time verbal. In the
close periphery of my breath, she spoke, "Okay." She continued to
hold her proximity as she continued, "But we must wait. There is too
much to do, too much to learn, in the few remaining days. I cannot
deny my feelings, Amir, but our day will come. First, you must secure
this future."

At the mention of delay, I was pained. Undeniably tortured by the
thought of denying myself this only connection. But she was right.
To ensure even the idea of Abigail, I was required to stow all but
the accompanying motivation. This was the only way to ensure her
preservation, and it was now imperative that nothing change, that
every small detail of her definition remain unaltered. Despite the
undeniable logic, I could not bring myself to utter an agreeance and
instead simply nodded to affirm the pact of patience. In stark contrast to the former day's dissonance, the remaining afternoon settled

into tattered cushions of routine to continue my articulations of the divine. At the summation of the session, she distinctly halted our departure to address me.

"Forty-six days. Forty-six days until you are passed through the distortion, Amir. I need to know how you feel. What lessons require review? Which words deserve repeated pronouncement? You have already trained for six hundred and eighty-four days, so forty-six is nothing. We need to evalua—" She continued on as the schedule applied weight in my chest. To this point, I had avoided the count-down, but now as anxiety fueled Abby's continued interrogation, I was infected.

"I . . . I don't know, Abby," I interrupted. "I think I know everything imparted. Besides the lessons yet to come, I can identify no hole in my training or omission in preparation. But who knows? Truthfully, I feel like a soldier. Carefully equipped according to the anticipated environment. Unfortunately, my destination is yet untouched, and I won't feel fully prepared until I stare into the mass's eyes and know we have committed the hoax and spawned belief."

She relented, as might a mother interrogating a son. With the subject of preparedness temporarily off-put, she deposited me in my room with whispered words and carefully timed glances. Films, viewed long ago in makeshift movie houses, had offered articulation of the consuming nature of love. As she walked away from the locked door, I listened. Her cadence was so familiar, I could perfectly picture her position in space.

I couldn't get her steps to stop echoing as I drifted to sleep. Perhaps a therapist would say the diminishing sounds seemed a good symbol for departure. Forty-six days. Forty-six days until I might as well be on a different planet from Abigail. Click. Click. Click. Even in my dream, the sound was becoming soft, almost too distant to hear, until finally, it did stop. And without sound or sight of Abigail, I was again left alone to dream of worries without such a beautiful form.

MARCH 12, 2087

Day after day of routine had left my awakening deliberate in nature. I would slowly allow my eyelids to part and confirm my unchanging circumstance. I would slowly pivot at the waist to sit up in bed. The movements, marked by the certainty of the day to come, carried neither enthusiasm nor anxiety but rather seemed inevitable. However, this was not the case today. This morning, as the curtains began to glow with the gentle morning sun, I bolted upright. It had arrived. The days had added one to the other and finally presented the one which I had long dreaded: departure. Today, I was to leave. To leave Mum and Hasim. To leave the dutiful gaze of Sterling. Most of all, today, I was to leave Abby.

As I emerged from my bed, I realized I was drenched in sweat. Indeed, beads of the salty fluid were still flowing down my face. I stripped my soaked garment off and replaced it with a fresh tunic. With the new garment in place, I stopped and stared at a small mirror balanced on one of Sterling's precious side tables. The brown-skinned traveler before me was not at all the boy who had been delivered here so long ago. My hair was long and roughly sheared in accordance with ancient practices. My eyes sagged from lack of rest, and my hands were thick and calloused from servicing machines. Even deeper than these superficial changes, foreign languages invaded my thoughts. As I finally pulled my eyes away from the examination, I couldn't help but feel again like an emptied vessel. Sterling said I was chosen for my characteristics. Now, after all the training, I wondered if I had any character at all.

I walked slower than usual to the parlor. In contrast to my own nervous energy, I found Sterling sitting glibly in the same chair he adopted every morning. As usual, he didn't grace me with an introduction but instead stayed engrossed in his reading. I had seen him in this position almost every day for the past two years, and the unchanging posture gave a good measure of his physical change throughout the months. Sterling was old when I had arrived at the manor, but now, as he slouched backward and reached for a nearby drink, he looked ancient. His skin was almost entirely occupied by pockets of discoloration. His hair, formerly bearing the white appearance of age, was gone altogether. Throughout the many months, I had increased as he had reduced.

Alternatively, Abigail seemed to have only grown in beauty. Her presence, which had always defined the room, enveloped the space. I couldn't take complete credit for her radiance, but her smile was truer than ever, and her eyes shown even brighter than at our first meeting. She strode immediately forward and walked beside me to the breakfast spread. To my surprise, there were a great number of morsels in addition to the typical rustic bread and fruit. I turned to Abigail, whom I expected had organized the exceptional last feast, but she gestured to Sterling. Sensing our glares, he turned toward us and cracked a smile before ruining the momentary illusion of sincerity.

"Enjoy, Amir. It seems only right. Even prisoners set to be executed get a final meal!" He chuckled as might an old, ornery uncle; only his breathy laughs seemed somehow deranged with too much truth.

I managed an uneasy smile and turned back to the table. Despite my initial excitement, as my hand hovered over one item after another, I realized I had grown accustomed to the simple ancient options. Finally, in a gesture that felt both strong and weak, I simply picked up the loaf and began to tear away the pieces. Turning so that Sterling couldn't quite see her, Abigail shot me an obviously worried glance concerning the choice. I just kept tearing at the bread. This was my reality now. Sterling had won, and part of me thought he offered the options just to finally prove it. He had taken even the idea of choice away. This was surely the purest depth of slavery, to control a man so thoroughly as to not require the cold steel of shackles. Regardless of how he had done it, the bread tasted good. It tasted . . . comfortable.

Brainwashed much?

They both watched me eat the loaf. Abigail continued to look confused, while Sterling confirmed my suspicion with a smug look of victory. After I finished the dense block, he slowly emerged from his perch. His cane had always tremored slightly as he shifted weight to the rod, but lately, it shook more violently. Nevertheless, he stood and beamed toward Abby and me as if to finally acknowledge the momentous occasion.

"Well, Amir? This is it. Days have gathered to years, and you have become Him right before our eyes." He rocked back and forth on the shining cane. My eyes reflexively drifted to Abby as he continued, "Look at me, boy! Don't you see? We've done it. Feel the rough leather of your hands. Tread on the callouses of your soles. Listen to the new language in your head. This is it, Amir. You are the Hope, and today we send you back. Now . . . are you ready?"

As he addressed every transformation, I couldn't help but acknowledge the changes. I curled my hands. I rocked on my heels. He was right: I was ready . . . physically. And maybe even mentally. However, as Sterling waited for my response, which was little more than a formality at this point, I couldn't help but soak in the only detail which urged me to stay: the sunlit profile of Abigail standing in my periphery. I knew her very existence was perhaps linked to my departure, but I felt frozen. Instead, I simply cataloged every detail of her appearance. The silence hadn't yet been so elongated for her to notice my lingering gaze, and I relished the moment of secret appreciation. Finally, just as she started to turn, my reservations turned to resolve, and I turned back to address Sterling.

"I'm ready."

At the announcement, Sterling shakily pivoted in place and began the walk to the cavernous space of the spinning distortion. The last time we had visited the room was years ago, when Sterling first demonstrated the machine. Accordingly, I barely remembered the series of turns which led to the shimmering door. There was no need to make any last provisions or cram any last-minute lessons; the last month's intense run-through ensured this. Instead, we all

Appearances are deceiving

walked in silent sequence down the decadent halls. The rich wood accents, which had once seemed a decadent passage to another life, were now understood to be thin veneers over a cold training ground. Finally, after several turns, we approached the shimmering door. It was just as I remembered, densely woven of intensely shimmering fibers. Every motion seemed to be in slow motion, partially because they were, as Sterling caressed the boundary to open.

Every so often, I felt Abigail's soft touch at the back of my arm. In between suspicious glances from Sterling, she would deposit a well-timed morsel of warmth. They were little more than assurances of displaced affection, but they made the procession both harder and easier. I was crippled with yearning, but propelled by a mission. However, just as I was sure the opposing effects would tear me apart, we emerged into the cavernous concrete vault. To my surprise, the small cardboard boxes, which had helped convince me of the mission's validity so long ago, still adorned the floor. Having now long considered the nature of time, the scene felt like a snapshot frozen in our story. A few dozen boxes remained strewn across the floor where I had lashed out in anger. Sterling had never touched the scene again. I shouldn't have been surprised. The paused arrangement was indicative of his singular focus. Cleaning up the discarded boxes had nothing to do with our success, nothing to do with his righteous mission. We walked by the moment in time and toward another.

I could already hear the deep, resonant churning. It was a sensation akin to driving with only one window rolled down. The pulsing air felt as if it had been cut roughly and without precision. The edge was now only a few feet away, and I stepped carefully toward the boundary to take in the distortion. Just as I remembered, the void was deep and lacking the assurance of ending. Instead, the column of air gave way to a churning blur of color. Despite the lack of discernable movement, I could sense rotation. Sterling was now to our rear at the control kiosk. I vaguely remembered the process and had scarcely prepared myself when the metal platform suddenly protruded from the void's wall only a few feet to my right. Abigail was still beside me, but as we were in clear view of Sterling, her only expression was a sharp breath inward. It was Sterling's voice that rang out from behind and cut the silence.

"This is it, Amir. I'm sorry I couldn't arrange more of a sendoff." He gestured to the platform as if his announcement rendered the process harmless. I looked to the metallic platform then back to Sterling.

"Mum and Hasim. Promise. Pro—"

"Amir! Please, my boy! We've already been over this!" he snapped back.

"Well, do it again! Promise me, no matter what happens you'll take care of them!" I screamed back over the deafening whir of dissonant air. For once, he acknowledged my request and stared intensely back at me.

"Okay. Okay. Amir, I promise you they will never want again. Look around you, Amir. Do you have any idea how much all this cost? Don't worry about your family for even a moment. Cheating them out of their due wouldn't save me anything at this point. Besides," he shifted his shaking weight upon his glinting cane, "you can inspect their condition for yourself when you return!"

His response seemed sincere, if only due to the acknowledgment of his own greed. He was right—buying a house for them was chump change compared to what he had already invested in me. Like a fighter pilot, the realization of my indispensable value was suddenly empowering. He couldn't touch me now; I was too valuable. The insight coupled with the heart-pounding anticipation of departure unexpectedly manifested in one deliberate movement; I turned to Abigail and squarely planted a lingering kiss. At first, she instinctively tried to turn from the view of Sterling. However, as she, too, realized my power, she drew me close in the embrace.

"Enough!" Sterling bellowed from the kiosk.

I let the warm touch linger a few moments longer out of both love and insurrection before turning back to view Sterling's fiery gaze. He turned back to the control pad in anger and forced the platform a bit farther over the distortion. The mechanical movement was a clear pronouncement: get on and go. Having embraced Abigail and enraged Sterling, I was happy to oblige and stepped forward onto the narrow surface. The protrusion was about three feet wide. As soon as I planted myself, it started to extend out over the churning blur until I was standing squarely above the mass. I turned as I waited for my final release and stared into Abigail's streaming eyes. This was it. I took in the scene and carefully recorded every detail for use at some later, perhaps harsher, moment. Just as I wondered if we had been paused like the boxes instead of propelled backward, I felt my small floor give way. The fall was quick and afforded no time for second thoughts. Instead, I simply stared up at Abby as I descended into the blur below.

APRIL 26, 29 AD

I emerged as might a lightning bolt: springing forth from the separation of the sky itself. I may have been delivered through the cleavage of gravity, but it felt more like arms were ripped from chest, legs from torso. The passage had been instantaneous, not marked by some tunnel or light as so often described in film. Instead, the experience was that of anesthesia. The only memory was of falling deliberately toward the deafening blur and emerging writhing in pain upon some dusty ground. I lay still and let the particles settle around me. With every moment, the surrounding landscape became clearer and my own perceptions more lucid. The immediate topography was gentle, marked by neither peak nor valley. Intermittently, short patches of vegetation sprang forth. Each fleshy leaf was a deep green, apparently a darker shade than any I had seen. Perhaps this was an illusion, but as I stared, the effect was striking. As if an engine gently warming, my senses were slowly recording more facets of the foreign setting.

I inhaled deeply and held my breath to discomfort. The air itself confirmed my journey in time. The atmosphere filled heaving lungs and left no stain. The taste I was so accustomed to, now recognized as impurity, was replaced with utter clarity. And indeed, as I stared above at the glaring sun, my freedom was fully realized. Here, displaced thousands of miles and even years, I was finally subject to only my own motives. Admittedly, as I stood from my position, Abigail's words rang forth and rendered me even remotely motivated to carry out the hoax. But other than these innermost inspirations, which no man can evade for fear of diluting his very will, I was free. Free to move without sanction. Free to appreciate the foreign horizon for minutes instead of moments. Free of Sterling. The old jailer's absence was so welcome as to spawn disbelief. I turned reflexively in place to verify his nonexistence. No stooped figure. No glinting cane. I was rid of him, at least for a time.

With all physical inputs seemingly adjusted to my newfound reality, I remembered my lessons regarding the initial setup. The first step in the glorified exercise in camping was to verify my location. The intended drop site was five miles west of Nazareth. Sterling's words sprang forth in my head, thankfully a product of organic memory rather than an unwanted invasion from the neural link.

"You will need to confirm your location. The intended basecamp was selected based on records of little traffic. However, if the distortion's coordinates were off or certain presumptions of shepherd routes inaccurate, you will need to establish a suitable alternative."

To evaluate my position, I was to first wait a short time for a delivery of provision, the first in a long series over the course of the mission. Within the pod were several components, including the automated excavation tool and camouflaged covering. But of immediate need was a set of ultra-distance binoculars. These ocular scopes were capable of glassing targets at ten miles. The surrounding topography would limit this distance, but the scopes would still enable me to locate any settlements from a distance. Sterling had warned that this first capsule would arrive some thirty minutes later than my own appearance, a necessary separation within the fabric of time. Sterling was unsure of the likelihood of interaction between travelers, but any contact within the distortion between me and additional objects posed a risk yet unexplored. Accordingly, I descended to the ground to await the package's arrival. I longed to stand as I waited for the bundle but maintaining such an erect profile risked unintended discovery. Instead, as if once again restrained by some invisible enforcer, I lay flat in the dust and scanned the horizon for any disturbances.

After what seemed an eternity confined to the uncomfortable pose, the air around me shifted. The atmospheric particles shimmered and loosened until, suddenly, the anodized pod sprang forth. I had never seen the distortion operate from this receiving vantage and was temporarily mesmerized. Finally, as the oblong container rolled unpredictably across the uneven ground, I gently ceased the movement with my foot. It took considerable effort to crack the vessel's seal, but eventually, the contents lay bare, all accounted for. I quickly scooped up the formed black binoculars and began to scan the horizon from my still-prone position. Nothing. Every direction yielded no visual feedback other than the obtuse, angular faces of ground cover. Considering the lack of discovery, protocol dictated I move gradually toward the presumed village until I was able to verify the town's position. As my eyes began to ache from the exhausting exercise, I thought of the lessons occupying my past but in fact in the future. I had questioned the redundant exercise. It had seemed overly careful and a painstaking imposition. Now, as I was faced with the real thought of happening upon some ancient native, the implementation felt prudent. As was undoubtedly the case with some practiced soldier, the actualization of preparation infused the all-important ingredient of adrenaline. The hormone was undeniable as I became distinctly aware of every bird traversing the sky above and every insect below. Finally, after two deliberate approaches without visual confirmation, I was greeted with the familiar outline of a man. I stopped as might a trained hunter, carefully constraining any audible exhale. The figure was ranged at six kilometers away, obviously out of ear's range, but the act of stealth was reflexive.

I cranked on the aperture to bring the walking figure to full size. Ragged robe trailed bent knee. He was short, even compared to my own short stature, but adorned with a ragged beard. As the man strode across the field of vision, additional movement beyond confirmed a community. Now several men and women traversed the landscape, their paths connecting a series of structures that extended beyond. At approximately eight kilometers west of the camp, the town was exactly as intended, and I was free to travel back and establish the concealed base. Before initiating the return trip, my vision stalled on the distant settlement as my reality stabilized. In an existential examination, the likes of which Sterling had often warned against, I realized it was true. Verses from Proverbs invaded my thoughts, reminding me that no man's experience should be applauded as ground-breaking. Instead, man only perceives his own actions as innovative, in truth another vestige of hubris. Shrugging off the consideration, I continued to pridefully marvel at my own pioneering accomplishment. First person to go back. Or forth, for that matter. I was at the center of the most important production in history, and the gravity of this role was finally evident. After a while longer of considering my own magnitude, I inched back toward the camp and began the process of excavation.

The tiny churning mechanism made quick work of the soil below. As the void was extruded farther and farther without malfunction, I mused at the eternal irony of preparation. I had trained so many hours in case this machine encountered unexpected issues, but now as its movement slowed to completion, it was clear the lessons were in vain. If I had no knowledge of repairs, the contraption would undoubtedly be laid up with some infirmity. I examined the excavation result. The depression was just as it was in training: about twenty feet across and eight feet deep. The edges bore an intermittent undulation, a tell-tale sign of repeated correction. With the hole complete, I turned my attention to launching a drone overhead to gather the aerial image for projection.

Command. Drone, elevate in place and record an aerial photograph at fifteen feet in elevation, I thought, imagining the sentence in a diction much different than my own, one much older and forceful. As commanded, a shimmering mass ascended above my head to record the image. The drone was typically concealed and only visible to the trained eye. I had become accustomed to the shimmering mirage and could now just make out the aerial silhouette lost in the blue above. As the drone gently descended, I began to unfold the rigid screen to fit atop my depressed station. The material had odd physical properties and could be unruly. Its tendencies were just rigid enough to resist most deflections but not so predictable as to simplify the process. Instead, the scene likely looked like an old man applying a fitted sheet. The interaction lacked grace and bordered on battle. Finally, after many manipulations, the screen lay flat and strong across the opening's breadth. I gingerly stepped upon the surface to verify strength. There was the slightest of deflections, but the degree of movement was consistent with training. Finally, as I had begun to wonder if I lacked some much-needed command prompt, the screen suddenly illuminated to form a seamless, natural blanket of sparse vegetation and sandy soil. Even I was unable to identify the boundary between reality and effect.

I withdrew a few steps to gain a complete perspective of the established basecamp. I was to spend the next two weeks gathering reconnaissance regarding the town's general characters and locate Mary and Joseph. To do so, I would daily observe Nazareth with the scopes. In addition to extreme range, the bound scopes were equipped with programs to read the movement of lips and audibly retort the Aramaic expressions. By slowly identifying interconnected social webs, I would eventually locate Mary and Joseph and research any close relations. However, now as vibrant blue gave way to darkened dusk, I retreated to the massive hole for sleep. As I descended upon a thin cot within my sanctuary, I longed to call Mum. For the first time, I missed Sterling's manor. However censored the calls had been, the signals had managed to transmit the essential soul of Mum. The inflections of each syllable were so distinctly her as to transplant me to the tattered riches of our flat. But now, as I drifted to sleep without any reminder of her voice, the distance between us was paining.

Intermittent sleep constructed the hours of night. As my back lay starkly still, slightly deflecting the canvas cot beneath, my mind reeled with thoughts of gravity. Not the physical force whose manipulation had delivered me to this era, but rather its aptly named metaphor denoting emotional weight. The task at hand, which I had so often minimized in scale, was now here and felt bigger than me. As was often the case with sleep, the moments intended for reprieve had replaced egotistical musings of grandeur with admissions of inner fear. Indeed, moments between slumber only articulated the foreignness of my setting. The camouflaged screen atop my bed offered an unrestricted view of the night sky above, and with no other source of light pollution, the stars shown bright as fire above. The numerical mass above was unlike any visual experience available in the urbanized future. My eyes darted from one speck to another, intensely trying to distinguish one formation from the other. The moon anchored the composition. The white round was truncated but only just: a gibbous, either waning or waxing. I finally descended to sleep with peculiar thoughts bordering on dreams, their strangeness unencumbered by the mental faculties of day. The moon, I recall musing groggily, was perhaps my most constant companion. Indeed, he was the only face present throughout the altered sequence of my story, observing both my window in Sterling's manor and my dirt dwelling of now. We fell asleep together, likely to wake apart.

I broke the impotent spell of sleep slightly before daybreak. The timing of my awakening was automatic, as I could hear the wretched bell droning despite its absence. The sky was a welcome reward to the engrained schedule. I lay still and watched as dark mass divided into blue and orange sinew in the growing light of morning. As the colors battled for domain over the coming hours, I ate some condensed sustenance sent in the first capsule. The tasteless mash was devoid of flavor, kept as simple as possible to conserve energy in the process of travel. I collected the day's provisions, binoculars, quill, and pages: a rudimentary set of tools to track and record the village's characters. As my legs finally extended to stand, I looked once more at the colors above. As each strand curled in tight exchange, I was reminded of the locks of Abigail's hair. In her absence, my light was off. The rays that had been perpetually filtered through her amber locks were now laid bare. The illumination of my new surrounding was bright and honest, lacking the intoxicating presence of love. In pursuit of only this, I stepped to the ground ahead.

The land between camp and recon point one was simple. The general form was defined by angular faces whose interactions were seldom extreme. Instead, one melded into another with a sneaky ridge and hidden valley. Vegetation scattered amongst the rocky terrain, its presentation neither invasive nor scarce. The height of each sprig was appropriate for the semi-arid environment and suggested scarcity of provision. I plodded, happy to examine the trace of every step and suck in the ancient air. Within minutes, I was back within range of Nazareth and prepared to sit as might an officer on a stakeout. During lessons, Sterling had devised a method to locate Mary and Joseph amongst the town residents. With a population of only a couple hundred, some initial observation of every member was necessary, with an intense focus on any connection to the divine couple. Accordingly, the procedure was simple: use the binoculars to observe dialogue. As long as I was positioned to see at least one participant's lip patterns, the device could actively report the words at hand. The scopes were equipped with recording and playback capability to provide for later study. As I encountered different individuals, the catalog would grow, eventually to overtake the few inhabitants of particular focus. The exercise would likely take weeks, and I was only to emerge once I was confident I could seamlessly operate in the small community as if I had been born and raised.

I gently rolled the scope's focus wheel and fidgeted to find a comfortable position. The view of the settlement below presented a few figures in a rigid morning routine. Three men traversed the dusty streetscape and halted as their paths converged, each apparently happy to stop and talk. I zoomed ever so slightly and carefully centered the rightmost man's mouth.

"Elam! Did you hear any wolves last night? I am going to move the flock because Heba says they were howling as the sun goes." The man extended an arm to point westward and visibly grimaced. "They've taken so many this season, and I can't afford another."

"I didn't hear any, but I also didn't hear the baby crying, or at least I pretended I didn't till she went to it," his cohort exclaimed in my first observed Aramaic humor. "So I guess I don't hear much at night."

Even through my remote vantage, the humor wasn't lost. The tempo of conversation was unlike the rhythm of the future. Each man spoke slowly, so leisurely, in fact, it seemed neither would be concerned if the exchange lasted all day. More differences became evident as the group continued swapping scuttlebutt. Judging from their general muscle tone, all the men appeared to be in their forties. However, the skin plastered over their strong frames indicated an alternate age. Their outer layers looked as if they had been stripped from bones and tortured. The dermal layer was so worn and creased as to suggest a much older man. Despite their youthful spirit, these characters were likely well past middle age.

Their garments had rough edges that trailed behind, very similar to my own—a victory for Sterling's research. The conversation meandered from one man's opinions regarding the town's leadership to the intestinal rituals of another's sheep. I carefully documented the men's names, occupations, and origins from within town. To record the location of each man's dwelling, I instructed the drone to fly high overhead, far above any means of sight, and take a photo of the entire village. I then sketched a simple version of the image on one page of my collection. Each residence was assigned a number to be referenced in documentation. As I drew a rudimentary version of the aerial image, with a considerable lack of talent, I was reminded of Sterling's words.

"It doesn't have to be pretty, Amir, as long as you can use it effectively. If perfection were necessary, we would simply print the image, but any unnecessary futuristic documents are more potential liabilities that can easily be blown away or haphazardly discovered. No, it is better to use simple techniques in case of discovery."

Day: 002
Time: 7:43
Name: Elam
Dwelling Number: 34
Sex: Male

Age: 40–50
Occupation: Shepard
Conversational Notes: Expressed frustration with local leadership about failure to provide a clear calculation of dues. He also mentioned a sick sister about whom he was worried.

Day: 002
Time: 7:43
Name: Heba
Dwelling Number: 26
Sex: Male
Age: 40–50
Occupation: Manual labor (digging trenches, wells, general construction)
Conversational Notes: Appears to be poor within the economic structure. His manner is quiet and only momentarily interjected with nods and affirmations at others' points. (May be worth following further, as he may have interactions with carpentry trades.)

Day: 002
Time: 7:43
Name: Joshua
Dwelling Number: 13
Sex: Male
Age: 40–50
Occupation: Sells culinary goods
Conversational Notes: Portly and jovial. Loved to mention the trials associated with raising four children. Seems to be extremely social and is likely close to every member of the community.

The sun arched low and sweet upon the ridge as I carefully recorded note after note. As the last hint of light marked the day's end, I cradled my hand, which seemed permanently contorted from the extended notation. I had recorded the conversations of fifteen separate individuals. The conversations themselves only took a small portion of the time but tracking each lead back to their individual residences proved taxing. Some members stalled for extended times at work or meandered the town's boundary in search of certain companions, only to return to their dwelling after several chores. I clutched my pages gingerly in my contorted hand. As I traversed the borderlands to basecamp, I considered the newfound characters within our elaborate charade: a baker, a builder, even a thief. To observe these lives from so removed a vantage point reminded me of my days of theft. Carefully and efficiently reducing a person's core character based only on a few samples.

As I approached camp, I scanned the ground for the fabricated vegetation. However, my pulse quickened as I discovered the first of, undoubtedly, many setbacks in Sterling's planning: the camp's camouflage was so convincing as to render it invisible to even me. After half an hour of kicking dust and pulling at weeds in an attempt to locate the hole, I finally made contact with the smooth, manufactured surface of the projected cover. Despite success, I was shaken. For the first time, I felt the adrenaline-pumped risk of failure. As Sterling had so aptly pointed out, the extreme separation from any support rendered me potentially ruined. Potentially stranded. Potentially dead.

The next morning, I did not leave camp at daybreak. Instead, I let the rays bask my camp in morning clarity and studied every surrounding detail that could be recorded. Perhaps the previous evening's confusion was the inevitable failure of one so unpracticed at wilderness survival as to lose his own camp, but I was now determined to study every crease of the immediate plot. Arid cracks extended in unique fractal patterns normally unnoticed. But now, as I grasped for any identifying structures, these terrestrial fingerprints were invaluable. Finally, I happened upon a nearby boulder, slightly longer than a forearm and angular in form. I heaved the stone within feet of the opening of my dwelling and at last felt confident in the library of landmarks.

Away from camp, the hours quickly settled into a lonely routine. I wrote and wrote of each member of the settlement. Some individuals constantly appeared, apparently eager to be rid of their daily chores. Others were seldom seen, quickly scurrying from one structure to another with little to no interactions along the way. These ghosts made the effort considerably harder and became high-value targets. I carefully traversed the town's boundary to attain the proper vantage point for all manner of interactions. On day three of observation, I had located neither Mary nor Joseph and found myself rapidly exhausted with the tactic. The sun, which had initially seemed beautifully naked as compared to modernity, was now realized to be a dangerous fireball. Its unstoppable slivers constantly bombarded my backside as I lay prone. The dust invaded every crevice of my form and caked my very anatomy. The true nature of this era was rapidly becoming known. The land was yet to be raped. The air yet to be soured. But comfort there was not. I no longer marveled at the natives' wrinkled, dirty appearance, for it was inevitable. Just as Sterling had intended, I was quickly becoming one of them.

Finally, on day five, I heard mention of Joseph. A squat, portly man pronounced the name in reference to some grievance regarding a carpentry bill. He bellowed at a companion with passion as he described the conflict.

"He charged that for just a table! Just a minor table. Joseph and Mary are probably eating well tonight with those prices!" He kicked the dirt in an exaggerated finish.

I had already followed the man for quite some time and knew this complaint was not unique. In the past hour alone, he had proclaimed the same complaint about three other proprietors. However, as I honed my vision upon his ever-moving mouth, any consideration of the statement's validity was quickly forgotten.

"In fact, when he delivers the piece tomorrow, I am going to refuse to pay. I will determine what is fair, considering his meager effort."

This was it: my ticket to exit the sunbathed hell of surveillance. For the next two hours, I tracked the man with such intensity that my eyes often burned from lack of blinking. Occasionally, as he slipped from alley to intersection, his rotund profile was momentarily precluded from vision. During these moments of terror, I scanned every perceivable outlet within the urban fabric, scared he had found some obscure means by which to slip away. However, every time I was convinced he was gone, along with my chances of graduation, his protruding belly would silently emerge and give away his position. Through a series of conversations along his travels, it became clear the man was an importer of sorts. He notified persons throughout Nazareth of when their goods might be arriving from surrounding centers. Finally, when his meandering path came to an end, it was clear his penny-pinching mentality was fruitful.

His residence was one of the largest in town. This was not a great feat, as, overall, the dwellings were humble in nature. Most consisted of small stone settlements or piles barely recognizable as homes. However, Matai's structure was considerably more elaborate. The stones had been honed and stacked with careful order. The walls were purposefully punctuated with cased fenestration. Even the trail meandering to his entry was neatly swept and appeared to be etched with hand-drawn designs. I couldn't help but scoff at his incessant complaints of price and quality, and as his profile became momentarily backlit from within, I was reminded of Albert Mustep. Indeed, I would not be surprised if the man whose watch had started this entire tale was a distant descendent of the asshole before me.

After an hour of watching the man traverse his estate, the sun gave signal of the day's end. I took one last look through the scopes, one last attempt to convince myself the positive development was more than a dream, and began the walk back to camp. This time, the natural surroundings easily gave my retreat away. The arid cracks presented an iconic pattern and led directly to the hefted stone denoting entry. After a quick dinner, I sat and scribbled my daily account to Sterling.

Today: the sun's rays were unrelenting. I sat atop a ridge and recorded eight new figures before finally happening on a mention of Joseph. According to the conversation, Joseph will deliver a table to the man tomorrow, and I have located his residence. I will spend all day tomorrow observing this location to catch sight of my soon-to-be father. I have amassed a record of forty-five townsfolk and am gaining a better understanding of town politics and structure. Actually, the community is not unlike those of the future. Each personality is quickly filling some familiar role: drunkard, gossip, old and deranged asshole (not that I have ever met one of those before . . .)

Tomorrow: I do not foresee needing additional supplies tomorrow. Despite finding mention of Joseph and Mary, I have many persons left to document prior to insertion and will only require the simplest of tools.

Yesterday: I remember a girl. Before my life was hijacked. Our words lasted so long the chairs became worn. She saved me from certain loss. In a moment of separation, we were joined. Most of all, I remember the light, ever filtered through amber strands. I have never been so aware of the power of light. Now, as I am subjected to the raw energy of the unchecked sun, it is this filtered glow I miss most. Memories of her have already sustained me in times of distress. To see her face again will be to live again.

I ended the letter and allowed the page to curl and fall to the floor below. My legs ached from the strain of the day, each toe screamed out with a personal blister, and my eyelids involuntarily closed after having been so long subjected to the bright landscape. This night, sleep was potent. The depth of my unconscious departure was so bottomless as to finally allow a total escape. Fortunately, my buried dwelling protected me from risk of a predator, passerby, or any other danger that might seek to attack my temporary vulnerability. The overnight temperature ensured comfort since I lay in an unconditioned space. Sterling had mentioned that he intended to send me back in the late spring to ensure agreeable temperatures until I was welcomed into Mary and Joseph's home. I was glad of the comfort and safety because tonight, I would have slept regardless.

I awoke early. I was still sore but somewhat refreshed after the long rest. One welcome side effect of the ancient lifestyle was more sleep. In lacking the modern convenience of electricity, I had gone to sleep relatively early. So, despite rising before sunup, I had amassed many hours of much-needed rest. As is often the case with days of importance, my stomach was knotted in anticipation. Hearing word of Joseph felt like another beginning. To this point, I had been observing characters that could exist anywhere. Although interesting, these personalities held no historical significance and would likely play peripheral roles in my performance. But Joseph. He and Mary represented the first glimpse of main actors. Interactions with these two necessitated a careful accuracy to ensure the same progression of reality. They were the first hurdle to ensuring the existence of Mum, Hasim, and Abby.

I walked, still concealed in darkness, and moved to a position to observe Matai's house. Joseph would likely not arrive for quite some time; I imagined most furniture deliveries did not occur at the crack of dawn, but I would not leave this location for fear of missing him. Knowing that this day would potentially include even less ambulation than usual, I located a large boulder missing a concave chunk on its foremost face. I wedged my hips into the gap and slightly furled my robe beneath my neck. It was the greatest comfort I had yet known during the long days. Finally, with feet set atop another convenient feature, I brought the binoculars to their eternal station.

To my surprise, the wealthy owner was already awake, scrambling to and fro amongst the many comforts. He tweaked the alignment of a vase placed at the mouth of his entry. He diligently swept the walk meandering across the front approach. As he worked, an equally portly woman emerged from within the dwelling to intermittently offer sustenance. Even in the minor interactions between husband and wife, it was clear his previously observed prickly attitude was equally applied to his family. He was a pain in every ass in town. As she offered him a crusty loaf of bread, he berated her regarding the lack of flavor.

"When did you make this!? It tastes stale. Why don't you make something that tastes good for once?! I make enough money to eat like a king, and yet you bring me this!"

His verbal abuse transitioned to physical as he punctuated the address by raising a hand. As his open hand pivoted through the air toward her cheek, I could barely constrain myself. My position was far too distant to reach her in time, and I knew I couldn't make contact yet, but the event was hard to watch. She took the resounding blow and turned her face downward in retreat.

"Go! Go make something that doesn't taste as old as you!"

She silently pivoted and walked along the freshly swept path. Despite being precluded from her husband's view, I could clearly see tears streaking with every step. I couldn't help but see my mum's face. Unlike many poor kids, I had never been subjected to such violence. My father had never raised a hand in anger and would have been disgusted by the display.

Now, as I lay in wait for Joseph's arrival, I had a newfound hobby to pass the time: imagining command prompts to punish the man for his brutal behavior. Careful not to begin the thoughts with the proper wordage, for fear that the vindictive musings would accidentally become reality, I ran through a gamut of possibilities. *Fly above and drop a boulder on his head. Fly close enough to slice at his groin. Descend and knock over his perfect statues.* The ideas became successively more elaborate and violent until I realized the man was no longer in sight. In my rambling imaginings of justice, I had lost sight of him, and it was unclear where he had gone. To get an even higher vantage point, I carefully stood atop my seat-shaped rock. Panning the site, I was still unable to locate him. Had I accidentally prefaced one of my imagined scenes with the word command? If so, the man was likely lying somewhere unconscious and emasculated. However, as I continued moving my eyes back and forth across the area, I finally spotted the familiar silhouette down the street. He was waddling back and forth while shouting commands at some companion yet to emerge from around the corner. In the moments which followed, the vertical line of visionary preclusion became the anchor of my anticipation. I stared at the corner with such intensity as to bore through the blockage. After what felt like minutes, the urban edge offered a gently swaying transport: the leading edge of a table. Following in close tow with his hands clasped firmly around the small wooden piece was a slender man in his forties: Joseph.

His hair was longer and straighter than most others I had observed. His frame was thin but not to the point of weakness. Instead, as he traversed the streetscape and gracefully heaved the table from one hip to the other, his practiced strength was evident. With every step, Matai berated him. "It's a simple piece! Who do you think you are, Joseph, Bezalel!? For the price you're charging, I should be lucky to get the Tabernacle!" Through every word, Joseph remained unphased. He stared straight ahead and never acknowledged the hateful sentiments. I felt a sudden pang of sympathy for his treatment as if I were already somehow connected to this transplanted father figure.

Sometime after entering Matai's ornate home, and likely after having received a less than deserved payment, Joseph exited the estate in the same direction from which he had approached. I scrambled to mobilize from my perch. Unsure of which direction he might turn and determined to discover the location of his home, I rushed to get ahead of him. However, as he continued his march across town, it was as if he knew he was being followed. His legs were swinging faster and faster, and every turn was taken suddenly. From my position, some four kilometers away, every minor move he made meant considerable action to preserve the viewing corridor. He turned a corner, and I hurdled over a rock and ran twenty feet. He walked between two taller structures, and I was forced to completely reroute. All the while, my eyes were still glued to the depressed apertures of the binoculars, a condition eliminating the much-needed perception of obstacles immediately surrounding me. Inevitably, I tripped and clawed my way through unexpected encounters as I tracked Joseph throughout town. It was unclear whether Joseph was walking with such purpose toward some pending deadline or was simply a naturally fast mover. Finally, just as I heaved a heavy breath of exhaustion, he slowed. He was now approaching a series of dwellings crudely compiled against the mouth of a rock face. I adjusted one final time as Joseph walked toward the farthest opening and was immediately faced with the sensation of falling. My leg had contacted something with enough force to send me flying forward amongst a series of small, angular rocks. The points and spades dug at my skin as I was forced to lower the binoculars to address my immediate condition. However, as the scopes separated from my face and finally allowed a glimpse of my surroundings, the rocks were the least of my concerns. Standing before me, eyes widened and staff drawn, was a shepherd.

MAY 3, 29 AD

One of the man's measly flock was shrieking and writhing on the ground between us. With the sheep's bleating, the angry shepherd, and the rock poking me in the ass, it took a moment to deduce what had happened. But as I slowly stood from the uncomfortable ground, I realized the object that I had impacted was the sheep. The creature slowly regained its footing and clung to its human caretaker. My eyes slowly traversed the length of the staff, which was thrust so close to my face as to cross my eyes. Unfortunately, the figure holding the crooked instrument was not of the old and wise variety often recorded in the Bible. Instead, before me stood the tallest Nazarene yet observed. Dark, shaggy hair rested upon broad shoulders, practically bursting from his primitive wrappings. He alternated between nearly growling at my face and peering down intermittently at my clutched binoculars. This couldn't be it. This couldn't be the end of everyone I loved. I scrambled to think of an Aramaic statement to remedy the situation.

"Please forgive my accident. I am sorry for any impact on your animal. Please allow me to go home for funds to compensate you for any damage," I gently requested in my first Aramaic uttering in the ancient world. Somehow, I had imagined my first words would be under better circumstances. After a long pause, the man, without lowering his staff, retorted in a forceful tone.

"Who are you? I've walked these hills my whole life, and I have surely never seen you." He paused and momentarily glared again at the binoculars. "And . . . what is that? Is that an idol?"

I digested his inquiries and searched for any answers to appease his appetite for truth. Sweat was now visibly dripping from my face, and my legs were slightly shaking. These physical manifestations were surely not helping the believability of my case. I searched for a name to provide. I couldn't say Jesus. Not before any of the memory insertions. Finally, as the silence began to weigh palpably, I could think of only one culturally appropriate name.

"I am Amir. I am a traveler by way of Sephorris. I deal in strange goods from faraway lands. These are an import from the far east." Initially his body language seemed to relax, but as he again spoke in a deep gravelly voice, my hopes evaporated.

"Amir. Hmm. I think you should come with me to town. The elders will want to meet you and discuss these details." He slightly gestured with the staff back toward Nazareth.

No, *no, no!* I silently imploded as he herded me like another member of the flock. For the first time in months, I reflexively turned to the sky and silently appealed to the Lord above. Having my confident control stripped away gave room again for such ridiculous musings. As is always the case with prayer, it mattered not. Without another immediate option, I trudged along in front of the hulking figure and raged against the reality. With every step across the arid terrain, a face appeared to me. Mum. Hasim. Abby. Mum. Hasim. Abby. None of the three would likely ever exist thanks to my screw-up. Mum. Hasim. Abby. The three apparitions continued to assault my consciousness the entire journey to town. All told, the walk took the better portion of an hour as my new master shouted directions to streamline our route. His instructions were so detailed, likely due to a lifetime of operation, as to lead me around particular stones and dusty patches. It felt as if the man were so used to protecting precious life, he couldn't help but ensure my safety regardless of any perceived threat. Finally, after many commands, we emerged at the boundary of Nazareth.

"To the left. Down that main road. There we will find the elders," he directed from my rear.

I turned as instructed and plod toward whatever aged council was to decide my fate. Tears began to well and collect on the quivering shelf of my cheeks. Mum. Hasim. Abby. We had worked for years to ensure my specific brand of future, and now it was undoubtedly ruined. As we traversed a few last turns, onlookers emerged to watch the unusual procession. I let my head fall, as I was not eager to saddle the disdain of others in addition to myself.

"Sit there. I will call to them." He pointed to a stone bench outside of several nearby dwellings. "Habar! Yasim! I have a stranger! He was in the hills."

As I awaited the emergence of these ultimate judges, I looked down at my hands that still clutched the binoculars and some sheets of notes. We had not practiced getting caught during training, and I now realized it would have been wise to throw these objects from my person during our long walk. Now, as several ancient figures emerged, it was too late to ditch the contraband. I raised my head to see three men who looked to be at least one hundred but were probably only fifty, stride slowly toward my seated position. The foremost elder addressed my captor as he strode with considerable effort.

"What is the meaning of this, Joram!? Who is this man? Why have you called us from prayer?" The man's voice was harsh and impatient. His gaze shifted from the shepherd to me as he awaited an answer.

"He says his name is Amir. He claims to come by way of Sepphoris. But he is strange, bearing strange trinkets and running amongst the stones. I believe him to be mad but wanted to bring him to you before passing judgment." Despite the extreme physical difference between the shepherd and the elder, he spoke tentatively and with respect.

At the final word of the shepherd's explanation, the leading old man stepped forward to address me directly. "Who are you? Why were you in the hills behaving like a mad man? Don't you know such things are forbidden? And what . . . is that?" He pointed to the binoculars. His tone was intensely negative.

I was not certain if I was being considered for some form of punishment, but I felt likely to be condemned based on these first words. I had no choice but to stick to my story.

"My name is Amir. I was simply traveling through your hills when I ran into the sheep. I have offered compensation for any damages and apologize for the intrusion. This is simply a rare good from the far east." I tucked the binoculars beneath my furled tunic to divert the subject of conversation. However, as another elder stepped forward, it was clear the concealment had the opposite effect.

"Give me the object which you are so keen to hide. We will judge its relative virtue." He stretched out a wrinkled hand and patiently waited for me to relinquish the evidence.

My mind was now moving rapidly, trying to imagine some alternative ending to the encounter, but as the delay began to appear as a challenge, I was forced to comply. I reluctantly unfurled the tunic surrounding the scopes and gingerly passed the object to the old man. I was now aware of many spectators. Some faces were familiar from my observations. Despite only knowing these personalities remotely, I felt an extra sense of embarrassment in their presence.

The elder snatched the molded form from my palm and began to turn them repeatedly in close examination. His quivering fingers traced the contour of the hard rubber casing. He rotated the wheel with extreme caution as if any sudden movement might cause injury. Finally, he seemingly noticed the glinting glass of the lenses themselves. In an action that proved the innate ingenuity of humans, he slowly brought the light-transmitting nodes closer and closer to his face until they were snuggly surrounding his eyes. At first, he was disoriented, looking at faces and objects in his immediate surroundings. However, as he continued to pan, he slowed on the distant peaks. I watched the exploration and tried to imagine what reaction he might have to the futuristic tool.

"This tool. Distance is no matter. I can see the distant peaks as if approaching their base." He paused his analysis to pan the horizon again, but continued speaking with the binoculars still raised. "These are the tools of a spy, undoubtedly sent to spy on us Nazarenes. You . . ." He lowered the scopes. "You are a spy. A snake in the grass, waiting to strike. What business do you have with us, snake?"

His hands were now quivering in anger at the thought of the supposed clandestine operation. I quickly considered all my cultural and historical teachings in search of some saving sentiment.

"I am no spy. No serpent sent to strike at your heel. I am simply a traveler. I have often heard of the hospitality of Nazarenes, but now I see you do not follow the scriptures. Do not forget to entertain strangers, for by so doing, some have unwittingly entertained angels. Do you not follow this teaching?"

I now lifted my head to stare directly into the man's eyes to fabricate any empathy possible. He stared back in unwavering intensity. After several moments of this direct exchange, he and his two aged cohorts suddenly turned to one another in private consultation. I could scarcely make out the rapid Aramaic whisperings, but their tones did not sound sympathetic. Their tunics intermittently curled in response to exaggerated gestures. One man pointed to the distant eastern horizon while another waved the binoculars as evidence. Throughout the entire discussion, I could feel the hot sensation of eyes, undoubtedly created by the many onlookers. The wait reminded me of my judgment for theft so long ago. In that case, I had been delivered from a harsh sentence, or so I had thought, but here I sensed no such liberation. Finally, after several minutes of discussion, the leading elder turned to face me.

"You have insulted us and used our holy texts to lie. You were discovered spying, crawling through the hills like the snake you are. Since you wish to test our devotion to the law, we shall treat you as the text prescribes dealing with a snake. As the Lord said to Moses, 'Make a snake and put it on a pole; anyone who is bitten can look at it and live.'" He purposefully caught my eyes as I had his, except he conveyed only disdain. "That snake was of sin, and so are you. You have brought potential wrath upon our settlement, and we must now act as it was written."

At the end of his profound judgment, two rugged men from within the crowd emerged, apparently his preordained merchants of force. As they surged forward to detain me, I pivoted in every direction, looking for an escape route. But as I turned, expecting a clear path of escape, I was faced with a wall of spectators. Their ranks were so tightly stacked as to allow no way out. I pushed forward in desperation, shoving at the mass as the two ancient jailers secured a firm grasp on my tunic. The force exerted from behind was immediately overpowering, and my weaker frame fell directly to the sandy ground below. As the tandem started to drag me through the clearing crowd, now happy to part, I cried out in desperation.

"I am not a spy! Please don't do this! Please have mercy as the father has mercy! Please . . ." I paused to gather a labored breath as my own tunic was pulled tight against my throat, "please! I speak the truth. I am not here to harm you! Ple—"

"Cease your hysterics. Your judgment is complete. It is required to perform this sentence as you have blasphemed and are surely deceptive. Do not speak again the name of our Lord. You will be detained tonight as preparations are made."

With this final word, the old, wrinkled trio retreated from the lively scene, apparently eager to be out of sight of my writhing form. My two escorts continued the procession and easily countered my incessant attempts at freedom. We rounded a turn, and I contorted to rip at my fatigued tunic. However, the woven fibers held fast and enabled easy control by my captors' worn hands. In a different tactic, I strained my neck to address the yet faceless men.

"Please," I spoke gently to the nearest controller. "I have a family. I am just a simple traveler. I beg for mercy."

Tears forged a path across the dust-covered contours of my face. The men were unaffected. Instead, they simply shoved harder at my back. My efforts were useless. My mind raced to consider any yet-unconsidered options. The drone initially supplied was not the larger version that could potentially lift me to safety. Instead, it was a much smaller apparatus intended only for aerial photography. With no technological companions to come to my aid, I was at a loss. Eventually, as the detainment sequence drug on, I stopped struggling in a clear manifestation of broken will.

Few observers remained as our steps finally slowed in view of a darkened depression carved into a low-lying mass of rock. Its jagged boundary cast an uneven shadow into the dim opening and rendered the orifice sinister in appearance. In my now-growing list of detainments, this was surely the most depraved. Without gracing the location with any words of explanation, I was shoved forcefully through the menacing boundary. I stumbled across the uneven rocks and turned quickly to attempt one last escape. I rushed forward to the illuminated exterior, but just as the intensity of exterior illumination suggested freedom, the environment was suddenly cast to utter darkness. Instead of springing forth into the flowing air of uncaptured scale, my outstretched hand was met with cold, solid planks: a wooden barrier placed and secured from without. I curled my fingers inward and beat on the face so hard my hand felt as if it were breaking. I was left alone. In the void of darkness. Awaiting death.

Just as with my previous detainment in modernity, I had no fellow detainees to distract me from the mental despair that took root. How could this be it? Me, sentenced to death in obscurity. The world deprived of hopeful redemption, and my three emblazoned faces erased. All of Sterling's stupid training had failed to account for the random interactions of reality. Or maybe it was all me. Too stupid. Too clumsy. Failing everyone again. Just as I had failed to provide any semblance of prosperity for Mum and Hasim, I was now failing to ensure even existence. The darkness of the cavern was so absolute as to prevent any potential of optical adjustment. I considered groping in the pitch black in search of some unconsidered means of escape, but with the jagged, rocky floor below, such an effort seemed ill-advised. Instead, I resolved to remain obscenely still. Over time, the intermittent messages of pain telling of the sharp rocks jabbing at my back were ceased. In their wake developed a radiant numbness, a distinct lack of perception. And without this sense, there were none left. No light with which to see. No movement to ensure the fresh feel of touch. No smells in the stagnant air of captivity. Only thoughts remained. Thoughts, the ethereal force of being, ascended to their rightful position of all and everything. These now-broken sentiments were me. Not my body, now realized in the dark to be only a physical carcass with no bearing on existence. My mind was all, and there was scant left unbroken within this vault.

With no perceivable reason to sustain such existential crisis, I descended into sleep, the sort of rest one might experience after a great row with a loved one. Dreams precluded reprieve as I was bombarded with reconstructions of sense. Here, Hasim's inquisitive voice forced me to hear, Mum's sunken eyes forced me to see, and Abby's gentle lips required feeling. It was impossible to escape the reality of failure. I drifted between the two states, awake and devoid of perception or asleep and bombarded with feeling, until finally, a sudden sliver of light broke the cycle. My arm reflexively rose to defend the penetrating rays as the sliver slowly enveloped the entire mouth of the cave. I could only spread my fingers enough to dimly filter the image, but it was enough to determine the time at hand: it was my jailers. Death, traditionally cloaked in darkness, had been pronounced in sudden light. It was time.

This time, I did not resist. I ignored, with newfound nihilism, the cutting rocks at my feet and surrendered myself to the hulking figures. They furled my garments into fistfuls and shoved at my back in a reverse procession of the day prior. As early settlers might flock to the hangman's noose, so too, a silent audience followed us. Their morbid obsession with defeat ensured the heavy weight of judgment. I was a great tool of measurement to their weary souls. I cared not. If I was them and they were me, I would stare too, embracing my relative position, if only for a moment, of having outperformed at least one other. Whatever turmoil might be ensnaring the day, it was at the very least preferable to my miscarriage.

Every step, and there were many, added inevitability. Hope minus hope reduced to nothing until we again stood before the council of three. Their faces were contorted in scrutiny as I was again pressed before their feet. I did not look up. In my final moments, I would not give these final and ultimate assholes the satisfaction of interaction. Even with my head lowered, the elder's short intake of air prepared me for his pronouncement.

"We are here to bring glory to the Most High. We Nazarenes serve the Father and have avoided His wrath by shunning sin. Yet, in our grass, we find you. A viper waiting with tools of hubris to bring sin to our ranks and wrath upon our people. Accordingly, you will be raised up, positioned in the sky so all can see that sin has no place here."

At his summary, I remained unmoved, sunken posture unprovoked. A rough hand impacted my cheek with a mighty slap and forced me to move.

"Speak, serpent! What do you say to these charges?"

I heaved in a desperate attempt at laughter. Yesterday, I begged. Today, I laughed. The gesture obviously worked, as his woven tunic curled tight when he pivoted away from me in anger.

"Bring forth the pole!" he proclaimed through gritted teeth.

The slow-moving trio strode to a distant seat, apparently to observe the proceedings from a distance. A portly man emerged from the crowd carrying a heavy shaft, whose bore was large enough to prevent any deflection despite its considerable length. As the tip approached my position, the sun glinted from large metallic nails protruding from the cylindrical face, my means of attachment.

Now, as my two captors again heaved me to my feet, I could no longer maintain the glib exterior. Tears surged, and guttural cries escaped without warning. Their heaving hands remained unaffected. One tore at my tunic to expose the inherently vulnerable cladding of rear. Another pressed at my neck with such might as to fold my weakened frame to a distinct ninety degrees. With my torso now parallel to the dusty ground below, I could feel the splintered face of wood shoved atop my exposed back. The rough grain intermittently caught and tore at the skin and triggered anguished cries of agony. After forcing the length past these epidural catches, a rudimentary mallet emerged from the ranks. This was it. I could still see them, however dimly. Mum. Hasim. Abby . . . Mum. Hasim. Abby . . .

"Stop!" a voice cut through the violent drive to death. "Do not lay another hand on this man."

The pronouncement impacted like thunder, a shockwave

traveling through every chest. Before the unseen outcry, there were the sounds of violence, ripping of cloth, and grunts of exertion as they heaved the timber upon me, but now, there was nothing. Every breath had stopped, and every hand held still until the voice again thundered.

"What is the meaning of this? Why have you condemned this stranger to be lifted up?"

The source of the thunderous decrees was apparently approaching as the crowds began to part from the rear. I strained my neck against the rigid backstop, trying to see the source. I could only perceive movement as the parting spectators formed a moving void amongst the crowd. Finally, the ripple erupted at the mass's boundary and presented a man. Unremarkable in appearance, he wore the same woven tunic, the same worn leather thongs, and bore the same wear of sun-drenched desert. Yet, upon his emergence, time had stopped. Only he was immune to the stall as he proceeded toward me. From behind me, the elder's now shriveled voice mounted an effort at resistance.

"He is a spy, found crawling like a serpent amongst our grass. He will bring wrath upon us and must be hung up as the Lord commanded."

His words, before so confident in righteousness, were now composed of quivering syllables. The newfound authority walked past my position without meeting my eyes. He strode to within five paces of the old man and stopped.

"How do you claim to know his heart to the point of death? What does he claim in the face of these accusations?"

I watched the man's tunic sway in the wind while he waited for an answer. I searched for some murmur amongst the crowd, some explanation of the man's identity. Despite not actually growing up in Nazareth, I knew the interaction was highly irregular. Who was this man, and why did his words command such influence? An effect not limited to the elders, but rather every soul within earshot.

"He . . . he . . . says he is a traveler. A simple traveler dealing rare goods," the elder finished and dropped his head while waiting for a response. The pace of the movement was reflexive as if he had accidentally stared at the sun for a moment.

"And why have you been so keen to dismiss his claim? Are you equipped to expose truth, be it yours or his? No. Only the Father can judge these truths. And even then, as truth is inevitably exposed to lie, He has mercy. Are you so holy to act differently, to refuse grace?"

The man slowly turned to finally match my incredulous glare. His eyes, like his general appearance, were unremarkable. Brown and clear, but not unlike my own. Yet, as he now stared back, I had the distinct feeling of being invaded, exposed, and laid bare.

"We should be apt to believe these claims. That he is indeed a traveler . . ." He distinctly paused after the word, seeming to denote a variance to the term's traditional meaning. "And is indeed here to deliver the makings of man. Nothing more. Another, not so unlike yourself, in need of grace."

I had now become so engrossed in the interaction to forget the heavy timber resting upon my bleeding back. But as he finished the pronouncement, time eased to normal operation, and I felt the ache returning. No matter the pain, my focus remained as the elder finally rallied a retort.

"Of what concern is this matter to you? This stranger is held in no esteem or even known to us. Why do you presume to upheave our will? You yourself command neither aged wisdom nor regard. Why are we to undo this ruling based on the simple words of—" his reinvigorated words stalled as he seemed reluctant to add a final insult "—the simple words of a carpenter's son?"

At the mention of this identifying relationship, I considered my minimal knowledge of the town's residents. Was there another carpenter? A woodworker other than Joseph? However, my deductions were interrupted as the elder continued.

"No, you have no word in this. It is already decided. Provisions already gathered. Your words have no authority over this matter."

Now quaking with either rage or fear, he turned to my executioners.

"Raise him up! *Raise him, as is required!*" he yelled to the hulking figures. Rough hands, whose presence had been temporarily forgotten, surged back to motion. I cried out as one held my writhing frame secure against the wooden face, and another brought back the mallet in preparation to strike. Just as the tool's momentum was set to reverse from backward to forward, my defender again interjected.

"Do not swing this instrument of death, and do not presume to question my authority! Surely, I tell you, every nail driven to this timber is another added to your coffin!" The thunder, which had been almost forgotten, again rippled through the crowd. "Do not presume to understand my authority based upon the heritages of man."

Despite the riveting happening, my body was palpably failing. Sweat rolled from my brow in waves, and I struggled to sustain the heavy load. My legs visibly shook as I fought for consciousness, determined to witness the ending to my story.

"It is not yet his time, and he must be released. This I command, in my name and that of the Father!"

Forced to divert any final morsels of energy to those organs required to listen, my legs gave way. The entire mass of the long shaft slammed atop my broken body and pressed my face to the dust below. Even through the excruciating failure, it was the quivering elder I heard as my reality turned black.

"As you command, Jesus."

MAY 4, 29 AD

My eyes slowly parted, and dust immediately assaulted my vision. I blinked off the particles and searched for further evidence that my ending had been in life rather than death. I was lying in a dusty patch of ground overlooking the scene of judgment. I pivoted in place to observe the different facets of my body. Ripped tunic where hands had pulled. Shredded skin where grain had caught. But no nails. No timber suspending my limp body for all to view. With the evidence overwhelmingly suggesting I was alive, I finally revisited the event's profound ending: Jesus. The divine character whose unlikely existence had necessitated my very presence had emerged. I remembered the first time Sterling had inquired of my feelings toward the supposed deity. "I believe He was just that," I had spoken, "a man. No more, no less." Now, as I remembered his physical presence, I realized our ignorance. No matter the arsenal provided or knowledge imparted, I could not assume this role. Shivers ran through my still-fatigued legs as I recalled His voice. God's voice. However, considering the newly understood danger of this ancient society, I opted to stow the implications of my encounter until a safer station was secured.

It was unclear how my body had been delivered to the clearing, but I had no intention of staying in the exposed post. Yet, as I strained to stand, it was not my legs that resisted but the commodity of breath itself. At the first sign of labor, my diaphragm panged out in agony. I crumpled to the ground to alleviate the sharp pain. The crushing weight of the timber must have broken the embedded workhorse. During training, Sterling had instilled some knowledge of anatomy in case of injury, but this stabbing sensation emanating from the crosshairs of rib and heart was beyond me. Left with little recourse, I sat still to control my heaving chest. Eyes closed, I sat immobilized and cursed in English. Every terrible exclamation felt like a piece of home. The comfort reminded me of the few times I had tried smoking. I dragged on the consonants like a Pall Mall until a swirl of dust kicked up from my rear. I pivoted fast, and the oxygen required practically split my chest in two. Standing silently, and listening to my string of expletives, was Jesus. As my eyes turned in their sockets to minimize the work performed by my torso, I was met with blinding light. I could know His identity from the periphery, but as is the case with the sun, His direct person was cloaked in intense light. This optical effect had not been the case before I blacked out, but I was glad to not meet His eyes. It seemed inevitable that this powerful creature, whatever His nature, would be enraged with our blasphemous plan.

"Hello, Amir," He practically whispered.

In an odd effect, which was likely a product of delirium, the voice was like that of my father. I could not help but relish every syllable as He continued, each bringing me momentarily to the long-forgotten presence.

"I cannot stay with you, Amir, for although one, I am sent for all. I can say little of what is to come except this: as the moon trails the sun, so you will be to me. Mirrored in track and linked in time, but never to meet until the ending of our story. Do you know why you were sent, Amir?"

I struggled with words as I tried to recover from the effect of His voice. And even once the mechanics of speech were revived, I could think of no suitable alternative to the blasphemous truth.

"I came . . . came . . ." My resolve faltered as the blinding light seemed to intensify. "I came to be you. To use tricks to fool them all because . . ." My next words needed to flatter. "Because of the hope you bring."

At my finish, I brought my eyes right to the precipice of burning, trying to perceive a response. However, the blinding core did not explode in anger as I expected, but instead slightly receded. I could now see His face in the light, warm brown eyes connecting with my own. His look was not of rage but rather concern.

"I'm sorry, Amir. I fear the path required of you has been bent. So manipulated by man to leave little clarity of purpose. Yet, as is the case with many creations, lucidity is not required. Just as Pharaoh's hardened heart was used to the glory, so, too, will your bent path. You did not come to be me."

"Yes, I'm afrai—" I tried to interject as I suddenly felt compelled to honesty, but His piercing voice overruled.

"You did not come to *be* me, Amir. You came to be *with* me. When I need you most. You cannot know of what I speak, but trust in me, and you will find deliverance." My mouth was now unhinged at the profundity of the conversation. "Amir, I must leave you now, and you cannot come again to me. We will speak again when Sun and Moon converge, but no sooner."

At the final word, the light suddenly intensified. Where His brown eyes had shown, only white-hot light remained. The skin on the naked reverse of my arms seared as I shielded my face from the unbearable heat. Finally, as I was certain the force would overpower, it was gone. I lowered my singed hands and stared at the spot which had been occupied. Nothing remained. No light. No man. Not even the blackened evidence of fire. Instead, only I endured, a crumpled silhouette amongst the rocky ground.

The interaction's effect was that of a long day of toil in the hot sun. Every muscle ached, and my lips wicked at one another for lack of moisture. However, as I finally turned away from where He had stood, one muscle was revealed to be healed rather than impaired: my diaphragm. The enigmatic pain completely vanished, and I was once again able to stand. I stared down once more at the place where I had skirted death. The scene below bore no evidence of the trial, but the violent exchange was all I saw. It was the first moment of real violence I had borne, and it was already hard to escape. Back tingled as if the timber was still in place. Legs suddenly quivered at the remembered weight. Having been reduced to a quaking mess, I forcibly turned from the scene toward the familiarity of camp.

The typically short walk felt long. The hot sun, as if eager to add to my pain, hung low on the horizon for the entire trip. Eventually, the steps totaled the requirement, and I recognized the subtle clues of the site. Even to pry at the invisible cover was a tax I could hardly pay, but after several attempts, my fingers managed to spring the mechanism. By this time, the sun had given up its heated assault and the cool moon had risen in its wake. Now lying in the suspended reprieve of my cot, I was finally forced to face the uncertainty of my future. The mission for which I had prepared. The reason I was trained, tortured, and even operated upon was worthless. But I could return. With a simple letter stowed away to Sterling, the portal home could be procured. I could explain Christ's reality and urge him to bring me back. Back to the warm filter of Abby's presence. Back to the tattered prayer mat. Back to home. Yet, as I considered the logistics of such a solution, a divergence emerged. Sterling's belief in our plan, however twisted, was sincere. He had obviously received no such letter in the most recent iteration of reality. The words of the only letter shared came rushing back. I, or some version of me, had only confirmed the ongoing success of the plan. I had written of disciples and faith, the rising power of a movement. How could this be? I could undoubtedly affect the conditions after my arrival, but those characters already present were presumably there in any iteration. Christ was there every time this reality had played out, and yet I didn't write of Him. I didn't mention, "Hey, God was here after all, you crazy asshole, no need to put me through hell." There must have been an explanation, but as my eyes constricted due to exhaustion, I abandoned the conflict.

Due to my injuries, sleep was as deep as death. I slept well past the engrained buzz and likely would have continued had a more alarming sound not resounded: footsteps. Even within my concealed fortress, the thought of being again discovered was crippling. A deeply held breath began to curdle in my seized lungs until finally, I could hold it no longer. The expired air tumbled with enough might to generate a cough, more than loud enough to be heard by the stranger above. The soft padding stopped, obviously straining to listen for more expulsions. Forced to inhale as silently as possible, I prayed the intermittent paces would trudge away from my location. After what felt like minutes, the faceless intruder reinitiated movement, hopefully shrugging off the isolated sound. However, as the number of steps grew to allow a mental map of the movement above, I realized the figure was rapidly approaching my exact position. Despite my previous failure with the technique, I reflexively paused respiration. To my shock, the next clue from above did not reflect the movement of a foot but rather that of a hand. The corner of my supposedly invisible cloak was being manipulated from above. I couldn't believe it; I could barely locate the disguised surface, and yet this local was about to pry it away and expose me. As the subtle fidgeting audibly grew closer to the required action, I was forced to act.

Prepared to face a hulking, growling figure, I heaved up the cover and jumped to the ground above. But as I pivoted to face the mysterious figure, the light around me gave way to a familiar hue. Standing before me, and providing much-missed filtered light, was Abby. I stumbled around the edge of the massive hole and practically collapsed into her outstretched arms. In a display of anti-masculinity rivaling any of my life, I burst into spontaneous tears in her outstretched arms. She, too, sobbed as we embraced without the constraints of the future. Her soft hands wrapped around my back but paused on the deep incisions of the day before. I could feel her hot tears on my shoulder as she strained to look over at the wounds. After many minutes locked in an emotional reunion not requiring words, I finally pulled away to address her unbelievable presence.

"What are you doing here!? Abby, this place is different than we thought. More dangerous. Harder to predict. And . . . there is som—"

My urgent message was suddenly interrupted as Abby again burst into tears. Knowing her mannerisms well, it was clear these tears were spilling forth from some undiagnosed source.

"Abby, I have to tell you something. It's not as we tho—"

Again, her sobs interjected. "Amir, there's something I need to . . . something I need to tell you." She stuttered between gasps for air,

"Sterling, he . . . he . . . he lied to you." She stopped for a moment to wipe away the waves of moisture to hopefully provide her words with more clarity. As I watched her dab at her reddened eyes, I was confident I already knew the untruth of which she spoke: it had to be Jesus's existence. Eyes dried and resolve stiffened, she attempted her announcement again. "He lied, Amir. He didn't tell you why he chose you, he . . ."

Now I interjected reflexively, "He did, though! I know why; he said it was because of my genetic traits. Pure Palestinian. Short stature. Angular face. He said I was as close to an ancient Nazarene as there was!" I exclaimed, confident this would qualm her unreasonably emotional concern with this point.

"No, Amir. This was probably a reason at the beginning of this recurring time loop, but this time, Sterling cheated. He knew he had already sent someone back to play the part, and so instead of trying to identify his main character by such a broad search, he looked for hard evidence proving who was to be used."

"What are you talking about!? What do you mean hard evidence!?" I asked, now legitimately confused regarding her entire explanation.

"The cross, Amir. He has a portion of the cross upon which Christ supposedly hung. Blackened and decayed, but it came with a pedigree. Every steward had carefully recorded the sequence, leaving little doubt of the relic's authenticity. And, Amir, the piec—" She wept heavily, approaching some emotional climax.

"Abby, please don't cry. Sterling lied about many truths! Don't worry, I know he lied about the whole thing!" I assured her, careful to portray my concern rather than any impatience.

"Amir, the chunk of ancient timber, knocked away under blows of a hammer had a stain. Deep black by the time Sterling acquired it, but there nonetheless. It was blood, Amir. Christ's blood. Your blood." Now a silent tear traversed the well-worn path across her cheek, but she maintained delicate composure. "He tested it, Amir, and searched every database accessible to find his traveler. And your blood, drawn when you went to prison, was a match." A multitude of tears now joined the lone descendent as she struggled at the pronouncement. I drew her close to my chest and clasped my arms around her shaking body.

"But the plan says I am to go back," I whispered softly in her ear, clearly exposed as her typically flattened hair parted due to her desperate condition. "He showed me the synthetic copy. The plan was for that imitation to take my place in the final hours. He even spoke of the switch in the Garden of Gethsemane. I promise it was all planned."

"It was all a lie, Amir," she continued from the warmth of my tight embrace. "He had no intention of replacing you with the imitation. He tested it, and it was unconvincing and unreliable in such a violent and unpredictable interaction. It couldn't be risked. Instead, its only suitable use was to alert the authorities of your position one day earlier than the time for which you prepared. You would be caught off guard and captured. Brought to trial and death just as described." I hugged her tighter still as her chest heaved for air at the thought of such a violent end.

"Abby. Please stop. Dry your tears. It will be all right."

She continued, despite my appeals. "Amir. It's not all right. It's not. You are going to die. You're going to die on a cross, and there's nothing we can do about it. Not without changing everything we know."

I patted her back as she gave up on trying to stand. "Abby. Please listen. Your father may have lied, but he also messed up. The training. The languages. The whole plan, Abby. It was all wrong. This is what I was trying to tell you. The whole reason we did it. It was wrong. Abby . . . He is here!" I practically shouted, eager to assuage her fears.

"Who is here?" She pulled away from my arms, looking puzzled. I waited a cruel moment as one often does before such an opportunity of profound announcement.

"Jesus. He is here, Abby. Jesus Christ is here." My lips curled upward as I waited for the revelation to impact.

"No, Amir. It can't be. It's got to be another person named Jesus. Just some ordinary man with the same name."

"He is no ordinary man, Abby. He is as described. He is light . . . and thunder! He saved me from death! He is God!" As I proclaimed my final words, I realized the sentences, all entirely physical truths, sounded like the insane evangelistic ramblings that used to be the butt of my jokes.

"But the bit of cross, Amir. The blood, the test. He can't be. Sterling had the proof. He was so sure."

"He was wrong! I don't know about his supposed relic, but that is not my blood. Christ is here. He is real. Everything we read. It's got to be real, Abby. Don't you see? We can go back! We can write the letters and go back. I don't have to die. I don't even have to act! We can write to Sterling to open the portal and go back!" I smiled and intensely waited for her expression to turn. Instead, she lowered her head to face the ground below.

"No, Amir." A tear dropped, its creation precluded by her drooping hair. "This was a lie too. There is no way to go back. He would have needed two sources of density, and only one such object is possessed. The portal cannot be opened in that manner. Only if there was such a machine here would it work." It was my expression that now turned. Disbelief quickly turned to selfish anger.

"How do you know all of this!? Did you know all along? Was it all fake? The talks? The kiss? Did you set me up for this? To get stuck in this dust bowl?" I yelled before stopping to consider that her very presence likely precluded these accusations.

"No, Amir. Please. I promise. I didn't know. After you left, he found letters I had written. One a day for a year. Realizing our connection, he tried to convince me to abandon the idea and finally revealed you were never to return." In a reversal of roles, she now strode forward to envelop my quaking frame.

"How could he do this!? Strand me here to die. And . . ." I paused as the ego of my words was realized, "Abby. Why did you come here? You are stranded too. Why did you condemn yourself to such a future!? Now you're stuck with me! You shouldn't have come. You should have left me alone."

"Don't say that. <u>You know why I came. I had to come. I love</u> you, <u>Amir.</u>" Despite trying to hold me in confident assurance, she heaved. "<u>I couldn't let you die alone. And I couldn't stand to live alone. Please</u>, Amir. We may <u>not be able to leave, but we don't have to die. We</u> can eke out a life together. Forge a <u>new path in this</u> time. <u>We can be</u> <u>happy.</u>" She whispered her final words with newfound optimism.

We remained locked in reciprocal dependence for some time. She, leaning on me for lack of resolve, and I her. The seemingly pathetic co-posture was one known only to those whose worlds had ceased to be. Perhaps parents suddenly robbed of a child or even those little ones deprived of parents. <u>Souls left without the aid of a</u> <u>well-worn path, instead left to strike out in search of another route</u> <u>yet unknown</u>. However, as Abigail leaned deep into my chest, the fog of uncertainty was cut by the most potent comfort I had yet known: a companion. And indeed, as Abby's arms slowly shifted against me, regaining strength and resolve, it was clear she felt the kernel of hope as well. She was right. <u>We weren't dead, only displaced.</u>

After some time in the interaction, which ran on warmth instead of words, we pulled away and nodded in understanding. We were to make a go of it. Past, present, or future, our love was unchanged. Now, Abby's expression turned to obviously more complex thought.

"How can it be, Amir? How is He here? It can't be. He can't be! And . . ." Her eyes rolled slightly upward as if suddenly aware of some predator above. "What if He is? You know it all, Amir, just as I do. We had the stories inserted and imprinted. Adam, Eve. Cain, Abel. Sodom and Gomorrah." She paused and panned her own person from toes upward. "Amir, all those stories of fall and pride . . . what about us? If He is here, and is as described, we are surely damned!" She was now practically shouting the implications of divine justice, but as she continued, she suddenly lowered her voice to a level so soft I could barely hear. "He is a jealous God, Amir. If He wiped them away for sculpting an idol from stone, how much more upon us will He bear? We constructed a god not of stone or wood but of our own pride. <u>Our plot is the very manifestation of sin.</u> 'The Lord detests all the proud of heart. Be sure of this: they will not go unpunished!'"

As she hysterically began to remember verses telling of our demise, I interjected to calm her down. "Abby, stop! It was Jesus, and He was definitely God, or at least something other than what we are, but he wasn't angry. Trust me. I was there. The moment when the hammer was set to strike, He arrived. He did not want to punish me but save. I don't know what it means that God is here, but I know what it means that we are here. We need to survive. Forget God. However potent, He is harmless, benevolent instead of violent. We need to focus on survival."

At the pronouncement of my words, an inner battle silently raged. Jesus's face, bathed in light, burst forth from within and shouted of his holiness. Despite my attempts to calm Abigail's anxiety, I, too, felt the singing conviction. He required it all. Heart, soul, and mind. But as I stared at Abigail, another voice, one far more ingrained than this newfound God, sprang forth and urged self-reliance. As in the case of some potent drug, it seemed unwise to dabble in the deity of God. Although I was confident in my current mental faculties to stave off the insanity of faith, if I let Him in, it was unclear how my mind would operate. I could be left as Abraham, driven to sacrifice the very one I had come to love. No. I could not let this force, no matter its truth, derail reason. As the battle was decidedly resolved, Abby interjected to carve an existence somewhere between pride and faith.

"Then let us write to Father, Amir, and tell him of Christ's reality. We can, at the very least, proclaim His name in the future and move on with our lives here. Surely, this is the very least required by God. Then we can find a life here and—"

I interrupted as the ridiculous debate of time and reality began. "We can't! Your father might default on the deal and cast Mum and Hasim from the house. No, we can't because they need this, Abby. And . . ." My own explanation stalled to understand the confounding logic. "And we didn't do it last time. In the last iteration, we wrote no such proclamation. I saw the letters, Abby. Your father believed the mission had been a success. I had written each day as if I were performing the role. He believed I had disciples. He believed I performed the miracles. And he definitely believed I died on the cross." I watched her features deform in processing thoughts. "No, we cannot send such a letter because we *did* not send such a letter. Our very existence is reliant upon this version of reality, and it is this version to which we must adhere."

Abby did not muster a retort for some time. From my knowledge of the scriptures, I knew, as did she, the choice at hand was not novel. Lose everything we loved to proclaim the apparent truth of God or retain our reality and shrug off duty. To me, the choice was clear, but Abigail's resigned posture revealed a truer spirit. She looked from feet to sky and peak to valley, anything to not address the conflict. Finally, with no sight left to occupy her vision, she met my eyes.

"I'll do it for us. I haven't known any reality worth preserving until now, but I will do anything for us. It's why I'm here, Amir. I love you." She maintained an intense gaze as she continued. "I haven't seen Him as you have, but we can only hope that God's grace can equal our betrayal. We both know the alternative reckoning."

"It can," I boasted. "It surely can. I saw him, Abby. He will forgive us," I proclaimed as I buried any doubt, but deeper than my equation would allow was a whisper: sinner. It felt like the moment so long ago when I had quieted the moral rumblings which objected to thievery, and again I found myself muttering the same phrase: "God, get over it, Amir!" This was no time for a moral awakening as I stared at the person I loved the most, now thrust into the dangers of the past.

"It's simple, Abby. We have to write every letter just as expected, both to preserve Mum and Hasim's reward and to preserve our existence. Luckily, we know the story."

Abby muttered something under her breath and turned in the direction of Nazareth.

"What?" I asked, eager to engage in a more collaborative dialogue after our disagreement over faith.

"We can just watch the story! Surely, regardless of the completeness of the training, it will be easier to spy from afar and record the daily happenings than to constantly imagine characters and goings-on to fill the letters. We will just watch with the binoculars!" She looked at me, or rather through me, and I could tell she was working through the logistics of our future. "The only thing is . . ." Her voice trailed into a whisper. I had learned during our time spent in preparatory conversations she hated to articulate difficult realities, an effect perhaps of having dealt with her mother's death. I waited patiently for her to rearticulate whatever truth upon which she had happened. "The only thing is water . . . and food. We can write to Sterling for a few more weeks of sealed meals, but eventually, you were expected to integrate into society. You would have gathered water from the town well, eaten at your followers' tables. We won't be able to write for these forever. Sterling will only believe the reconnaissance lasted so long."

She was right. I couldn't believe it hadn't occurred to me yet, and I began to ponder solutions out loud. "Then let's integrate. Let's go to another town, Sepphoris perhaps. We can make up stories and get jobs. We can write our correspondence to Sterling in secret at night and become one of them. We know the language, are culturally educated, and will have to become part of society eventually if we are to stay. Then we can drink of the well and eat of the table!" I confidently exclaimed the answer, but Abby's face indicated she again was far ahead of my reasoning.

"The letters, Amir. They may seem simple correspondence, but you know as well as I Sterling is expecting to provide provisions to specific locations. Fish and bread. Ointments and medicines. No, Amir, at least for the next three years, we will have to coordinate these drops. Imagine trying to ensure believability, to satisfy Sterling, and obscurity, to ensure some local doesn't happen upon these goods. The fish alone, Amir! He expects to send thousands of pounds of fish to feed the hordes. We will have to deal with these loads. Also, Sterling knows the general route of Jesus's ministry. He will be suspicious if all your letters are buried in Sepphoris instead of dotting the countryside as described in the text. Perhaps . . ." She paused with a mild rise of optimism. "Perhaps we should simply join Jesus and His followers. We can observe His ministry firsthand each day and escape to the hills when needed to deal with the shipments."

As she finished the musing, I could hear Christ's words ringing despite lack of mental invitation. *We will speak again when Sun and Moon converge, but no sooner.* Now it was my turn to whisper the spoiling truth.

"We can't." I could only mutter the concise response as it felt like our options were hopelessly exhausted.

"Why not, Amir? I know you're not ready to face the reality of Jesus, but this might be our best option."

I racked my brain for some explanation other than the cryptic words of Christ. It felt as if acting according to His words acknowledged the very power I was reluctant to face. But in searching for an alternative, some reason more rooted in my own will, I could feel the truth: even I was fearful of violating His providence.

"Because . . . because . . . because He told me not to!" I exclaimed, exhausted by the internal struggle. "He said I couldn't be with Him; it wasn't part of the plan."

"What plan!? What do you mean, Amir?"

"I don't know! I don't know what He was talking about, but He said we couldn't meet again until the Sun and Moon meet. I don't know what He meant, but He said it and . . ."

I tactfully trailed to silence to avoid articulating the power His words were now demonstrating over my life. Abby stared hard at me to determine what end I was trying to avoid and, revealing our familiarity, her expression quickly softened. She knew me, and she knew what I was trying to avoid, who I was trying to avoid. Finally, as if stepping into the dusty print of my past, I reluctantly admitted the only remaining option.

"I can steal it. The food, the water, and anything else we need. I will sneak to the village at night and steal it all. It's what I do, Abby. It's who I am."

I allowed my eyes to drop away as I finished. I could barely admit the reality. The ramification of Christ, which was most impactful, was not His identity, but mine. Despite being stripped of everything, Sterling had provided one asset long forgotten: identity. I had been thrust, however violently, from a position of obscure delinquency to that of Messiah. For the first time, I was able to provide not by cheating and stealing but by saving. Despite the falsity of even this role, I had come to realize prideful existence for the first time, and however temporary, the feeling was fulfilling.

"I'm sorry, Amir. It's not who you are. I know it can't be easy to go back to this, but no matter what you might do, I know who you are."

She stroked my long shabby hair, now caked in blood and dirt. I accepted the comforting touch as if to admit my crisis. Her warm touch did somehow make the ache lessen. The apparent truth of her love, regardless of my external identity, anchored the deeper humanity of life. It didn't matter to her. What we did. Where we lived. None of it mattered. We were reduced to the truth. We weren't thieves or travelers, orphans or outcasts. We were souls, thought-producing cores bound to each other in the endless space of being.

We stood there, clinging to the only reality known until the pounding sun seared at our backs. Carefully pulling away from one another, Abby turned to face my exposed camp. With the invisible film cast aside in my defensive exit, she could see into the rudimentary pit.

"So, everything worked according to plan?"

"Of course," I chuckled, "not one problem! I could take that stupid thing apart with my eyes closed, but of course, nothing went wrong. The only real issue," I walked over to the boulder I had placed to mark my spot, "was the utter perfection of the camouflage! It was so seamless I couldn't even find camp the first night. That's why I added a few homey touches to give it away." I nudged the stone with my toe to indicate the subject of my humor.

She smiled and looked back to the horizon. The distant line where sun met earth was bending to the will of heat. I watched as her face slowly slackened when she thought I wasn't watching. This new world was setting in. The endless dust. The glaring sun. The danger. Abby was obviously encountering the truth that had very nearly taken my life. This was not the manicured training ground cradled in her father's mansion. This was to be the foreign extreme.

"Here." I tossed her a water bottle sent with Sterling's provisions. "Drink some. It's easy to become dehydrated here."

She nodded and downed the reservoir as I carefully repositioned the camouflaged screen. Under normal circumstances, I exited through a small, hinged flap at the membrane's edge, but in my mistaken alarm, I had thrown the entire face with such might to cause folds and ripples in the perfect surface. I secured the center point with a concealed clasp and worked my way around the outer edge. With every metallic pronouncement, the surface tautened, and the image grew more seamless. Finally, with every connection reestablished, the mirage was rendered.

"Wow. It really is invisible!" Abby exclaimed. I was down in the pit, still fiddling with the last calibration but could sense she hadn't moved from her position at the hole's mouth.

"We should probably get in for now," I hollered from the belly of my fortress.

"Already!? It's not even dusk yet!"

I popped my head out with something close to lightheartedness. She jumped and giggled, equally willing to escape the gravity of our predicament.

"I know, but it's too late to get to Nazareth and back, and you do not want to get caught without a plan." The deep gashes on my back ached as I continued. "Trust me. I thought it was simple until I ran into a sheep!"

Perhaps due to my previous tone of humor, or because my head was still comically protruding as might a turtle from his shell, she started laughing at my odd warning. And indeed, for the next several minutes, she uncontrollably chuckled as I recounted the amazingly clumsy encounter with the shepherd and his flock. However, as the story slowly shifted to my detainment in the blackened cave and eventually to the timber itself, she stopped laughing. Her metered steps slowly descended into the depression, and she addressed my wounds, the physical evidence of the account. Her fingers traced the boundaries of each raised fissure, and her eyes watered at the evidence of my account.

"Amir, these are terrible." She gasped. "What should we do?" I pondered her vague inquiry for some time before finally admitting ignorance.

"What do you mean?"

"These are deep, and . . ." she paused, likely in anticipation of some negative prognosis, "and dirty. They could very well become infected."

She was right. For the first time since my injury, I diverted the sensory energy required to perceive the wounds' physical input. I could feel the odd sensation of flaps of skin rubbing with rough dirt. The feeling was akin to that of a splinter but more diffused and far more disturbing. Foreign agents were infiltrating, and infection was sure to follow. I stared into Abigail's downturned eyes and considered our predicament.

"A letter," I finally exclaimed with a sudden jolt of energy.

"What?" She gently lifted her head.

"A letter. All we need is a letter to Sterling to procure antibiotics and wrappings!" I immediately began rooting through the camp's piled provisions. After a few moments, I uncovered the pad upon which I scribed my daily correspondence. "Actually, we need to write a couple of letters for the days I was detained. Here," I beckoned to a seat fashioned from a large rock I had placed in the subterranean camp. "Sit down and help me write for the supplies."

I couldn't help but intensely watch her form move throughout the cramped space. It was a sight that I would have never seen again had Sterling's plan been realized. With her lithe frame now rested in the most comfortable apparatus available, I began to pen the letter. The roughhewn writing utensil was encased in an ancient-looking wood but housed a fluid engineered to last the test of time.

Sterling,

Today: I traversed the hills with binoculars drawn close to acquaint myself with the town residents. I was able to locate Joseph's dwelling and plan to further investigate his close ties tomorrow. Although today's reconnaissance was fruitful, I did, unfortunately, sustain a deep gash after falling amongst the jagged rocks. Please send topical antibiotics and oral antibiotics and wound dressing materials to this location. Ensure that they arrive at approximately 18:00 on day six of the mission.

Tomorrow: I will be evaluating close relatives and contacts associated with Joseph and Mary. The only provision associated with this observation is two additional sets of binoculars. When I fell, the first such set was rendered useless, and I feel it best to always carry a backup in case of another such accident. Include these items with the immediate shipment of antibiotics.

Yesterday: I remember Hasim's lyrical joy of learning. Each day I arrived at our small and dingy flat to find him engrossed in texts too large and old for any normal child to entertain. Nonetheless, his knobby knees punctuated his joyful posture along the brick wall. Bridges. Buildings. Inventions. No development or marvel escaped his inquisitive spirit. Often, the endless lessons inevitably brought forth after his readings grew tiring. But now . . . after being thrust so far from his presence, I can only dream of his voice again.

As I carefully laid down my instrument, I was aware of hot tears gliding across my dirt-caked crevices. Hasim. The short, required recollection was too much to bear as I now realized I would never see him again. Never hear his voice lecturing Mum about some fascinating new development as light gave way to shadow in our old flat. The entire reason I was here was now forever gone. I was only snapped from my lamentation by Abigail's gentle touch on my shoulder.

"Amir? Amir, are you okay?"

I blinked through the tears to find her departed from her monolithic seat and so close I could feel her hot breath. I mustered all the resolve I could in some semblance of masculine fortitude. I couldn't afford to cry. Our lot was dealt, our path unchangeable. I would have to mourn the loss of the future at a more convenient time, one less consumed with the present.

"I'm fine. Don't worry, just dust in my eyes," I proclaimed unconvincingly.

I leaned forward through a palpable atmosphere of doubt and deposited the newly minted letter into one of the shining canisters. After much tinkering, the lid audibly pronounced closure with a metallic affirmation. It was so tightly sealed, I remembered Sterling lecturing; it would not allow a single grain of dust for the next two thousand years. At the shining pod's front, a helical bit extended forth in an ominous peninsula. This was the component that enabled the vessel to burrow deep beneath the ground and remain undiscovered for so long. I carefully positioned the tiny auger's tip to the ground plane and initiated the rapid rotation necessary to send the companion down, down, deep below the surface, and into the ever-realized future. One day, Sterling would collect this and many other vessels to ensure the necessary provisions were delivered for our supposed encounters. The first test of this correspondence would now unfold faster than I ever imagined.

"How will we know if he got it?" Abigail inquired as the autonomous digger burrowed deep into the ground.

"It should be obvious soon," I assured her, "assuming our measurement of time is accurate, the goods should arrive within min—"

Before I could finish the sentence, I became acutely aware of an overwhelming sensation in the air surrounding me. It was the distortion. I could feel the particles composing the reality around us, heaving in apparent submission to Sterling's future force. Despite the unsettling nature of the distortion, I remained unmoved due to my experience with the force. Conversely, Abigail, who had no such familiarity with the sensation, was obviously frightened. She practically leaped across our dusty foxhole and landed squarely in my arms.

"What is it!? What's going on?" she whispered, concerned about the fundamental pulsing which was most manifest in the beat of our very hearts.

"It's your father's answer." I gently held her away, just distant enough to shine a satisfied grin. It was the first notably positive development since my arrival, and I couldn't help but revel. "He found the letter we just wrote and sent back the provisions. I requested the delivery be made only moments after I penned the letter and behold—an instant response!"

I stood, arms still crooked to hold Abigail's momentarily frightened frame, and searched for the goods sent from far in the future. Left of our encampment lay only the singular stone I had heaved to denote our position. The right yielded a similar condition: no visible additions. My outstretched arms, which I thought could never complain of Abigail's touch, were starting to ache as I nervously craned my neck through the small opening to examine our entire surroundings. Finally, just as my heart had begun to signal concern, I saw the shining pod.

"There," I exclaimed, "there is our answer."

Abigail outstretched her legs and slowly removed herself from my arms, noticing my quivering weariness. She hopped up the embanked mouth of our depression and addressed the pod. I watched her familiar yet almost forgotten figure stoop to grasp the object. Every step. Every flick of her shining hair. Every pronouncement shaking the air between us was a mighty reassurance of comfort: I was stranded but not alone. I had been given the gift of love. Displaced love, but love nonetheless.

"How do you open this thing?" she inquired as she strode back to my unmoving position.

As I watched her tinker with the seamless exterior, I recalled how separated the instruction had been at the manor. She had little knowledge of the technological aspects of the journey. As Sterling had said, "the preparation would have been untenable with just one person. Luckily for us, fate had provided him a worthy co-bearer in the load." She knew only the historical and cultural aspects but nothing of the space-aged device now at hand. She practically tossed the heavy case to my still-quivering arms and watched intently to learn how to breach the casing. I smoothly let my index finger rest at the fore of the container, then moved my hand laterally down the container's length, the finger all the while gently dragging behind. Instantly, the path blazed by the lazy digit illuminated with a deep red glow, and the pod audibly relented.

As the metallic fixture separated, a series of wrapped components spilled forth. Abigail bent quickly to gather the goods.

"It's all here, Amir! Antibiotics for the gashes. And . . . two new sets of binocs!" she excitedly pronounced as she held up the new scopes. I nodded and managed to upturn a semblance of a grin as I was now aware of the growing pain. The forced gesture wasn't lost on Abigail. "Lay down, Amir, and I'll put this on your wounds and dress them."

I obeyed her sincere command and lay face down on the singular cot now cast in shadow. As I prepared to feel the hot sting of palpation, I couldn't help but think of some motion picture inspired settler biting a belt in resolve to enormous pain. I was unsure of the validity of this makeshift technique, but as I sensed Abby's hands descending to address my upturned skin, I quickly furled my robe into my mouth. To my surprise, the fleshy canyons had gone numb, perhaps from already being caked in dirt, or perhaps this was the reality of such wounds. The only palpable effect was the quietly audible lapping of ointment as she spread the heavy lathe upon the area.

"Am I hurting you?" she asked, bringing her shining eyes within inches of my own.

"Not at all," I groaned, as might a tired man at the touch of a masseuse. Even in this unorthodox exchange, the energy between us was tangible. If two persons had a stranger first evening alone together, I had never heard the tale. This was not the amatory encounter I had envisioned, but it was nonetheless supremely satisfying.

With my confirmation of no pain, she ripped open a large adhesive dressing sent along with the ointments. Careful to avoid contacting the central bandage with her grimy fingers, she pressed the rectangle firmly onto my epidermal schisms. I slowly flexed my back muscles to test the adhesion. The excellent quality ensured by Sterling's research was once again manifest as the covering remained firmly attached.

"Take these too." Abby outstretched a rigid palm bearing two large tablets. "The bottle reads, 'fast-acting oral antibiotic.' Hopefully, it helps prevent any infection."

I downed the pair without even considering the colorful casings. The pills' notable size would have, under normal circumstances, rendered discomfort. But, as I was now becoming aware, real pain and fear rendered such discomforts impotent. Abigail was now shuffling to and fro to stow the leftover provisions with some logic in our tiny dwelling. I looked up through the projected cover. The burning intensity of day had given way to placid night. Twinkling nodes only visible in our newfound rurality punctuated the endless black. It was arresting, and the distraction was decidedly welcome. However, as my mind revisited the ingrained contours of Mum's face, I was suddenly aware of Abigail's now-penitent posture.

"Abby! Are you okay?" I practically yelled, as might a toddler concerned with his mother's condition.

Her global form remained unmoving, but her lips whispered into the darkness. I could only make out certain words, but given her posture, the action was unmistakable; she was praying. Her knees were pressed hard into the dirt below with such pressure to denote the same fervent faith to be exhibited by my mother someday long from now. Now realizing the action, I recoiled my further inquiries and waited silently for her final word.

"Amen," the pronouncement rang in our tiny quarters, and she finally turned to address me.

"What are you doing?" I asked gently. The inquiry, succinct in verbiage, was nuanced in undertone. I knew she was praying. I had been easily able to deduct the physical act. I was asking why.

"I am just talking to Him. It seems the least we can do, considering the situation." She examined my stoicism. "Don't you think?"

Honest retorts abounded within, happy to remain only ideas yet unarticulated and unjudged. *No. I don't think. So, I've seen him. Seen God. Perhaps if you weren't here, and I had little to lose, I could trust in this strange new force* . . .

The truth was I was still more confident in the age-old pride of self. I had failed to provide for Mum. I had failed to provide for Hasim. But so had this God. At least in preserving the unclouded purity of my own steerage, I was allowed an illusion of control. The realm of these musings, one composed of only neurons and electricity, failed to muster speech when paired against Abigail's deeply sincere eyes.

"Yes, of course," I finally mustered. It was such a familiar act; one I had performed hundreds of times as Mum emerged from pleading with God. "As you said, it's the least we can do." My voice died, lacking the energy and not provided an environment to resonate. Its feebleness did little for believability, but she nodded in meager satisfaction.

Sleep was hard to come by in the desert heat. Unlike the previous evening, the searing pain was quelled just enough to ache rather than disable. I turned both physically and existentially. Abby's words floated in the half slumber, swirling into the profile of her penitent prayer and finally transitioning to the face itself. His face. Christ. As before, the outline, though distinctly palpable, was composed of blinding light. The darkness of sleep, the cloth typically thrown on the flames of daytime life, was obliterated in the light of His face. Abby was right. God was real. I had seen Him condensed to the form of a man. And as much as I wanted to discount His deliverance, He had already saved me. However, just as the burning face grew ever closer and my defiant spirit began to crack, an old force puffed and bellowed to spring forth whatever darkness required to quell the intense union. I couldn't relent that which was required.

MAY 25, 29 AD

The days, cruelly defined by the desert heat, added one to another to form weeks. Each cycle, we set out in the cover of the dark and nestled into the rocky hills to gaze out over Nazareth. The experience, as is often the case with life's profound moments, felt oddly mundane. I had encountered the exhilarating truth of Christ's identity, but now as we watched Him perform the routines of a carpenter, it was hard to keep our eyes open. As I sat in the jagged crook of a rock ledge, I looked over at Abigail's similar position in a nearby contour. Without her unexpected arrival, I would have surely died of boredom. Actually, if she hadn't shown up, I probably would have eventually killed myself. It was a morbid thought, but now as I considered this reality without her presence, it seemed a perfectly reasonable act.

"Amir!" Abigail's whispered exclamation forced me to re-engage my glazed eyes. "Amir! Look! I think He's getting ready to leave for something."

I jerked the knob on my binoculars hard to the right and panned to capture Christ in the doorway of His rudimentary dwelling. We could not see His face, but slung across His shoulder was a small rucksack. It was a small detail, but after becoming so familiar with His typical movements and routines, the sack was alarming. He shifted his weight from one foot to another within the opening. Occasionally a shoulder would lift as if to accentuate some point. He was talking, likely to Mary and Joseph concealed within the dwelling. The rapport between these three had been a rare source of entertainment amongst our hours of observation. Despite having undergone the extraordinary, to put it mildly, experience of a virgin birth, Mary and Joseph often seemed to have forgotten Jesus's true nature. They would constantly inquire of his plans to make a living or pester about when He would finally find a woman. Each time Christ would answer with some existential proverb that seemed completely unrelated. Joseph would nod as if he understood perfectly, but as soon as Christ left, he would turn to Mary and share his real thoughts.

"What did he say? He has grown under our watch, but I fear we have failed him, for He is surely one of the strangest men yet known."

The couple's sentiments, when coupled with our understanding of Christ's life to come, created immense amusement. "Jesus Christ!" Mary would occasionally yell in rebuke rather than blaspheme. They didn't know, apparently couldn't know, what was to come of their "strange" son. But now, as Jesus's body language grew more animated, I wondered if this inevitable future was finally becoming known. Just as I could scarcely wait to see, Christ turned to emerge completely, and our scopes could see His lips to record the interaction.

"Yes, yes I will." He shrugged in Mary's direction. "But I can't misrepresent these truths. I am not to return. Not in the way you desire. From here, I must be . . ."

I pushed my binoculars' wheel, desperately trying to gain more magnification. Despite having reached the scope's maximum aperture, I could see tears streaming down Jesus's cheeks.

"Just as a bird builds to the point of flight, I can never again return to the fold of your bosom. You have been . . . true. True to your love. True to his love. As sure as the fostering of an orphaned soul, your love for the son of man will never be forgotten." He concluded His typically biblical-sounding pronouncement and strode forward to tightly embrace Mary.

"I think this is it!" I finally addressed Abigail's initial question only now that the facts were obvious.

My heart, perhaps atrophied from stagnation, palpably pounded within its ribbed cage. After a long while spent in Mary's arms, Jesus turned and began to deliberately plod away from the pair. Their arms, now left void of Jesus's body, found new refuge around one another. For the first time, I felt like an intruder. This was not a story from the Bible. Not some carefully recorded excerpt to confirm divinity. This was a family torn apart. A father deprived of his life-long friend. A mother robbed of a child. This was a moment defined in value by the scarcity of participants, and our gazes had cheapened it. As if confirming my thoughts, Christ suddenly turned as He strode. His eyes swiveled to starkly address me through the scopes.

"Aghh!" Abigail cried out as His face was basked in light. His human features, seen only seconds before, were instantly burned away and forgotten. Even from our distance, I had to turn away. With her hand outstretched to block out the impending light, Abigail shouted, "What is that?"

"It's a sign," I coolly retorted. I couldn't claim to know God or even His earthly manifestation, but this seemed a clear message. "That's Him. That's the real Him. It's beginning."

Finally, as my joints ached at being contorted amongst the rocks, the light faded. I turned back just in time to see Him trudging down the dusty trail. We carefully leapt from our monolithic perches to follow. Having learned a painful lesson, Abigail led without peering through binoculars and called out any obstacles before I arrived.

"Rock, two-o'clock!" she pronounced as if a member of some breaching tactical force.

Due to the amplification of distance, we struggled to keep up. Every step Christ took through the village, we had to jog an offset perimeter. Finally, it became clear He was exiting the settlement and heading north. We weren't certain exactly which direction He would journey. The biblical text, still ringing in my head, only mentioned He traveled to the settlements within Galilee. According to the script, He would come back to Nazareth only to be driven from town by the same characters who so warmly welcomed me. Once out of town, we were able to match the speed and walk in distanced parallel. Imprinted with a mental map leftover from training, I considered possible routes. Abigail, who had even greater stores of historical account, did the same.

"Probably stopping in Cana."

"Yep," I eructed. Cana was only a short distance north of Nazareth and seemed a likely first step in Jesus's teachings. The procession was scriptural. A profound beginning to change the world. However, as Abigail strode forward, obviously engrossed in the historical amble at hand, I considered the journey's more immediate implications. Sterling had carefully planned for my movements.

Firstly, I had to command my technological companions to pack up camp and follow at a distance. *Command. Stow all basecamp items and track my position from a distance.* I could feel the prompt filter through my internal connection. The other major change, besides locale, was a source of provision. Starting tonight, we would write letters informing Sterling of the initiation of ministry. Accordingly, he would no longer expect to send food and water to sustain. And so tonight began my reemergence to the delicate dance of theft.

———

That night, in a moment of déjà vu—an odd sensation made stranger by being displaced in time—my palms began to sweat in anticipation of performance. A thief. It was a vocation rarely sought, and yet I found it in every time and locale yet encountered. For some reason, I couldn't help but imagine some white-collar asshole boss telling me I had been transferred. *Amir, you're our top performer. Your numbers are the best we've seen, and so we're going to reward you with a transfer! How does theft in Nazareth around 30 AD sound?* It was a stupid scenario, but the kind that I imagine all people entertain.

Despite the momentary escape from reality my musings had provided, I was suddenly snapped back by a noise below. I brought my binoculars to my face, now caked in dirt and discolored from sweat. I was perched two hundred yards away in the crevice of a large boulder. Now, stirring in the pitch dark, was a small, portly man I recognized as the importer who had berated Joseph. He stumbled in front of his dwelling, obviously groggy with sleep until the purpose of his excursion was made known. He suddenly lifted his tunic high in the air, a boy-like gesture reserved for times of extreme solitude, and began to urinate. Not knowing anyone was watching, he relished the experience. Finally, after what must have been the product of many glasses of wine, he stowed his boyhood jolly and returned inside the gaudy residence.

This was it. The time had come to enact my clandestine acquisition. The truth was, I had come to this spot with this man in mind. He and his dwelling had several characteristics that cried out to my senses. The home had a detached food store, a rarity in ancient Nazareth. Also, the man owned an enormous water vessel. The ceramic container was at least as wide as my outstretched arms and the same dimension in height. Similarly impressive was the man himself. His enormous girth, almost as rotund as the vessel, ensured an easy getaway should we meet in the darkness. All were accounted for, and all sat idle and asleep in the night before me. I started to traverse the rocky minefield between my position and the house. The angular faces of stone had come to represent the greatest threat to my existence. In addition to my dramatic encounter with the shepherd, the rocky points constantly scratched and clawed at my foreign skin, eager to leave an impression. After a few minutes of carefully plodding along, I stepped into the back corner of the man's property. In most cases, it would be difficult to determine where a villager's property line stood, but in this case, the boundary was denoted in a series of hewn stones set end to end to appease an insatiable vanity.

The storehouse was secured with a rudimentary lock. Its steel face, although highly imperfect in finish, did represent a significant obstacle without the proper tools. However, through a recent shipment from Sterling, we had been provided an adaptable tool to breach such circumstances. The thief's best friend, as the device should have been named, consisted of a small angular extension with a great number of extendable teeth. The multitude would gently emerge and fill any void with the requisite form to spring the mechanism. I carefully inserted the instrument and waited as the internal process was performed. My eagerness turned to horror as the lock sprung open with such force to launch to the hard ground below. I groped at the mass without prevail as it cut through the night and impacted the surface. A resounding "clang" rippled through the sleeping settlement and left little chance of secrecy. I bolted to the shadowed side of the structure. Even the white glow of the moon might accommodate the vision required to spot me. Yet, as I strained to hear the slightest sound of stirring, I was met with only unspoiled silence, the favorite medium of spies and thieves alike. After a few more moments of bated breath, I emerged to address the storehouse door, now pivoted open without the latch's restraining force.

I stepped inside and perceived the contents with the dim lunar light that had followed me through the opened door. Risen loaves, salted fish, and sacks of grain prevailed. The shelves were full, and I began to gather a sample of the items to stuff into my rucksack. I was careful to gather an amount great enough to sustain us for a few days but not so greedy as to draw immediate attention. I shuffled the adjusted contents forward within their rows to ensure no visual clues as to the new absences. With my bag heaping full of sustenance, I replaced the padlock and turned to the nearby water vessel.

The bulbous form, whose gentle striations were evidence of some creator's hands, was not graced with a modern valve. Instead, any person wishing to harvest the life-giving fluid had to remove a matching ceramic lid from an angular outcropping. The protrusion, jutting out to provide an ergonomic aperture, greeted me as I approached. I removed the lid and began to scoop water into a container previously sent back by Sterling. "One. Two. Three . . ." I counted softly to myself in the dark. I wasn't sure why, but it seemed prudent to know how many measures the exercise would require. Finally, after seventeen dips, my container was full.

Carrying all the components of daily success in hand, I began the walk back to camp, now unfortunately located near Cana to the north. The provisions, particularly the water, weighed enough to elongate the journey's effect. I had estimated the distance to be four miles, and judging from the significant time taken, this was accurate. Yet, in the rare moment of solitude, I was allowed the opportunity for displaced self-consideration. Abigail, although providing love and life, also suddenly imposed the relentless company of marriage. For the first time in my life, I was afforded neither privacy nor singular will. Instead, every experience and plan were filtered through our dual existence, a process both treasured and tiring. Now, in the darkness, I considered those thoughts only entertained alone and in the dead of night. Thoughts of where I had been. Beginnings. Musings of how things could have gone differently. Alternatives. And, lurking never far below the surface, the burning face of Christ. The emblazoned contour was another constant companion and one far less welcome than Abigail. He had whispered as I sprung the lock. Tapped as I plundered the vessel. *Wrong, wrong, wrong,* a chant erupted. I mustered my own seething form and extinguished the image. This was no time for impediment and certainly no time for morality.

Tired and ragged, I approached the boundary of our new camp. I sucked in a full volume of air and slowly whistled the imagined tune of a nighttime bird. It was our practiced sign of entry. An audible pronouncement of arrival to ensure ease. Abby, obviously not asleep, immediately emerged from the concealed depression.

"Amir!" she whispered with force to denote exclamation. "Thank goodness. It was starting to feel like too long. How did it go? Are you okay?" She walked forward to relieve me of the heavy sacks. As soon as she transferred the full weight, she practically crumpled under the weight. "Wow! These are heavy!"

I nodded in affirmation with little energy left for mutterings. "Let's stow them and take advantage of what little dark is left." We heaved the sacks into the corner of our hole and lay down on the singular cot. Abigail's body was warm. It was an effect likely known to all spouses. The warmth of the one first in bed. The other, preoccupied with some errand, climbs in to find the familiar curled heat of sleep.

———————

Morning light accumulated upon our biological shutters until the lids naturally sprung open. It was later than usual, not surprising considering the busy night. Out of reflex, I turned to verify the food and water sacks were still there, to make sure they were real and not the product of some engrossing dream. The bags were still crumpled in the corner, and with my fears of imagination conquered, I rose, eager to taste our efforts.

"Do you want some bread?" I hollered to Abby, who gazed up from the taught canvas. I was excited to eat the bread and meat, considering the bland goo sent by Sterling.

"Oh heavens, yes!" she retorted with equal vigor.

I pulled a hardened loaf from one of the sacks and tore at its rustic exterior. It was remarkably like the version produced by Sterling in preparation for our journey. The rotund form was heavily sprinkled in a dark flour, and when bent to the point of submission, it emitted a loud crackle. I tossed a large hunk to Abby and immediately bit into my own. The leavened white webbing was ripe with flavor, and the crust provided a much-missed resistance. For several minutes, the only sound between us was that of chewing.

"It's so good," she stammered through bites.

"It's just like your dad made," I said in a rare allusion to the now despised character.

I was unsure how Abigail thought about him, but I had come to hate our unseen provider. We devoured the rest of the loaf and staved off thirst with a generous portion of the water. Finally, with stomachs full and mouths wet, we emerged from our hideaway, ready to observe Christ. We were a couple of miles from Cana, and the rocky desert was already warmed to the point of perspiration. We walked and discussed predictions for Christ's day.

"Cana is where He turned the water to wine, but this will surely not be today. No, today will probably be a simple lesson at the synagogue. Nothing earth-shattering. A lesson about Moses, perhaps. An Old Testament tale directly alluding to the son of man."

She speculated for the entire walk. I often forgot that, unlike my accelerated acquisition of knowledge, Abigail had also developed a passion for history. Eager to confirm the validity of her forecasts, we nestled into a dusty outcropping just in time to see Jesus emerge from the home that had welcomed him the previous night. He strode with the estate owners in close allegiance to the synagogue. This religious temple was notable amongst the sandy structures. With little time to consider design, most of the structures were a result of circumstance. Built crooked to avoid a large stone. Lopsided for lack of care. The synagogue was the only form that had obviously warranted careful consideration. Its walls had been carefully milled to a perfect surface. The doors hung square and swung without derivation. It was a reminder of priority. Religion, however corrupted, as Christ was about to suggest, was precious in the narrative of life.

He and His newfound companions walked confidently through the doors and disappeared into the darkened interior. There were few openings in the building envelope, and Abigail stumbled to and fro to gain a view.

"I can't see anything, Amir! I can't see what he's saying!" She ran erratically amongst the rocks, much as I had before my accident.

"Abby! Slow down. Don't run with your scopes up!" I bellowed, as might a rebuking father. "Look there," I pointed to a square opening intended to let light into the fore of the temple. It was high on the wall, but considering the topography, it seemed a view could be acquired from the adjacent hill. "I think we could probably see in from there!" I gestured toward the scrubby face.

She bobbed her head enthusiastically, and we set out, walking forward against the kerf of the cut until we stood atop a monolithic projection. The vantage point was perfect. Positioned squarely within the bounded opening was Christ. He was standing proudly erect and grasping the edges of a massive copy of the Law. Abigail quickly nestled into the comfiest spot possible, which was still incredibly uncomfortable, and took in the scene. I quickly fell asleep.

Hours later, judging from the reddened tone of Abigail's skin, I awoke to her gentle whispering.

"Amir! Amir!" Even in my groggy state, I could sense her disappointment in my slumbering lack of enthusiasm. "He's done. You missed it! He used the story of Joseph and weaved in a series of proverbs to address His authority!" Her voice projected with such excitement that I almost worried someone might hear.

And indeed, as I looked below, I realized her vigor was shared. Dozens of people filed out of the synagogue. Small groups intermittently clumped together out of eagerness to discuss the happening.

"This is it, Amir. The beginning of Christianity. The beginning of Jesus Christ."

Even I couldn't help but tingle at the profound sight. Mum and her personal brand of religion sprang to mind. All those people to come. This was the start.

"I'm glad you enjoyed it," I stammered. Wrong words. I could see it on her face.

"You're *glad* I *enjoyed* it? Amir. You can't tell me you don't feel it. You have to fee—"

She stopped short, perhaps remembering our past conversations, and wishing to avoid a row. I afforded a gentle nod. I agreed. I really did. I wanted to be swept away in the magic. To be rid of self-reliance. But it wasn't happening. Still stewing in the awkward dissonance, we journeyed back to camp, the sun now low on the horizon. We spoke in short spurts, but I could sense she was only eager to talk about the day's events, and I had nothing to offer. Instead, in my periphery, I could see her mouthing quotes undoubtedly from the day's readings and grinning. Faith was already affording her some of the hope we had intended to preserve.

Dinner, composed of preserved fish, brought a reprieve from the subject. Instead, we munched on the salty flesh and laughed about memories of secretive lust during training.

"I thought you were gorgeous the second I saw you!" I admitted. "I actually worried you guys were some kind of perverts at first. Especially when I saw the pictures of the disciples on the wall. I just thought they were twelve boys that looked just like me. Past victims, perhaps!"

We howled with laughter at the thought.

"I told Father to just come straight out and say it instead of his dramatic theatrics, but he insisted on a production . . ."

Her voice diminished to nothing at the mention of him. I measured her face to decide whether to turn away or hug her. Her watery eyes urged the latter. I smothered her solace in a warm embrace, and we quickly transitioned to sleep. Our bodies shrugged at the first semblance of rest, and we had little energy to resist.

JULY 6, 30 AD

M arked by the arched movement of sun and moon, our days assumed a routine. We woke early each day and trekked to record the actions of Christ. Unlike the condensed and accordingly action-packed accords of the Bible, most of each day was spent talking. Occasionally, He would reach out a hand and cure some ailment or disfigurement, but most times were spent simply talking, eating, or even laughing. Abigail, perhaps through her willing faith, had no problem remaining engrossed in the lack of action. Christ's words were more than enough to firmly anchor her worn feet to whatever rock or outcropping we found each day. However, as she strained and scrambled to carefully record every divine uttering, my mind wandered. Failing to muster the love for this figure that might manifest in unrelenting focus and boundless energy, I did anything but focus. Often, I was jarred awake by gentle prods from a disappointed Abigail. My back aching from having been carefully wedged in some spot of shade, I would emerge groggy to face Abigail's discerning gaze. It was painful to so utterly fail by a measure that now drove Abigail at an essential level. And so, today, as we settled into the crooked monoliths, I newly resolved to focus on the growing number of disciples below. I slowly rotated the ridged rubber wheel atop my scopes to bring Christ's ever-moving mouth to tight focus. He was loosely draped over the village well, and a few people surrounded as He launched into one of many parables that never made it to the Bible.

As His words weaved between the reality at hand and carefully crafted metaphors, I became aware of a slight movement around a nearby corner. It was an odd effect of such an elevated vantage point: the individual paths of so many, often thought to be private, were rendered visible. Often as we honed in on the developing nucleus of Christ, we couldn't help but watch the villagers' private lives as well. Quarrels between spouses, back-alley deals, and tender caresses prevailed in the concealed corridors between structures. Sometimes I looked away, either reluctant to engage in more of the overwhelming emotion that constitutes life or simply uninterested in the clichéd scenes. However, occasionally I couldn't help but relish the timeless drama. Now, as I reflexively turned toward the glint of movement precluded from public view by a well-placed corner, I was surprised by a small and remarkably dingy child.

Through the countless hours of observation already performed, I had developed an intuitive sense of relative wealth. It was a form of perception not reliant upon a biological endowment but rather upon a catalog of experience. In my own time, the decades still home to my beloved Mum and Hasim, I could instantly discern a person's wealth based on every tiny detail. Shoes, pants, shirt, cleanliness, gait, and a plethora of other distinctions often revealed one's disposable income. Based upon this developed sense, it was clear the child now hunched behind some riff-raff was obscenely poor. His braided hide shoes were fraying at every corner, and the soles were so reduced as to lack identity. His tunic bore more evidence of poverty. Large, jagged holes peppered the woven surface, revealing the brown skin beneath, and even through the intermittent openings, the shadows of ribs were noticeable. Even the styling of the robe was unusual compared with the typical version worn by the ancients. Most of the flowing garments had a stitched collar to prevent continued unraveling. But this boy's version was devoid of this feature and had long ago relented the boundary.

I rocked forward to emerge from my elevated perch and moved slightly right to assume a better view of the new target. In my periphery, I could see Abigail smiling as I scrambled to the new position. My uncharacteristic enthusiasm had been noticed and mistakenly applied to Christ. I was happy to accept the misappropriated approval as I gazed again at the filthy child. His general form was so diminished as to leave every joint a knobby outcropping. As he sat back to the wall, I was reminded of Hasim's knobby knees always pointed to the sky as he read his books. The dingy boy moved very little and, at first, it seemed he was embracing a moment of reprieve. However, as I continued to watch, small movements punctuated the pensive posture. I finally understood the timing of the nods and smirks as they correlated with the oohs and ahhs of Abigail as she watched Christ. He was listening to Christ. Ashamed to emerge but desperate to listen, he remained in the alley throughout the sermon. I couldn't help but watch every expression mustered by the tiny figure. After almost an hour, it became clear Christ was done with His lesson. The onlookers began to mill about and exit through the surrounding urban corridors. My newfound subject heard the movement and sneakily bound from one obscured position to another. I blinked a couple of extra times to allow for a longer session of unobstructed sleuthing. He tucked carefully behind one of the elder's homes, then around the side of an old woman's storefront. He kicked up dust at every turn but was careful to stay hidden. Abigail started to stir to my left as the proper subject of our observation was long gone.

"Well, that was an interesting one," she said, turning to address me. I was so determined not to lose the strange character that I didn't hear her. "Amir! What are you looking at!? I thought for once you were watching Him."

"Hold on! Just a minute!" I practically barked. The rude tone was less than becoming, but even a momentary lack of focus would render the figure lost amongst the dusty structures.

Finally, as Abigail's carefully orchestrated movements indicated she was losing patience, the boy slowed and stopped at the boundary of a shadowed valley at the edge of town. He approached an opening somewhat akin to a door, and I, finally confident I knew where the boy lived, turned to address Abby.

"Well? What are you looking at?"

Her tone was uncharacteristically sassy, overtly peeved at my previous treatment. I waited an awkward second to consider my response. The truth was I wasn't sure what I was looking at . . . or why. A ragged boy. Unrelated to the focus at hand. And yet, I couldn't help but watch him. I opted for the simplest truth first but knew inevitable inquiries would follow.

"Just a poor little boy," I said, gesturing down toward the boy's dwelling. In fact, at the distance we were from the village, the gesture provided little information as to the boy's location.

"Where?" she asked, pulling her own binoculars tight to her face. I was amazed as I silently watched her expression scanning the horizon. She required no further information to manufacture interest. Just the idea of a poor child was enough to compel action. Her instant compassion, perhaps a result of faith, was admirable.

"Northwest corner of the village. At the base of the jagged cliff running along the rearmost row of structures."

After all the time spent following Christ, we were like two seasoned cops on a stakeout. Descriptive directions had been streamlined via trial and error, and Abby had no problem finding the boy. I could tell she had acquired a view of him, and I, too, gazed down to share the experience. He had reemerged from the rudimentary dwelling with two feeble figures following close behind. He was carrying a small loaf of bread in his palm and turned to share the morsel with the other two in the shadowed curl of the terrain. Even through the perception displaced by distance, it was obvious his companions were his parents. All of them were so thin as to allow easy comparison of bone structure. Just as the boy's, the man's jaw sprang forth long and angled and left no doubt of inheritance. His mother was crooked over. The angle formed by her back spoke to some forgotten injury, leaving in its wake a broken life. She shuffled after her young son and sat feebly as the three shared the meal only suitable for one. Having eaten his portion quickly, the boy now regaled the couple with the words of Christ he had heard from his alley hiding place. He jumped while informing them that the meek would inherit the earth. They steadily nodded and occasionally flashed a halfhearted grin, but from our vantage point, we could see his mother turn to wipe away intermittent tears. Regardless of what he had heard, they were starving, and she was overwhelmed. I couldn't help but think of Mum, sobbing in our own kitchen as she struggled to feed Hasim and me. I could feel tears welling, hot and defiant at the feeling, but I strained to contain the response and turned to watch Abby.

To my surprise, she was already watching me. Apparently less reluctant to express her lamentation, her dusty cheeks were actively washed by the streaking tears. I felt stupid for forcing us to watch the pitiful scene. We had a clear directive to ensure our own loved ones' futures, and I had entangled us in the emotional exchange of some equally unlucky family. I pulled in one last deep breath to bury the image once and for all before turning to stand up. Abigail didn't move.

"Amir?" she meekly pronounced, still seated. I turned back to address her unmoving person.

"Yes?" I retorted with a slightly shaky voice. "We really should get going to get back to—"

Before I could finish, she interjected, this time with distinctly more determination.

"Amir, we have to help them." She let the statement hang low and sweet without extraneous words.

I waited for some time, then addressed her. "We can't. I know, I want to, we just can't. We have to focus on our future, not theirs. If we mess up and don't coordinate the letters and shipments, every-thing we know could be lost."

She sat in sullen silence for minutes. It was a terrible victory to attain. My point, however valid, had reduced us to hollow shells of duty in place of moving souls of action. We were trapped. Trapped by my love of Mum and Hasim. Trapped by our selfish version of the future. Even trapped by each other. The choice at hand was cloaked in the glamour of time travel and its accompanying trials, but in truth, the question was one as old as time. Staring down at the disheveled scrawny boy before us, the timeless test was clearer: us or them. Our happiness or his. Our comfort or his. Our life or his. Once, in what felt like another life, I had witnessed a boy standing in the path of a careening car. The silent electric motor had given no warning of the device's course deviation, and the small quivering figure was frozen in view of certain death. At the moment that divides a decided reality from its unknown alternative, another figure entered my vision. An old man, mustering what little physical prowess remained, thrust the boy from the path and absorbed the blow himself. Lacking the proverbial car, I wondered if we were now letting the boy before us die to preserve our own reality. The memory, a terrible one under any circumstances, had now rendered me limp and unmoving in our perched observatory. However, as I turned to address Abigail's presumably equally sullen exterior, I was met with gently upturned lips and the tender smile I so loved.

"I've got it, Amir!" she exclaimed, voice reverberating in the dry desert air. "I know how we can do both, preserve our destiny and theirs." She paused and gazed back toward the boy and his family. "We are getting close to the first feeding, Amir."

She stopped, apparently expecting a reaction. I stared back, still trying to understand any implications of her statement. Based upon Jesus's movements, we were certain the first mass feeding described in the Bible was mere days away. The monumental event would represent a great deal of work to conceal the massive load of fish and bread sent by Sterling. We had decided to bury the massive load of food using the excavation tool. Unable to reveal the truth to Sterling and concerned about the stench of thousands of pounds of rotting fish, burial seemed the only option. However, as Abigail again brought up the miracle, I couldn't yet see her point. Likely aided by the consistently lagging expression I now bore, she pressed on to explain.

"All that food, Amir. Wasted. And these people, so many left wanting. Let's not bury it; let's give it to them! I know we can't just go into town and hand it out, so we will have to find a way, but we have to, Amir . . . for them . . . for him . . ." Her voice trailed off as she looked toward the ethereal deity that now compelled her.

I had to admit, the idea was enticing. She found motivation in the people we had watched Jesus heal. I found inspiration in those He did not. For every poor soul lucky enough to cross the path of God, I could see another across town. The boy, still sitting with his parents below, was exactly this. Jesus, for whatever reason, traversed the countryside and graced only a certain precious few with the deliverance promised. It was these forgotten ones that sparked the form of empathy rarely felt and often claimed.

"Okay," I stated simply, partially because the sun was now quite past its mid-day apex and partially because I couldn't resist the climactic syncopation of the unassuming phrase.

"Please, Amir, why don't you . . ." she started to reply, not yet registering my unexpected response. As her lips continued to speedily denote more appeals, she slowed. She finally realized my agreeance.

Instead of altering her streaming dialogue, she sat silent and stared intensely into my sunken eyes. I was reminded of interactions with Mum, an unspoken discussion between those so attuned to each other's tells as to render words less effective than the air between us. Just like Mum, I could tell she was waiting to address my words to examine a force far more potent: motive. I knew she was motivated by her growing love of God, and she knew I was still struggling to accept Him. Finally, I could stand the inspection no longer.

"Look, don't get excited. I'm not ready to just start following Him blindly. I know you feel a . . ." I grasped for the proper word. "A duty because of Him. I'll do it because I feel a duty to them."

Her cheeks, previously held in a high position and telling of a slight optimism, relaxed in apparent disappointment. The expression was subtle but felt like a shockwave traveling to my chest. However, as she finally added words to the overture, I realized I was mistaken.

"Do you really think me to be so callous, Amir?" I strained hard to hear, as her voice was softer than before. "Do you really think I want to help these people . . . that child . . . because someone, even God, said it was right? I want to help them for the same reason you do. Just because I grew up rich doesn't mean I haven't felt pain. I'm not so far removed from the condition of being human as to not imagine his life and his obvious loss. I don't believe He said charity was good to manufacture some sense of duty. He said it was good because it momentarily exposes the shared condition of man. To imagine the life of another . . . the pain of another . . . briefly binds us in spirit, and such a union feels to me to be the point of everything."

Her words were an elegant reminder of her superior perception of just about everything. It was the sentiment I had longed to hear from the faithful, but had yet been deprived. Realizing the limits of my speech, I now opted for less corruptible communication and leaned forward in an embrace. The resolution, to aid the poor villagers below, further warmed the touch of skin between us. It was a resolute sense of purpose that had been unknowingly lacking in our relationship. The objective of our daily duties was often so displaced in the preservation of future existences, like Mum and Hasim, as to leave us wanting for traditional fulfillment. Had our relationship blossomed out of some mundane encounter and grown in the precious confines of a single time, we might have been considering having a child, but now even this feeling of extreme charity was enough to bind us more tightly to one another.

Eventually, we broke from the embrace and began the walk back to our ever-migrating camp. Due to our delayed departure, we walked in the white iridescent moonlight instead of the shimmering red sunset. The topography of today's route was miraculously smooth and allowed me to stare up at the glowing white crescent. As instructed by Sterling, I nightly logged its phase in the dark sky. Tonight, the distant sphere was heavily precluded by the earth beneath our feet, leaving only a thin celestial sliver. Considering the slightly larger condition of yesterevening's orb, this was a waning crescent. I cursed Sterling's name, as his lessons once again provided a newfound insight. However sinister his plots may have been, he had prepared me well. The moon's condition, when considered with some of Christ's recent movements and speeches, meant we had about three days before the massive feeding. Tomorrow, Christ would move on from the people we saw today to be closer to Bethsaida. While He was to be some miles south of us, we would sneak back and deposit the stores of fish and loaves sent on from

Sterling. Thinking about my past interactions in this time made me dread the risky exercise. Only able to think of this maneuver, I finally forced us to the conversation.

"How are we supposed to get the fish and loaves to them, Abby?" I asked between steps.

I slowed slightly in anticipation of a complex answer. She kept moving, neither slowing nor choosing to address the question for some time. Since she had arrived, I had provided most of the leadership. Although my arrival was only weeks before her own, the brutal encounters had made me immediately feel like a weathered captain. However, as I now pensively waited for Abigail's answer, it felt the roles had shifted. This was her idea borne out of her passion, and at least temporarily, the relational dynamic had shifted. Finally, as her silence started to feel like an abuse of power, she graced me with an answer.

"As far as I can tell, those that would need the sustenance are all right there. Forced to nestle into the rockiest crevices at the outskirts of town." She gestured in the darkness. I couldn't make out the movements, but I could hear the swift movement of skin through air. "The truth is, in this particular case, I think we've been lucky. Think about His route, Amir. They are so isolated and ignored we don't need to worry about some righteous elder or pompous Pharisee. So . . . let's not make it complicated. Let's just bring it to them."

Not concerned about Abby seeing, I contorted my face in the dark. The idea of encountering people again made me cringe.

"And what if they have the same reaction I encountered before? What if they want to stone us?"

"They are hungry, Amir. Surely their bodily needs will have erased the mind's hate. And if it hasn't . . . it is simply a risk we will have to take." She ended the statement with the simplistic naivety only found in the faithful.

The conviction in her voice left no room for argument, and I pursed my lips tight to keep from retorting again. Perhaps she was right. All the same, my dreams that night were a tumult of jagged stones heaved by brutish men.

JULY 7, 30 AD

The next morning, Christ moved, as expected, toward Bethsaida. As usual, we followed hundreds of yards back in the group's periphery. Every step taken with little burden today was another that would have to be conquered carrying the many loads of food tomorrow. Despite the relatively short distance, the trail was a particularly rocky one. To remain obscured, we carefully remained in the rocky unconquered crevices which bounded the distance. We would be forced to take the same route tomorrow. Despite the arsenal of drones and technologies already sent, we would have to carry the loads in makeshift packs. Remembering the punishment my binoculars had brought, we had resigned to never use technology unless absolutely necessary. Although the path would be arduous and the loads heavy, we could perhaps explain our actions if caught. Alternatively, a drone invisibly carrying me or the baskets through the desert would be as difficult to explain as had been the binoculars.

Christ spent the day preaching in small groups around Bethsaida with no indication of tomorrow's miracle. Abigail listened intently as usual, and I continued to formulate a plan for tomorrow's dispersal of food. The legendary fish and loaves that were so pivotal to the biblical account were described in almost no detail in the story. It had been easy for Sterling to create a rustic version of the bread likely used, but the fish had required more trial and error. The first question was one of the species. The Sea of Galilee contained about twenty species of fish. Only about eight of these were consistently eaten in the ancient dwellings on the sea's banks.

The next criteria I remembered from Sterling's speech was more technical. I couldn't remember the exact wording, but it was something like "genetic drift." Sterling had wanted to identify which species had undergone the least noticeable genetic change.

"After all," he said, "the illusion would not be very convincing if we revealed basketfuls of fish looking nothing like any they had seen before." This criterion left three candidates who had undergone little aesthetic change over the timeframe in question: Musht, Biny, or Kinneret Sardine. The final question which facilitated analysis was preparation. In all the biblical passages, there was no mention of how this massive catch was prepared. It was hard to imagine the crowd of spectators savagely chewing on raw fish. And yet, they were distanced from home and hungry. Sterling had decided the carcasses should be salted and cured to accommodate immediate consumption, or packed so as to be sent home. After trial and error, he determined Musht provided the best portion size and taste to perform the illusion.

It was the salted preparation which now seemed an opportunity. The truth, which I had been reluctant to articulate to Abigail, was the path just traveled was too arduous to perform with massive loads of fish many times in a day. However, considering the semi-preserved nature of the fish, I now realized we could simply carry comfortable loads each day to whatever poor population we desired. We would store the initial load in our camp. This would also allow me to stop performing the dangerous task of intermittently stealing food each night from wealthy villagers. We would simply use some of the sustenance for ourselves each day and deliver most to the wanting locals. The only concern left was storage. The fish and loaves, although stable, would give off some odor. We had never encountered any hulking predators amongst the rocky hills, but there was a plethora of small conniving creatures that frequented our camp. Ultimately, after considering many options to mask the smell, I determined we should write to Sterling for some form of sealable containers. We would need to carefully craft tonight's letter to convince Sterling of the normalcy of our request. After all, he needed to believe all the fish and loaves were to be distributed at once. After many hours of watching Christ and a brisk walk back to our camp, we sat down to craft our nightly correspondence.

Today: I traversed the outskirts of Bethsaida and spoke to small groups regarding God's oath to deliver man from bondage to sin. The disciples listened closely and even helped to address separate groups when the numbers were too large for intimacy. It was difficult to maintain supposed naivety regarding Judas's character, as he is already showing signs of deceit. He is the least eager to participate in outreach and is often angry at our impoverished style of living.

Tomorrow: I will be the feeding of five thousand. Please send the loads of fish to this location at daybreak within the false bottom baskets. Also, considering our travels within this region, the biblical number of five thousand does not seem possible. Although Bethsaida is a significant settlement, we are not drawing crowds of this size. This figure was likely the work of suggestive counting. The disciples, who are to eventually record this number, are not well educated in mathematics. Accordingly, when the moment comes to speculate of the crowd's size, I will suggest, with the added effect of deity, that the number is five thousand. However, in terms of provision, I would like to prepare for the possibility of five thousand in case the figure is somehow fulfilled. This provision will likely result in excess supplies. Accordingly, I will need some form of sealable containers within which to store the extra portions. Please send enough containers to house most of the load. This will allow flexibility regarding the required amount. By storing the excess, I will be able to offer food to starving travelers. These events may not make it into biblical accounts, but I assure you such micro-miracles will not go unnoticed.

Yesterday: I remember being gently enveloped in Mum's soft embrace. Each day, until the day I fatefully left, she curled her arms around me as if to bottle the warmth between us. When I was small, she stroked my hair from above as I only measured to her stomach. Eventually, in the years before I left, it was I who stood tall above her. Sometimes I would stroke her hair as if returning the favor from my youth. Sometimes, when I felt too

old or hurried to participate, I would try to wriggle free of her
awkward maternal gesture. Now, I look forward to the day I can
again wrap up the small woman and momentarily understand
her love as only touch allows.

It took all my resolve to write the last line as if I didn't know the
truth of Sterling's plot. The truth that I would never see Mum again.
Never hold her slender frame. Never stroke her hair, and certainly
never get to understand her love so perfectly again. I wanted to hurl
every expletive known to the old man. I wasn't certain of my own
understanding of the afterlife, but I longed to tell Sterling of Christ's
presence if only to prove that Sterling would undoubtedly be going
to hell. Instead, I sat in the dim light of our excavated camp and
trembled with the completed letter clutched tightly. My anger was
so intense I might have given in to my desires and revised the document had a hand not slid softly onto my shaking shoulder. Abigail
drew me to her from behind and whispered a quiet assurance. She
reached forward to grasp the letter, now slightly crumpled in my
grasp. As I tried to release the page, it was clear that the object had
become a token of my soul. Letting go and sending the words without revision was an admission. An admission that I was powerless
to punish the man who had taken everyone I loved. I could sense
Abigail understood the document's implications, and she was careful to apply pressure but not impose a sudden exchange. Finally, I
relented and recoiled to my cot to simply imagine Mum's face as I
faded to darkness.

All nights are the same, but this one felt long. I had turned about
within our small structure, perhaps looking for some escape from
the memory of Mum and Hasim. I was not aware of the passing hours
and was yet left tired and drained of energy. Nonetheless, I rolled
from my canvas cot to find Abigail already scurrying to and fro. The
sun had not yet crested the craggy horizon, but there was a sense of
energy in the air around us that suggested it wasn't far off. I had to
admit, the day felt significant compared to many in the past spent

sitting among the rocks. This day, like the letter penned the night before, seemed an admission. An admission of our circumstance. We were here to stay. After thousands of hours spent recording the actions of another, we were again ready to engage with our own lives. Feeding these ancient people with the provisions sent from the future was perhaps not a sustainable life, but it was at least the beginning of another life. The redemption of personal mission. An admission. That this dusty, savage, and God-touched time was ours.

I stepped forward and calmed Abigail's frantic movements with a simple gesture to the looming sun. Many miles away, across expanses which always separate man from light, the sun was cresting. It was unclear how close Sterling's shipment would be to the actual event. Typically, the old bastard was fairly accurate, but it was admittedly not a simple exercise. As the boundary of the orange globe became more pronounced, we started to see the telltale shimmer. The matter that was all around us was shaking. The shipment would have to come in several portions as not to overload the distortion. The first objects to silently materialize in front of us were three size-able baskets. I had seen the containers during training, but those memories were now distant, foggy images. We strode forward and dragged the woven cylinders toward the rim of camp to allow room for more arrivals. The ensuing barrage of baskets left little doubt of the scale of the operation. In rounds of three, they came for over an hour. Sterling believed I was storing these vessels tactfully near the feeding site and demonstrating that each was empty and then filled. The baskets themselves were quite clever. Each was woven using reeds which were sourced surrounding the Sea of Galilee. The weave was coarse, typical of the cheap construction which would prevail in these times. However, nestled into the curvature of one of the courses of reed was a very small projector. The item was so well concealed even I couldn't spot it. When initiated, it would project an exact image of the basket's bottom to create the appearance of an empty basket regardless of the contents. It seemed simple at first, but unlike the projector aiding our camp's camouflage, this one was not afforded a screen upon which to deposit light. MIT had developed this new type that could deposit the colored, layered light at programmed intervals to still produce an image. The device was activated using my neural link. I knew we wouldn't use the baskets, but I couldn't resist activating each as we staged them around camp. *Command: initiate basket cloaking.* Immediately, the basket, heaping with fish, would instead display an empty bottom. It was a fun trick, but now, having watched the effortless nature of Christ's real miracles, I was happy I didn't have to perform the act.

Finally, when our backs began aching from the countless baskets, the air stopped shimmering, and the matter around us regained validity. We were exhausted, but I was more concerned that no additional sealable containers had appeared. Just as I turned to Abby to point out the absence, I sensed the sequence beginning again. However, as I turned to assess the drop location, there were no sealable vessels. Instead, there lay a series of plastic bottles housing a deep black fluid. I leaned forward to examine the bottles. Each was about one foot in diameter and had a very specialized threaded nozzle at its top. As if the air itself could sense my bewilderment, a small paper letter materialized next.

Amir,

The fluid-filled bottles that preceded this correspondence are to be used to create a suitable storage area for excess fish and bread. The nozzle at each bottle's top threads onto a rear port on the mini excavator. After digging a suitably sized depression to hold the goods, thread the vessel on and command the excavator to "coat the excavated region with Polybond." The excavator will traverse the cavity's walls and deposit this self-hardening watertight casement layer. Then, simply seal the hole's top with the included membrane. This is a far more efficient system than a series of containers as requested.

-Sterling

Not having noticed the membrane referenced in his letter, I turned back to the spot and found a small sleeve containing a shimmering rolled sheet. The material was not unlike the cover of our own camp, as was the entire system. We were essentially creating an additional camp excavation which was sealed to water and elements with this membrane and the hardening fluid. I took the items back to Abby, who was still draped over one of the baskets, breathing hard. She nodded after reading her father's letter but made no move to initiate any further action. I, too, was completely exhausted and dripping with sweat but was not eager to leave the provisions in the beating sun for too long. Instead, I immediately initiated my mental instructions to the excavator.

Command: initiate containment excavation. Ten feet wide by ten feet long. Four feet deep. At the summation of my thoughts, which were internally narrated by a deep, strong voice that was certainly not my own, the small digger sprang to action. It started the mesmerizing series of passes, each time removing a tiny layer of dirt. The robotic labor provided just the reprieve needed, and by the time it was finished, Abigail was up and ready to inspect the hole.

"Do you think it's big enough?" she inquired, leaning over the striated wall.

"Probably not," I admitted, "but let's fill it and see if we need another."

I turned back toward the now restful excavator. Grasping one of the new bottles, I located the rear port on the excavator and attached the container.

Command: coat the excavated region with Polybond. The machine emitted a series of clicks and audible reactions before again entering the hole. It traversed the fresh walls and floor, depositing a thick layer of the black membrane. I bent down to touch a completed portion and found it already completely solidified. Once the little workhorse was finished, we began dumping the baskets into the cavern. To our surprise, and obviously demonstrating the irrationality of volume, the hole was able to fit almost all the fish. Considering the smell and moisture of the fish, we performed the process again for the bread loaves. Finally, five hours after we had begun the process, we sealed the storehouses with the camouflaged membranes. Sterling was right again. Considering the sheer number of fish and loaves, this method was far preferable to smaller containers.

As I collapsed onto my cot, Abigail shouted in from above, "So . . . when do we leave!?"

"Leave?" I croaked without looking up. "What do you mean?"

"I mean," she slowed on the word to add obvious sass, "when do we leave to bring those people some food?"

I moaned from the cot. My body ached from head to toe, and I felt as if I was deserving of a medical leave of absence. However, looking up for a moment at Abigail's beaming face, I saw her beautiful enthusiasm. She was as sweaty as me, and her posture had been visibly diminished by the series of loads, but unlike me, her eyes were still vibrantly pronouncing victory. I let out one more groan for posterity and pulled myself back out of the shady encampment. She beckoned to a couple of makeshift rucksacks. I hadn't noticed, but she had loaded the reused tunics with some of the fish and loaves. Before I could protest again, she strode forward and hefted one of the packs to her back.

It was impossible not to be inspired by her tireless compassion, and I leaned forward and grasped my own pack and flashed her a smile of admiration. She displayed a wide grin in response and stepped out north toward the impoverished encampment. Trailing behind, I could sense her passion in every step. Each was strong and bore little evidence of the morning's labors. The packs, which were not constructed to assist in bearing the heavy loads, dug into my shoulders and were surely leaving large blisters on the bony bearing points. The walk felt endless, and indeed even Abigail's pace eventually slowed. Finally, we began to see familiar rocky outcroppings that let us know we were near the boy's home. We stopped at about the spot we had been previously and pulled out our scopes to make sure there were no obvious threats in the rocky valley. We quickly located the boy talking to a neighbor. He was as wretched as remembered, and the old woman to which he spoke was obviously blind. I had worried we would arrive, and I would lose my nerve to approach the people. However, now I was surprisingly invigorated at the sight of the people below. This time, it was I who stepped confidently forward to traverse the last rocky distance to the valley below.

The final descent was quite treacherous, but eventually, we emerged into the settlement. As if sensing a new presence in the collective consciousness of this outcast network, the residents, one by one, emerged from their rugged dwellings. Some were visibly infirm, limping on misaligned legs or dragging deadened feet, while others seemed to be mentally impaired. Either way, the multitude of conditions read like a testament to modern medicine. For the first time, I felt rich. Hasim and I might have been endowed with little compared to some spoiled cohorts, but at the very least, we were given an opportunity of health. We had received vaccines, mysterious elixirs staving off the conditions I now saw. Some of the infirmities might have been inflicted at birth, but I had no doubt many were preventable.

As we strode forward, each inhabitant stayed in front of their residence. Sunken eyes were opened wide in obvious surprise at newcomers, especially ones bearing no sign of disease. Considering the residents' silent greeting, I had no idea who to approach or how. I imagined beginnings but encountered my own disability: eloquence.

Um, we brought this for you because . . . well . . .

Even in my head, I stammered and looked up and down their broken bodies.

Before I could think of an alternative to this grossly inadequate line, Abigail broke from our procession and moved toward an old woman whose strength had long ago abandoned and left her draped over a crutch made of a meandering stick. I stood stark still, not eager to interject my own greeting. I strained to hear how Abigail would preface our deliveries. However, as she hefted her pack off her shoulder, I was surprised to hear no such pronouncement. Instead, she silently reached into her pack to grasp a loaf. As she began to pull the length out, the woman flinched and shielded her face. I grimaced, imagining the many past blows that could manufacture such fear. Abigail didn't waiver. She slowly lifted the loaf and held it out close to the woman. The old, crooked character slowly lowered her defensive posture and stared incredulously at the offer. Finally, I heard Abigail offer an explanation.

"This is for you," she gently proclaimed. The woman still looked skeptical.

"Why?" The retort was powerfully brief. Encompassed in the one word was the opposite and equal of my constant question to God: why not? Whereas I had been trained to demand an explanation for absence, she had been so beaten down as to demand one for provision. Abigail continued to balance the crusty loaf while she formulated an answer.

"Because He is here," she said. The answer was elegant but cryptic. I could tell she was speaking of Christ, but I was unsure whether the woman would understand. I awkwardly gulped in some air and held it while the conversation continued.

"I've heard of Him." The woman subtly looked toward the little boy who had told everyone of Jesus's message. "Now He sends this . . . for my loyalty? So I will . . . *glorify* Him?" The phrase was pronounced carefully to denote disdain at the idea.

"Not for your loyalty. For your body. Not for you to know His glory. For you to know His love." The woman's posture was starting to visibly soften, but she had perhaps one more inquiry for Abigail before accepting the gesture.

"Why didn't He come Himself?"

"Because I . . ." Abigail gestured to herself. "I needed something too: you." She waited a moment for effect. "He could have come Himself, but I needed to meet you. To see you. I needed more love."

I couldn't see Abigail's face, but I could see her shoulders subtly rising and falling; she was crying. And now, as I leaned to get a better view, I realized the old woman was too. No more words were exchanged between the two. The woman reached forward to grasp the loaf, but in doing so, lost the support of the homemade crutch.

Abigail caught her and prevented disastrous fate. She slowly walked her into the ramshackle dwelling with the loaf tucked into the woman's arm. I, like the rest of the residents, was completely engrossed. My mouth remained agape for quite some time until Abigail's prolonged absence let the onlookers' eyes fall back to me. Feeling the hot sensation of observation, I addressed the nearest soul.

Deciding to rely on the eloquent speech of Abigail, I said nothing as I offered each a loaf and fish. Apparently satisfied with her explanation, they readily accepted and offered grateful nods in return. Most were the definition of meek. One after another, they clutched the unexpected gift and retreated to the ramshackle shelters. After all that we had been through, I happily accepted the silence. Perhaps some men defied the urgings of testosterone to avoid conversational emotion at all cost, but I was at the supreme mercy of this influence. Surprisingly, it seemed I would escape the valley without uttering a single word until the original intent of our charity revealed himself. I was almost through the entirety of the valley when his awkward yet energetic silhouette swiped across my periphery. By the time I had managed to swivel my head left, the shabby boy was already at my right side.

"Do you know Him?" He intensely whispered without introduction. It was a conversational beginning that would normally seem disconcerting due to lack of context. However, having covertly watched the boy's observation of Jesus, I understood his inquiry.

"Not exactly," I retorted. I couldn't help but flash a quick smile at the boy. He reminded me so much of Hasim. His mannerisms were so akin to my brother's that I could practically see him thinking.

"They're saying he's going to lead an army," he sort of whispered while stretching upon his toes to be closer to me.

I watched him carefully as he rocked back to his heels and waited for the impact of the statement, which he apparently understood as quite provocative. It was a sentiment I had almost forgotten from my lessons with Sterling: Jesus was anticipated by many to be an emerging physical king rather than a spiritual one.

"Is that what you think?" I prodded.

We were still striding down the dingy corridor of impoverished dwellings, but he now paused to seriously consider my question. He furrowed his brow as if to denote intense concentration.

"I'm not sure . . ." he started but paused again. "He speaks with authority, but . . ." He cut his thoughts short with a truncated pronouncement that was obviously practiced from being told to stop boring people.

"But what?" I gently urged, trying to convince him of my genuine interest in his thoughts.

He had already resigned to look down but emerged from the preemptively broken posture with life. Part of me was afraid of what conversational damn I had compromised.

"But I think He speaks too much of love to be a king. Kings don't need love. They need power. Might to impose their will. And He talks about the poor. The meek. Like us!"

He waved his arms to the broken people standing each in their preordained spots. As I looked from face to face, it felt like they had stood in these locations since the beginning of time. It was hard to imagine them moving. Some were physically unable. Others were so old that any major movement would undoubtedly occupy an entire day.

"Kings need to speak to people with power. Perhaps a general with earned loyalty. Or a wealthy man with slaves. Not . . ." Again, he turned his head from side to side. His eyes lagged in the rotation and seemed to be verifying that I was following in the motion. "Us. Some say the army of the meek could overtake by sheer number. Perhaps they have never met the meek."

He flashed a smile at the wisecrack, and I couldn't help but chuckle. I watched as he basked in the comedic success. I could tell he wasn't used to being met with such youthful acceptance of smart-assery. He reminded me so much of Hasim as to make the entire interaction both painful and addicting.

"So, if He isn't a king come to deliver you from the pressing stone of Rome, of what deliverance does He speak?" I had already stopped my long strides to allow for his signature stationary contemplation.

"Perhaps . . . we are all in bondage." Any comedic relief entertained had now vanished as he stared deep into my eyes. "But we're the only lot that knows it. We've had nights of hunger. Days of thirst. None of these," he gestured again to his aged cohorts, "has any illusion that we are free. Maybe this is the revolt He came to lead. Not against Rome, but rather pain itself." His eyes visibly watered at the thought. His insights would be impressive for an adult, let alone some punk kid. I nodded subtly before providing some half-hearted assurance of his claim.

"I think you're probably right," I muttered.

The boy was brilliant, just like Hasim. Although, his cleverness was more intuitive and less technical. He could discern intent more than Hasim and seemed to care less about the theological technicalities. Had Hasim attempted such a discussion, he would have analyzed hundreds of genealogies. Despite the obvious differences, the figure before me was the first semblance of comfort I had yet uncovered in this old world.

By now, I had dispersed all my provisions and had turned back toward the valley's entrance. Before stepping into the mouth of the passage, I turned back to the boy.

"What's your name?" I asked in a rudimentary Aramaic phrase. He didn't answer for a moment in reflexive suspicion, but eventually, he admitted the essential title.

"Levi."

I gently nodded and eventually offered him the reciprocal information. "I am Amir." Now he nodded, but I could already sense a sadness growing as my exit grew imminent. "And I will be back."

At this, he again shrugged off his defeated posture and seemed to float off the ground with effervescence.

Throughout my discussion with Levi, I had become completely unaware of Abigail's movements. Perhaps by the mathematics of our similar loads being dispersed at similar rates, she almost simultaneously arrived back at the valley's mouth. I crooked my arm in a kind, and indeed even jovial, invitation of squiring. She looked ecstatic at the gesture, believing servicing the wretched poor had impacted my mood. I curled a smile which I imagined the generous person of her dreams might. It was not a toothy grin but subtle and sweet. Just enough to confirm her suspicion of emotional impact. I felt like a fraud, but perhaps it was true. The boy had altered my understanding of these foreign peoples. I had, for the first time, recognized a familiar nature other than judgment and interrogation. I had seen just enough of Hasim in his face to remember the tingling sensation of family. The feeling, despite being a mental phenomenon, manifested in every muscle of my being. As we walked the distance from the forgotten valley to camp, my steps were lightened. The meaty sinew of leg which trudged ever onward felt as if it had been restrung in purpose. Judging by Abby's similarly affected gait, the experience had impacted her in the same way. Together we walked with such careless joy that we might have been mistaken for two souls found instead of lost, and upon arrival, drifted gently to sleep with energetic dreams of resolution.

———————

I awoke to the sound of guttural heaving. I bolted upright and found Abby kneeling on the dugout ground, violently gagging. Her arms were straightened to support her bent frame, and in the moonlight, sweat visibly glistened on her forehead.

"Abby! What's wrong?" I rolled off the cot and slung an arm over her to help support her weight. Her arms gave way, and I immediately assumed the small load. "Abby!" My voice was now breaking as one's does in situations lacking control.

"I'm okay, I think, just don't feel well . . ."

She sputtered before heaving again. Now her body started to shake and quiver. The movements were minor enough to suggest a fever rather than a seizure, but the tremors were nonetheless alarming. I hoisted her shivering body atop the cot and gathered her discarded modern clothes into a makeshift blanket. She continued to

ATTICUS MULLON

shake, but after a while, her movements slowed to a sweat-drenched sleep. I sat with the stillness only allotted to those awaiting a loved one's recovery for hours. Her brow occasionally quivered, and her breathing sounded more labored than usual, but sleep was granted. Without another violent episode, my own will to stay up eventually gave way, and I, too, left my watch in favor of sleep. I had always scoffed at the lack of discipline exhibited by those sad saps on TV that fell asleep next to their loved one, laid up ill. However, now as I was faced with the circumstance, I, too, failed for lack of resolve.

The morning sun announced my weakness as the first rays shown over the lip of our hole and illuminated my position.

"Agghh," I muttered, realizing I had fallen asleep.

I immediately turned to Abby, eager to assure myself my worry was for naught. However, as I peered over the rim of the cot, her skin, just yesterday reddened by the sun, was stark white. Her breaths, which had been loud and labored, were now soft and barely audible.

"Abby! Abby!" I cried out, so close to her face to ensure a response. She quivered slightly and turned slightly toward me, her eyelids fluttering.

"Amir. Amir, I'm sorry," she whispered without moving.

"No! No, no, no! Abby, don't do this. Don't say that. I'm sor—"

I struggled to finish. The effect of her state was arresting. Her eyes were closed again, but her subtle breaths still prevailed. I drew her close and alternated between sobs and angry exclamations.

"Always. For all the talk and preaching! *And bullshit!*" I shouted toward the sky.

It was for Him. For Christ. The fact that I knew God was real had only infuriated me more. At least before, I could find solace in the anonymity of misfortune. Now, such events had been given a face. A burning face, so selective in fortune and righteous in position as to allow my people to die again.

With no thundering answer from this deity, I turned again to consider Abby's state. How could this happen? I was fine, but she had been reduced to quivering overnight. Then the distinction dawned on me: the membrane. The membrane Sterling had fused to my sputum to prevent native germs. She had never received this treatment. My mind flashed to Abby's loving embraces of the day before. I could see her in the wavy image of memory holding the old woman's face close to her own, absorbing every foreign germ she had to offer. I immediately began a letter to Sterling.

> Sterling,
>
> I must forgo the typical format, for I am in a desperate state. Despite the sputum membrane, I have contracted a disease. I cannot identify the pathogen except to relay my symptoms. Vomiting. High fever. Intermittent consciousness. Labored respiratory function.
>
> Please send any potential remedies that could help immediately to this date and location.
>
> -Amir

I messily scribbled the writing in both haste and an effort to convince Sterling I was ailing. Just as before, as my hand slowed, the air surrounding gained a sheen and began to quiver. To my right, and this time so close I could practically touch it, appeared another metallic pod. I lurched to the container and dumped the contents next to Abigail's paled figure. Plastic bottles, small boxes, and even syringes spilled forth to the ground along with a note from Sterling.

> Amir,
>
> Enclosed are a series of provisions aiming to address your described sickness. Unfortunately, it is impossible to diagnose the specific pathogen at work. If this infection is the work of bacteria, the enclosed antibiotics will quickly improve your condition. However, if the cause is viral, we stand little chance of targeting the particles and will instead be forced to simply address the symptoms.
>
> Due to the unknowable nature of the disease, administer one

of each pill, capsule, and injection marked with the number 1. These components will not negatively compound and will cast a wide net for potential culprits. After twelve hours, if no improvement is noted, administer the components labeled 2. Proceed with this numerical progression every twelve hours until the trials are exhausted.

Although the remedies enclosed may seem extensive, there is little chance we will identify the pathogen. Instead, you will likely only be allowed to ease the discomfort until your immune system prevails. Please write of any developing symptoms immediately to aid potential diagnosis.

-Sterling

I quickly read the correspondence and began rifling through the pile to find all items labeled "1." One syringe, three capsules, and two pills filled the breadth of my cupped hands as I again addressed Abigail's strained breathing.

"Abigail . . . Abigail," I whispered so close to her face that even the weak exultations moistened my skin. "Abby, I have medicines you need to take. Abby? Abby, please, I'll bring water to take the pills." Finally, her placid limbs started to acknowledge my address as I turned to gather a reservoir of water.

"Amir . . . what do I need to do?" she whispered.

"Nothing, sweetie. Just hold still and swallow when I say."

I grabbed the first capsule and placed it in her opened mouth. Her jaw visibly retracted to swallow, but I could see the action lacked potency. I held back tears as I was forced to shove the tiny, coated pill back deep within her mouth. Despite knowing the effort was to heal, it was overwhelming to fight against her gagging reflexes.

Finally, after several such terrible administrations, she had taken all the first round and was now recoiled deep into the cot. I mirrored her action in despair. As the sight of her reduced state was now overwhelming, I selfishly averted my eyes. However, the effort was ineffective. Even with my eyes judiciously trained to the dirt floor below, the smell of wasting remained. She had sweat through every layer applied. Indeed, even these typically mundane functions harbored the stench of illness. Ambiguous as only smells can be, it was unclear what gave away Abigail's condition, but the odor made evident her worsening condition. With no measure left to take, save letting the medicines take effect, I lay my head upon her heaving torso and slept close.

As the bright middle hours turned to a dim ending, her condition only worsened. Regular breaths began to syncopate, leaving gaps devoid of much-needed air. No perspiration was now present as all moisture had evidently been voided. The pills, capsules, and even shots had done nothing. According to Sterling's instructions I was now to administer the second round of possible remedies and wait another twelve hours. However, as I stroked Abigail's typically vibrant exterior, I knew we would not be afforded such time. There was only one chance to save her, and it required addressing the very person that had thus far abandoned: Jesus. However reluctant my acknowledgment, He had exhibited power. His regard for us was perhaps harder to determine, but if anyone could save her, it was Him. We just needed to force His hand. To stare into the eyes of God and force empathy.

As true darkness replaced the meager attempt of dusk, I prepared for the pilgrimage. Abigail, although gaunt, would represent a significant load in the desert trek. I knotted several tunics tight and formed a sling to arch over my chest. With the fabric sling in place, I bent over the cot and began to tug at her limp body. Without raising to wake, she slipped into the rudimentary apparatus. The friction between my cloth and hers made the operation more difficult than anticipated. I could barely stand to play a part in the scene as I was forced to heave her more violently. Finally, she was secured to my breast, and the load was as manageable as was possible. She still made no sounds, and I began to move with great haste as I bounded to our cave's opening. We had to reach Him.

The passage, from our camp to Cana just north, was so quiet as to amplify my thoughts. Abigail, pressed tight into my heaving chest, was everything. In the pitch black, it was clear that the shriveled creature now clinging to life was all that was left. All that was left of my loves. All that was left to confirm my lost soul was found. The dust swirled with each quiet plod. I couldn't see it, but I could feel the flowing particles caking my feet as I jogged forward by the guiding stars above. The venture might have represented a physical challenge under normal circumstances, but the adrenaline-fueled potential of loss quieted any pain.

It was difficult to perceive Abigail's weakened breath as I ran, and whenever my sense of worry overpowered that of urgency, I was forced to stop and listen for the belabored sound. Each check brought some much-needed verification that life remained and immediately gave way to a freshly hastened gallop. Run. Hasten the normal loco-motion to the point of exhaustion. Anything to save her. Run.

I churned my legs so hard, the friction between sole and earth wasn't enough to hold. I slipped forward with Abigail's extra weight cantilevered in front. I turned as I tumbled through the air, an effort to shield her precious and vulnerable form. My attempt at rota-tion, weakened since I was already in the air, was just enough. My own hip hit hard but luckily was welcomed by smooth dirt rather than jagged edges. It hurt, but not enough to stop my progress. However, as long as I was momentarily ceased, I strained to hear Abigail's breath. I operated the fleshy valve that halted my heaving expirations. Nothing. Even in the utter silence of the desert night, I could hear no breath.

I smashed my face to her chest, pleading the silence was an effect of distance rather than truth. Nothing. I moved back to her lips and pressed my ear in the shriveled gap where breath might escape. The opening, usually preserved for the warm moist air of life, was cold and dry. Nothing. She was not there. I could see in the black of her eyes that the warmth of life had departed. With no facet of her being left to which I could cling for signs of life, and still a great distance from Cana, I turned for the first time upward. Upward to address Him using the remote method of which He so often boasted.

"Why! Why did you have to take her? What do you want?" I sobbed uncontrollably as I bruised my hands on the earth below. "She loved you. I don't. She prayed to you. Don't you get it?"

I was now screaming so loudly I was certain someone could hear. I didn't care. Saliva was spilling down my chin from the unbridled pronouncements, and I had surely broken my wrists from pounding the ground. I didn't care. I raised my head to scream again, but a cry displaced the focused air necessary. I collapsed. Without the will to sustain the anger, I begged, as any man does when faced with loss.

"Please. I'm sorry. Please. I'll do anything. I'm sorry."

Nothing. I shrugged over her and lay still, at least to be close as my reality receded.

"Amir."

The voice was my father's again, but the speaker's identity rippled in the matter of existence. It was Him. With every word, the invisible particles surrounding us vibrated until it felt like I would dissolve from the radiance. It was still dark, and there was no visible sign of Jesus, but still, the mutterings sprang forth.

"Amir. I am sorry."

This was it. I hadn't made it to Cana, but this was my opportunity to burn it all down.

"Bullshit! I know the stories. I have seen you do it. You have the power. And yet . . . And yet my father is rotting in the ground. And she is . . ." Considering the lack of physical form, I didn't know where to fling my primal grievances. Instead, I swiveled in place, determined to address any direction the form might occupy.

"Amir, I am sorry. This was the only way. To subject man to death was the only way." Again, the air stirred with every word, and I couldn't help but quiver.

"What the hell do you mean? How could this be it? You don't die. If this is for sin, you don't sin. It didn't have to be this way. You could have made it better; let us live like you." I was reminded of Job but was determined to get more answers than these meager reports.

"Amir, you have come to believe there is no reality outside my control. In fact, there are some truths woven to the very fabric of being that are not a question of might, but rather of being." The deafening pronouncements coming from the black paused before posing a gentle question. "What makes you Amir?" I could sense the wording had been simplified for my own comprehension, but the ambiguity still left me confused.

"What?" I yelled back to the night.

"What makes you Amir? Is it your name? Or is your specific consciousness defined by characteristics?"

"You killed her. You kill everyone," I interjected into the cryptic sermon.

"*Quiet!*" For the first time in the conversation, the voice erupted with the proclamation. The energy rippling through my chest was not angry, but instead urgent. "Amir, I was alone. Not even in darkness, as your ancestors claimed. Alone to only my own thought and existence. Darkness was not. Words were not. Only my own being persisted, palpable no matter how void of form or unarticulated. But I wanted you. All of you. Sprouts of more life to share in the oddity of existence. So I breathed it so. Ethereal forms equal in potency and will to me and infallible. But no addition was made. Just as you, I am God not because of the word given to denote my existence. Instead, I, too, was defined by my characteristics. Never-ending. Perfectly willful. Just. So, when I manufactured another existence with these attributes, it only added to my own consciousness. I was forced by the very pinning of identity to vary the additive characteristics. And the only way to vary from superlative was to introduce deficit. Weakness. Limits. Ultimately, death."

I sat still in the blackness. At some point during the faceless soliloquy, I had stopped turning about and instead stared at the sky above. If they were only uttered in my imagination, the words would never be enough to qualm the pain, but language was not the only force at hand. I could see the truths expressed. Not imagine. Not create my own plausible scenes. I could see from the beginning void. As described, absolutely nothing was felt. No men. No animals. Not even words sprang from within to bring form to the feeling of being. And yet . . . I remained, or rather, He did. I could feel, as if radiating from my heart, an energy quelling within. The ripple quivered until finally it sprang forth, endowed with the mission of creation. It expanded in all directions and exploded into light, the first physical manifestation of the force which composed my core. But the light dissipated. Instead of propagating, the spherical energy heaved and breathed before rushing back to its center, my center. This was it, the moment described. The energy of perfect existence was only reabsorbed to its characteristic self, destined to require deficit for identity.

I snapped back to the darkness at hand. Moments ago, I would have thought of the sky as utterly void, but now having seen a true absence of matter, I realized the rich feeling of being. This was no void, no lifeless, formless emptiness. Even this black was more comforting than the fabric with which He was endowed. My eyes were streaming tears at the overwhelming vision of true creation. I still could not comprehend the universal laws at hand, but I felt His pain in the utter absence of a companion. Yet still, as my previous rage seemed quelled and turned to tears, I felt the limp corpse of Abigail at my feet. The pain rushed back, and I again collapsed atop her, now robbed of even my focused anger. Instead, I resolved to live in pain. No one to blame. No war cry to muster. Only tears to manifest my own radiating energy. The small droplets pooled on an unmoving crook of Abigail's neck.

After minutes, or perhaps longer, I was startled to a more conscious state. The surface below my flattened cheek was quivering. Fabric draped over skin was furling, a visual homage to movement. She was stirring! I took in a massive breath to ensure an uninterrupted analysis. However, as the minute quivers gave way to an overt reawakening, I let my bottled breath escape. Her lips, previously darkened and cold, had regained color. The sinews that typically ensure the palpable poise of one's hands were regaining lost ground. And finally, her eyes, which I now realized validate all life, sprung open. The dark brown orbs were bright and fresh with no evidence of the temporary extinguishment. The simple movements, which would normally garner no attention, sent a tremor through my being and even seemed to stagnate the surrounding air. Now it was I who was arrested.

As sequential moments were apparently allowed, my first movement was involuntary. I fell forward to Abigail's now outstretched arms and openly began to weep. As is the peculiar effect of hugs, we were united via the warm grain of skin but isolated in the preclusion of view. I could only imagine the position of Abigail's soft cheeks, which were now nestled upon my shoulder. In the ironic privacy of embrace, I lifted my eyes upward to the clichéd imagined perch of God. I could feel Him. No words punctuated the space, even telepathically, but I could feel the consolation. He had delivered her. Without explanation, He had delivered Abigail back to the time at hand. She was delivered to me, and I was at least logically indebted to Him. Calling the act an intervention seemed to suggest the very selective compassion against which I had so railed. Instead, I remained decidedly confused at the deliverance. Regardless of my meager understanding, I found myself silently mouthing to the imagined presence above, "Thank you. Thank you. Thank you . . ."

We staggered together as the sun crested to our left. Minutes into the journey, Abigail still had not uttered a word. Feeling that both of us were in a state of shock, I didn't attempt to dissolve the sanctity. But as a few quiet steps turned into a journey of silence, I began to worry Abigail had been struck mute by the encounter with death. Finally, as I found myself carefully peering intermittently from my periphery, I could hold off no longer.

"Abby?" I managed to keep my interjection to the graceful minimum. The addition of words could perhaps express my concerns more aptly, but it seemed each would only pollute the pure question of unaltered identity.

"Yes?" she retorted softly without shifting her focused gaze ahead.

I again examined her expression from the corner of my left eye. The observation was so peripheral as to cause an ongoing strain because of the obtuse angle. Her eyes were still wide, and unlike the Abby I knew, she seemed absent. Her answer, however brief, forced me to the very inquiries I despised after tragedy. I couldn't help but remember after my father's death. Every person who ever knew me came forward with a clichéd pronouncement of insight. "*He's in a better place. You'll get through this. You have to be strong for your family.*" I would stare absently forward and force my mutinous lip not to spring forth with the raging response within. And so now, as I walked beside another who had encountered the unknown end, I was not eager to deposit nonexistent wisdom.

"Nothing," I whispered more to the soil below than to the beauty beside me.

Now it was her eyes that I could feel stealthily invading the space between us. Her steps suddenly halted.

"Amir, stop for a moment. Please."

Her final word of the statement seemed unnecessary until I realized I was still being propelled forward by the rugged blocks of flesh below me. Perhaps, as Abigail was now hinting, it was I who was unprepared to address the extraordinary happening which had befallen her. It felt like resisting a flywheel to slow the emotionally devoid churn of my legs. When I finally did as she asked, Abigail was many yards behind, planted firm in the desert sand.

"Amir, look at me," she announced with more force than before.

Finally, I turned my eyes to the shrunken beauty at hand. Her tunic, already rudimentary in nature, was filthy, bearing signs of the harsh experience she had undergone. Her skin, typically smooth and soft, bore marred chasms telling the brutal record of illness. Every mark was another reminder of the absence nearly imposed, which I was afraid might still be imposed.

"I am here, Amir. I'm not dead." She strode purposefully toward me as she continued. "Please, Amir. I am here."

The final distance between us was bridged not via the movement of feet but rather of hands. She outstretched the appendages, far more expressive in their elegant extension than the previous steps. They seemed to float as each finger gently furled into my tunic to convince me of the claim of physical presence.

"I am here. I am here."

I relished the force, carefully stowing the sensory perception of her strong hold. She was here. Every crooked finger drew in a breadth of fabric until I was pressed tight to her chest. She knew. Her sparing words had so easily articulated the fear which had taken hold: the fear which always took hold. Even so, I couldn't help but continue to mutter quietly to myself.

"Never again. Never Again. We can't go back," I whispered.

However, as Abigail suddenly held me at arm's length, it was clear my words had been heard.

"What are you talking about? Where can't we go?" she inquired. The hoarseness of her voice was so pathetic as to demand an answer for fear of feeling completely heartless.

"The Valley," I honestly exclaimed. "We can't go back to the Valley."

She immediately looked both confused and downtrodden. "What does the Valley have to do with this?"

"Don't you see," I explained, "the people, however needing, made you sick! See . . ." I pointed and gagged at the back of my own throat. "Sterling put a membrane in my sputum. It helps prevent sickness. We've never seen these viruses, Abby. These versions are thousands of generations before those we know. Every pathogen has the potential to kill us . . . to kill you!"

Until this point in my explanation, my eyes had bounced from point to point, but now I looked straight to her tear-streaked face.

"We can never go back."

I knew the announcement would devastate her, and I prepared for the worst. However, as I watched, she again surprised me.

"Amir . . . it's okay."

"No, Abby, it's not! You don't have the membra—" She cut me off.

"Amir! Stop! I'm not going to get sick anymore."

"Yes, you will. Although I would like to believe that eternal sentiment of humankind, how could you possibly know that?" I inquired. My tone, despite best efforts, was now sounding less lovingly concerned and more pompous.

She waited some time as my breaths slowed and denoted a reduced intensity.

"Did He," she looked upward, "talk to you when I was . . . gone?"

"Yes," I succinctly answered, not eager to transition to some sort of praise.

"He spoke to me too, Amir." She smiled, perhaps at the recollection of the experience. It was a smile unlike any I had seen. The facial expression was so peaceful and yet intense that I couldn't possibly imagine the state of being it denoted. "He said I wouldn't get sick again . . . ever. He said that love had saved me. His love. Your love. Even my mother's love. Even my love. Amir, don't you see? We have to go back to the Valley. As long as we love, He will protect me."

I couldn't believe it. Part of me had unavoidably started imagining a clichéd meeting of Abigail and Christ amongst backlit clouds. The other, more sophisticated part was overjoyed. The truth was I didn't want to stop visiting the Valley. They needed the fish. They needed the bread. And most of all, I needed them. Some semblance of identity was the only component of sanity I still reserved. And so, as if joining some jovial cult, I slowly allowed the same goofy grin to overtake my stoic face. Again we regained the shared mission of outreach, and again we were more tightly bound than ever. As we finally began to recognize the telltale features of camp, I involuntarily looked up. As was the case during my initial training, I found myself whispering, "Thank you. Thank you. Thank you." I wasn't sure what the autonomic reflex revealed of my own state of faith, but I decided, for once, not to care.

APRIL 13, 32 AD

Our days had added one to another to form a life. Each day, we traversed the jagged hills to record the evolving mission of Christ. Some days were cloaked in mundanity, leaving little evidence of His deity other than profound soliloquy. Others were marked with fantastic miracles, surprisingly similar to the accounts of the Bible. The accuracy of the script's progression left little doubt: the days left of watching God amongst men were few. We never articulated this insight to one another. Having trained together in the biblical, we were both confident in the other's understanding. Accordingly, each morning we watched, riveted as God lovingly marched to His own demise. Our moods were only lifted in the afternoon as we packed up our standard load of fish and loaves and marched onward to the Valley. Today was no different, and as we efficiently heaved the risen loaves into our packs, the solemn morning turned to a hopeful afternoon.

"I wonder what Levi has been up to," I casually muttered to begin the shift in focus.

"Hmm . . . if I know Levi, he has probably been running between Mica and Nasir, debating some obscure fact! I bet he has quite a row going between the two."

She was right. Ever since we had begun addressing the Valley's physical needs, new life had emerged, and Levi never got tired of seeing it. He ran from one resident to another and poked and prodded until they erupted at the mention of some deeply held belief. Sometimes Levi legitimately disagreed with them, but other times, he had admitted to me he simply wanted to see the intensity of life now regained. "It shows in their eyes," he claimed.

The truth was that Levi was not just compelling because of his similarity to Hasim. He was compelling because of his own fantastically naïve nature, and I wasn't the only person subject to his effect.

Abigail, too, had long ago adopted him into our unspoken clan. His parents, although more vibrant than before, were obviously still precarious at best. Almost every day, they pulled us aside when Levi was occupied with some discussion. "Please," they whispered, "when we go, please take care of Levi."

We constantly retorted with the ridiculousness of their concern, but we all knew we were just being polite. They were very sick, regardless of the provisions we brought. We had come to love everyone in the Valley, and the potential loss was difficult to imagine. However, the thought of taking care of Levi was of no concern. Our love for him was organic, without pretense or mission. He was consumed with a thirst for God, but his faith had little to do with our affection. He was a character worthy of letters—prose written back and forth to describe some newfound love.

As we walked the familiar path from our desert camp to the rocky valley, we laughed at stories of Levi. I recounted a recent instance when he had run covertly from one dwelling to another and carefully unearthed a difference of opinion. He had revealed each position so tactfully, as to leave the two yearning only to argue with the fire of sincere belief. Meanwhile, Levi sat concealed behind the corner and relished the newfound energy. He was a troublemaker of the best kind. Abigail recounted her own tales of his mischief, and our cackles resounded throughout the secluded procession until we reached the telltale signs of the Valley's mouth. One rock always articulated our arrival. Its striated form arched high above us like a forgotten cathedral entrance. I lifted my eyes to examine its monolithic underbelly as we passed. Abigail, too, shifted her gaze upward until suddenly stopping and lowering to the ground. I turned back to see why she had stopped. The pace of her movement didn't suggest an injury but rather the need to adjust some unruly piece of clothing.

"You okay?" I inquired.

She casually waved an outstretched hand forward toward the Valley as if to spur my movement on without her. "Yeah, just need to fix this blasted shoe."

She began to tease one leather cord through another until the shoe started to look composed again. The rudimentary weave had been a constant annoyance throughout our travels, and she had been forced to stop often to address its unraveling.

"Go ahead!" she exclaimed, again beckoning to the Valley's entrance only meters away at this point. I conceded and strode forward to the opening.

The Valley, as we had come to call it, was the perfect reprieve for the many forgotten souls it housed. The jagged rocks and shrubs peeking from darkened crevices shielded the outcasts from the prying eyes of an ancient society eager to eradicate them. Even so, when we had first arrived in the crescent, bearing our biblical sustenance, the residents were reluctant to even leave their dwellings that blended well into the ramshackle hills. With each day, and every additional calorie provided, they gained both strength and vibrancy. Now when we emerged into the shadowy terrain, we were met with a procession of slow-moving villagers. Of course, one figure moved faster than the rest, traversing the chatting statues and attacking at first sight of our arrival. It was with this ritualistic greeting in mind that I finally broke through the entrance and prepared for the onslaught of Levi. However, as my first shoe struck the dusty earth below, I was faced with silence. The air, devoid of the resonant vibration, was immediately disturbing. I scanned the settlement for the familiar wrinkled faces that had become our family. No one. No old woman weaving together the strands of some nameless weeds. No disheveled old men discussing the unrelenting requirements of marriage. And most noticeably, no Levi surging forth to greet me with an unwanted fact. However, just when the stagnant air was beginning to seize in my lungs for fear of their fate, I heard a shuffling to my right. I turned just in time to see a tall man with several others in tow emerge from the nearest dwelling. Their tunics were distinctly new. The cloth was so white that it left little doubt of ever having worked. The only color purer in the muddled environment was the deep black of their tightly groomed beards. As they approached, I covertly looked over my shoulder to ensure Abigail hadn't followed yet.

"You there! Who are you?" They addressed me with an air of authority and strode confidently within arm's reach.

Just as I thought they would surely walk right into me, they separated their ranks and surrounded me. Not all of them were taller than me, but their general condition, as compared to my recent company, was enough to ensure intimidation. My heart quickened as I turned in place to address the hardened gaze of each. As my pivot provided a view of the Valley's entrance, I strained to see any sign of Abigail, hopeful that she would not walk directly into the ominous scene. Initially, I saw no sign of her shining brown eyes, but as I drew my eyes tight together to filter the bright sun, I saw her face shadowed between two rocks. Her mouth was obscured by the presence of a small dirty hand: Levi. He had apparently stopped her from making the same mistake and was now holding her back from any pronouncement. Careful not to stall the pace of my turn and give away their position, I again faced my lead interrogator.

"I am just a weary traveler, come to seek refuge in this . . ." I beckoned to the disheveled dwellings, "this Valley of the forgotten. Please. I am very tired and wish only to take my place among them." I stood stark still and bottled my breath to hear any audible tells of reaction.

He emitted no sound, and his eyes remained unblinking. As is often the case with villains, he seemed superhuman in focus and ability.

"What's in the bag, traveler?" he retorted without any inflection to reveal his intent.

Sweat was now dripping in large noticeable droplets from my furrowed brow. My palms were equally moistened, and I was fighting to control a noticeable twitch. I swallowed a bolus of air and addressed his inquiry.

"The few trappings of a poor man," I managed without making any move to open the rugged sack.

His eyes drifted and stopped upon my package, which was apparently of great interest to the group. Just as I was certain his intense gaze would burn through the sack and skip the formality of opening, he turned away toward the dwellings.

"These . . ." he grasped for a word, "people. It's my job to know every one of them. To insist on behalf of Pontius that they submit their dues. I don't come any more than required for . . . obvious reasons." He wiped some minor dust from his tunic as he pronounced the vile assessment. Now he turned sharply back to me. "The last time I came to this cursed place, these wretches were wasting away, their ribs being their most defining feature. But now . . . now they are fed. Their filthy faces show evidence of smiles, and it seems death has been staved off for a time. And yet. And yet, they still have no money for the empire. So, traveler. I'm afraid I have to insist. What's in the bag?"

I grasped for some clever response in my repertoire of languages, but before I could present a verbal offering, the man sprang forth and grabbed the sack. He pulled it violently toward himself with such force that the makeshift strap stood little chance. Its fibers instantly cleaved, leaving me no recourse to attempt a struggle. I did reach instinctively through the air, which always seemed to be of a particularly thick variety in such interactions, only to be flung backward by one of the onlooking goons. I landed hard in the dirt and sat helpless as my original accuser gently opened the sack. I had grown accustomed to the anatomical conditioning of the ancient peoples, and even from this distance, I could perceive the smoothness of his unworked hands. As the top of the sack unfurled and revealed the dozens of fish and loaves, his eyes seemed to erupt in elated confirmation of his theory.

"I knew it! I knew these putrid beggars couldn't manage this alone! I knew they must have adopted some thief to join their pathetic ranks."

He dumped the contents out before the group to show the improbable amount of food. I began to open my mouth in defense but couldn't help but remember my early encounter with the ancient justice system. There was no use. Having watched a great deal of them from the lenses of my scopes, I knew the impossibility of such a man, worn and tattered yet carrying a storehouse atop his back.

There had never been such a man afforded the improbability, and I was not to be the first.

"Grab him and let's go," he beckoned to his henchmen.

Again, I imagined struggling. Punching and kicking. Biting and scratching. However, with Abigail and Levi just around the rocky point, I wanted any movements to unfold slowly and deliberately. If some chaotic fight ensued, it seemed possible they might be happened upon. Instead, I allowed my arms to be secured without tensing a muscle. I allowed every sinew to dangle limp and submissive. These men's hands were not smooth like their master's. Their muscle-bound instruments constricted around my wrists and biceps until I thought my thin bones would snap. They heaved me toward the Valley's mouth. Our path would come dangerously close to Abigail and Levi, and I began to shout to give them a clandestine warning.

"Please! Don't take me away from these people. Not away from this Valley."

The content of my speech was rudimentary and practically unconsidered. I was only interested in its reverberation throughout the rocky surroundings. The sound would both let them know we were coming and conceal their scrambling attempts to evade.

"Let go of me, you heathens!" I continued yelling, but my mind had already recoiled to a place reserved for upheaval and now unashamedly turned to prayer.

Please. Please don't let them find Abigail. Let them hide amongst the rocks. Protect them. My mental pleading repeated these basic requests over and over. I had always wondered why the faithful's desperate soliloquies sounded so stupidly redundant, but I now realized that our most basic desires are rarely complicated. Regardless of the message's eloquence, it seemed to have worked. Whether by divine intervention or simple luck, we saw no sign of the pair as we curled around the jagged opening. As we passed under the arched outcropping that had greeted me on our way in, I stopped my senseless yelling and fell into lockstep with my captors.

We plodded slowly westward across a particularly barren stretch of desert. The men's pace was deliberate. It felt as if they had performed this procession many times. I imagined that each step was slipping into a familiar track left from the day before, and my own footsteps were aligned with some other poor captive who was lying imprisoned at the end of this sequence. After thousands of these cloned steps, we began to see the telltale signs of settlement. There were intermittent grooves in the impervious desert floor, perhaps where some tired donkey had dragged a scraping wagon full of goods. And there were remnants of long-forgotten homes. I had seen this in many of the villages: old dwellings abandoned as their creators managed enough funds to move onward or decided to simply seek a more hopeful existence. I wasn't sure of the small town's name, but it was clear this was our destination.

"Lock him up," my main captor exclaimed before peeling away from the group, apparently close enough to home to pursue his evening. He turned back to the others as he walked away. "Tomorrow, we can bring him to Jerusalem. I've never seen him, but the Romans will pay for a thief."

My mind raced. These characters, unlike the characters in my last painful encounter, were focused on money. It was clear their allegiance lay in the Roman government, and they made no attempts to cloak it in righteousness or piety. The other men retained their stifling grasp throughout the length of the small town. As I passed, people emerged one after another to watch the happening. In a strange leveling, even my captors seemed exhausted by the journey. I could sense they knew the onlookers and wanted to appear strong despite their own exhaustion.

Accordingly, their tight grasps also leaned with a silent weight as the whole group used me as a makeshift crutch. Finally, after having been dragged through the entire town, they turned to address an extremely short structure. The only recognizable portion was the packed roof, which was maybe two feet from the shadowed earth below. As we drew close, one man released his hand from my arm and placed it firmly on the back of my head. Then he pushed down with such force to insist my frame crumple toward the low mouth of the lean-to. Indeed, as I relented, there became visible a makeshift opening in the stacked rock walls. This being the second ancient prison I had entered, I now knew each had its own distinct form of torture. My last cell had been dark and dangerously jagged. This new home was so small as to not even afford enough room to roll from back to front. As I shuffled into the space on my stomach, I realized I wouldn't be able to turn around due to the tunnel's size. Instead, as I heard some makeshift cover being secured behind me, I was forced to face the space's dark and menacing end. I couldn't perceive its conclusion due to lack of light, but it seemed inevitable that it was the ideal home of hostile creatures that would be unhappy to receive company. My arms were still bent at the elbow from having shimmied in, and I now had to decide where to rest the bruised appendages. I could force them back underneath my stomach and leave myself completely unsupported in the dirt, or I could extend them forward into the dark crevice to be devoured by whatever angry cohort was lurking. I tucked them under me and turned my head as far as possible out of the dirt. And here I was again, the familiar imprisonment of unconstrained thought.

It felt like I had been here countless times. In the cell after stealing the watch. In the cave after running into the shepherd. Never afforded the common decency of a cellmate with whom to commune and now seeing the inevitable faces again. Abigail. Mum. Hasim. Even Levi now invaded the darkened existence. Their faces cycled with such speed as to merge together to one general form of a silhouette of value. Everything I had. Finally, as the painful images became almost unbearable, I started to consider my circumstance with logic. I had been here twice before and had somehow been delivered in both cases. Once by a madman hellbent on delivering the world and once by God Himself. It was the latter that now gave me hope. Prayers intermittently objected in my darkened silence. However, as seemed to be the story of my life, self-reliance cried out in competition. Now a new image dominated my thoughts: the drone. Since my last imprisonment, I had new tools. Perhaps the concealed drone could link to my magnetic tethers, still firmly anchored in my shoulders, and lift me from this prison. I considered the structure around me as best I could. I tilted my neck to and fro to examine the walls and roof. The walls were stacked with heavy stone and bound with rudimentary mortar. The roof, however, was more skeletal in nature. A matrix of thick wooden trunks supported a dense thatch of reeds. The grid, although less imposing than the stones, was stout. Just as an initial test, I arched my back as much as allowed and pushed upward. My bony spine wedged into a small orifice between trunks. At first, I could feel the grid deflecting, but almost immediately, it stopped giving. It wasn't clear whether the drone could apply the force needed to pull me and the roof upward, but it was worth a shot.

I waited until darkness had consumed the village before summoning my technological aid, *Command: Deploy concealed drone to my current location. Initiate tethered magnetic connection and initiate max load lifting.* I finished the thought and began to wait, feeling as I imagined a mental patient might after speaking in their own head. However, just as I began to wonder if there was some malfunction with the interface, I felt the long-forgotten sensation of tethering. My shoulders, previously slouched upon the dusty floor, began to forcibly arch backward toward the roof immediately above. They rapidly contacted the wooden framework. The timbers, which lacked the hewn surface of a future component, dug into the skin as the force continued to strengthen. The timbers noticeably began to flex upward under the painful direction of my anatomy. With every moment, the force became more unbearable, but finally, the timbers started to crack audibly. The sounds of vulnerability grew louder and louder until I was certain the roof would explode in a shower of splinters. However, my bones were also signaling weakness. Their communication was not audible but instead took the form of an overwhelming wave throughout my back. I was now perfectly pinned at the shoulders to the roof, and it felt as if the unusual condition would rip my scapula from their very underpinnings. I cried out in agony as unconscious pain overcame my paranoia of discovery. Finally, these joints did add to the cacophony of cracking, and after one particularly loud pop, I could withstand the force no more.

Command: Disengage magnetic tethers and stow the concealed drone at camp. In this case, I would have welcomed a slower reaction as I was immediately dropped to the floor below. The roof, which had, in fact, been only slightly deflected, remained relatively stationary. It was clear that the force had been absorbed in many unseen cracks, likely permeating the members but providing no clear escape. I lay on the ground below and heaved. My arms had crumpled beneath me upon release, but I could no longer move them, perhaps due to injury, or more likely extreme fatigue. And indeed, now I found all resolve for the day gone. Before all of this, I might have reflected on my own misfortune, but now as I drifted in and out of consciousness, I could only think of Abigail. I hoped she had stayed with Levi. She knew the way back to camp, but the thought of her traversing the desert-scape alone was too much to bear. The truth was, I had no idea what she would do in such a situation. I hoped she wouldn't follow me in misplaced bravery, but she had, after all, followed me through time. I prayed to Jesus as I finally relented to sleep.

The morning was announced with labored grunts as the robust metal gate was released from behind me. The sun had not yet crested the meandering horizon, but as I was roughly pulled from my living mausoleum, it was clear yesterday's goons were early risers. They lifted me to my feet and took hold of my arms. In a welcome surprise, I was able to feel their grasp and mildly react despite the extreme forces of my attempted escape. In the absence of defining light, I could only make out the men's contours: the sharp bridge of a nose, an angular jaw, or the occasional protruding ear. The man to my right presented a smaller and somewhat softer outline than the other giants. He was shorter than me, and while the others made crude jokes and violently prodded me, he remained silent. Even his grasp on my arm felt more measured instead of simply being as tight as possible. In a trend that apparently persisted in all times, their boss was the last one to show, even though he had retired first the night before. Judging from his oblong gait, he was still recovering from some tonics of the night before. As he reached the group's periphery, he snapped, and the men initiated the same deliberate march as before.

With every step, I subtly swiveled my head back and forth to search for any sign of Abigail. I prayed with every turn that I didn't see her amongst the onlookers. Each face we passed presented a different account of my condition, like a series of distorted mirrors at a carnival. Judging from some faces, I must have looked quite injured and pathetic, enough to garner sympathetic nods. Others expressed only contempt and seemed to be quite happy with the judgment cast. We passed one after the other in a long line of reflections before I saw her: Abigail. No one else would have seen her, but I knew from the very way she moved. She was draped in a long dark tunic that covered even her face, and she ducked between buildings at the rear of the crowd. From this distance, I could just make out her shining brown eyes. Even from here, I could see that they were slightly reddened from crying. I silently mouthed to Jesus to keep her concealed. I begged not to let her be discovered. I was careful not to let my eyes linger too long on her for fear my escort would notice. After one last flash of her flowing cover, we were out of town. My stomach turned at having seen Abigail but having to stay silent. Everything besides reason urged me to call out to her. However, with every step, we distanced ourselves from the town and settled into the slow pace of inevitability.

I tried to recall the map imparted during training but couldn't figure out exactly where we were. An even bigger question was what was waiting for me in Jerusalem. During one particularly barren stretch, the group strung out, and I found myself only held by the shortest, gentlest man. I took the opportunity to meekly beg for information.

"What happens when we get to Jerusalem?" I whispered without lifting my head to address him. He didn't answer and made no sign of having heard me. Thinking perhaps he hadn't, I added a few more decibels to the inquiry. "What happens when we get to Jerusalem?"

"Shhhh . . ." he scolded softly.

"Please," I pressed, "please, I just want to know what I'm in for."

He waited until the others broke out in a raunchy conversation before finally addressing my question.

"Look, I don't know. I don't even want to be here, but we need the money to eat. All I know is the Romans have people there for stuff like this."

"Stuff like what?" I asked, curious of what all they claimed I had done.

"Stealing. Stopping the coins from making it to Pontius," he replied. There was notable disdain for the system, and it was clear the man was not excited to be involved.

"What will they do to me?" I asked, finally happening upon the most basic question of all men.

"It depends. Throw you in one of their prisons. Make you a slave to one of their generals. I don't know . . ." He sighed deeply before continuing. "Please, just walk."

I complied. I had gleaned all I could from him, and now the other members of our party grew closer to assume their holds. We walked for many hours more under the desert sun. It beat down upon us without reprieve until the journey felt like a lifetime. The men would occasionally stop and take long draws from their water bladder. They only afforded me a small gulp, and I was certain I would collapse from thirst. Finally, as the terrain started to blur together in a mirage of dust and stones, we saw the city: Jerusalem. Until now, I had stuck to the small outposts of the region. Villages inhabited by the poor and organized around the town well. But as we approached, it was clear that Jerusalem was entirely different. The land broke into angular faces that alternated between shadowed valleys and sunlit hills. Every monolithic face was dotted with hundreds of simple molded dwellings. Smoke billowed from some, perhaps denoting the baking of some tasty loaf. People strode everywhere, and the sounds of busy commerce overwhelmed. Here, no one stopped to observe our progression. This was apparently a daily occurrence and not worthy of even cursory observation.

The venomous leader of our party meandered through the alleys and passages at a dizzying rate. Now that we had arrived in the city, he seemed quite eager to get paid. Despite the circumstances, I couldn't help but marvel at the ancient metropolis as we passed. Intermittently, merchants would emerge in our path to assail us with their offerings. Whatever member of our party was closest would shove the store owners aside with little concern for their landing. I found myself saying a silent prayer for each as they landed in various states. Finally, after countless turns, we slowed at the sight of a semicircular enclosure.

Stone walls formed the boundary of the enclosure, with the interior a series of iron gates. The components were tightly bound, obviously having been composed by more expert hands than I had yet encountered. Behind each gate stood dingy men. Some let their arms dangle through the bars, while others shriveled in the dark corners of their rooms. In the center of the radius stood an enormous man pacing back and forth. He was dressed far differently than those I had yet encountered. A striated leather skirt obscured his legs, and he wore a formal tunic across his chest. The architecture, in conjunction with the formal guard, made the Roman outpost obvious. The large guard strode toward us immediately and addressed my captors.

"What's this?" He pointed toward me with a rigid outstretched arm. The leader of the crew pushed me forward to be more visible.

"A thief, sir. We found him delivering goods to a great many debtors. More than they could afford in a year, and yet not one has paid taxes to the empire."

The man walked forward to inspect me. No one was physically holding me anymore, and none seemed concerned I might escape.

"What's your name, thief?" he barked into my face.

I started to consider what fake name might be best when a hint of movement caught my eye on a roof several structures behind our position. I squinted in the glaring light and struggled to see what the shape was. I couldn't make out the outline, but it looked suspiciously like the dark tunic Abigail had been in at the last town. Just as I relocated the shape, the guard hit me hard in the stomach with a tightly clenched fist.

"No name it is!" he cried as I doubled over in pain.

He grabbed the conveniently presented back of my neck and pushed me into the most adjacent open cell. I fell to the ground and tried to regain my breath after the hard blow. The guard walked back to my captors and started to negotiate a price.

"You will be paid according to the prisoner's final verdict," he announced.

"And when is that? We just made a day's trip to bring you this thief, and I don't intend to leave without our money!"

"Relax," the guard said with an air of condescension, "the governor is hearing cases tomorrow, and from what I hear, they're eager to send a message of taxes and theft. Your boy might be a perfect no-name to make an example out of." He flashed a toothy grin to the gentlemen, indicating their good fortune. "You can't leave town anyway. You'll have to present the circumstances before the governor."

The men conferred with one another then shrugged in agreement before leaving. The guard's words about my future sentencing were concerning, but with my breath regained, I first stood and scanned the rooftops for any sign of the figure. Nothing. The small glimpse of fabric furling in the wind was nowhere to be found. Hopefully, it had been a mirage: a shape conjured in my own recessed longing. Nonetheless, I remained at the gate with my hands firmly clenched around the rough bars and continued to watch for a reemergence.

Our journey had stolen almost every hour of daylight, and now darkness approached quickly. I was starving, having only received water throughout the trip. Despite still wanting to look for Abigail, I could no longer muster the energy to stand and instead curled up in the dirt toward the front of the enclosure. Most of the prisoners had long ago stopped any chatter, and the compound was surprisingly still. I could barely see the darkened exterior when a small object descended into view. I opened my eyes wide to look incredulously at the item. It was a loaf of bread! A small, dingy string was tied around the morsel and trailed up above my cell. I peered out to the center guard station. He was asleep and not aware of any of the happenings. I hadn't examined the complex in detail, but I remembered only one story of cells, leaving the source of this lifeline still a mystery. I had eagerly taken the loaf in hand and began to untie the string when I heard the familiar voice.

"Amir!" Abigail's whisper cut through from above. "Amir, did I get the right cell? Are you okay?"

I breathed in sharply in contradiction: half-elated at the arrival and half-horrified for her safety.

"Abby!" I whispered upward, always keeping an eye on the slumbering watchmen. "Abby, you shouldn't have come here! It's too dangerous!" I tried to carefully meter my tone to convey concern but not anger.

"We had to, Amir! We're going to get you out of here. Do you know what they're going to do next?"

"What do you mean 'we'?" I quickly retorted, hoping she had misspoken.

"Hi, Amir . . ." Levi reluctantly acknowledged, also from above.

"Abby!" I scolded. "He shouldn't be here either! Both of you need to leave now. I will get out of here. Don't worry."

"I told him not to come, but he wouldn't let me go alone," she whispered back.

It made sense. Although Levi and I had developed an intense bond, he was fiercely protective of Abby. I couldn't help but smile at his grit.

"Where do you go from here?" she pressed again.

"I don't know," I honestly responded. "They said I go before the governor tomorrow for a verdic—"

Before I could finish, the guard let out a loud snore and seemed to stir.

"Get out of here!" I urged. Convinced by the stirring guard, I heard their light footsteps shuffling away atop my cell. "I love you!" I announced just loud enough to carry them away to the night.

Just as the sound of their steps grew too faint to hear, the guard stood and shrugged off sleepiness. I immediately dropped to the floor and descended to sleep: at first fake, followed quickly by the real thing.

I woke to the sound of more voices inspecting the prisoners of each cell. Again, the sun hadn't yet risen, but a trove of troops was walking to and fro in the compound. They rapidly arrived at my enclosure, and the night guard recounted my information.

"He was found transferring stolen goods to a group of debtors. None have paid taxes, and no one knows his identity."

The group immediately erupted into hushed discussions. I could barely make out the mutterings but caught intermittent words. They seemed to be fixated on the allegation of thievery and my unknown name. Finally, after a few minutes of deliberation, one nodded to the guard and gestured to the lock on my iron gate. The guard produced a large flat key and immediately sprang the mechanism. The largest of the men, all clothed like the guard, took me by the arm and led me to an elevated cart. The wooden frame of the cart had rusted connections and was firmly tied to the tired ass of an ass. As I stepped up to enter the cart, I realized I was the only prisoner yet taken. The troops were still outside and made no movement to set out with the cart.

"We just need one more," they said to the guard, gesturing to the yet unexamined cells.

They continued the exercise and quickly moved out of earshot. I sat stationary within the cart until they gestured to another cell. Just as before, the guard opened the cell door and stepped back to allow the captive out. For a few seconds, it wasn't clear if there was a man within. Then, from the darkness, a figure emerged. His hair was matted, and his eyes looked bloodshot. He looked as though he had been in the dark corners of the cell for years. Upon exiting the cell, he stared up at the bright sun and stretched before turning back to the troops. I watched as he stared at each of them with his fiery eyes before resolutely spitting on the nearest one. I gasped at the man's impertinence and could barely watch what would undoubtedly come next. The soldier swiveled his hips before launching a fist firmly into the prisoner's grimy face. It knocked him to the ground, and the troop took the opportunity to thrust several kicks to the man's ribs. The other soldiers watched and laughed for the first few strikes before finally pulling the two apart. They roughly grabbed the man and dragged him toward the cart. As they approached, I scurried toward the cart's front, not eager to encounter the bloodied man so quickly. My isolationist strategy of cowering away from the entrance turned out to be futile as they practically threw the rugged figure directly to my position. However, as soon as he landed, he bolted upright to the bars to fling a final insult at the Romans.

"Godforsaken snakes!" he cried through the bars as they rounded the sides of the wagon to whip the donkey to movement.

After it was clear they were gone, he finally turned back to me.

"Goddamn snakes. They say I stole from them. What about them! They take everything we have. You steal too?" he inquired while carefully examining my face.

I nodded in what I would imagined would be the manner of a hardened criminal. This seemed enough to him, and he sat back against the side of the enclosure, roughly over the wheel's bearing point. I scooted forward to see the city as we traversed the narrow paths. The night before, there had been many people meandering between the storefronts and dwellings, but now there were absolute hordes. The crowds were so massive that the soldiers had to part the numbers for the donkey to crawl forward.

I turned back to my fellow captive and inquired of the crowd's size, "Is there always this many people?"

He barely looked up, and the tone of his answer denoted a realization that I was perhaps an idiot. "Passover."

I took in a sharp breath. He was right. The sequence of my capture had left me disoriented to the calendar, but Passover had been mere days away when we were taken. I looked back out to the crowds. There was a palpable energy binding the people into excited clumps. At every turn, they were hunched into groups, and hushed whispers vibrated in the air. I strained to hear what they were saying, but the cart's wheels were too loud against the uneven streets.

To my disbelief, the crowds only grew larger as we entered a large courtyard and came to a stop. I peered out the sunlit opening until one of the soldiers came around to unlock the gate. The mechanism sprung with a mechanical clang, and we filed out of the cart one at a time. The new morning sun was directly in my eyes as I exited, and I squinted to perceive my newest surrounding. As the sunspots faded from my vision, they were replaced by a mass of people loosely formed into a circle. In the center of the radius, there was an ornately constructed mass carefully crafted of wood. Its many facets each led to the next in a gentle taper until all that remained was a small platform with an even smaller man perched atop it. He sat rigid and unmoving and looked down upon my savage companion and me. His attire, although still militant in nature, was far more ornate than the Roman troops yet encountered. The trim of every segment of his battle skirt was articulated with golden rivets, and his breast bore several medals of apparent achievement. His hair was carefully manicured to fold neatly to one side, and his eyes beamed with intelligence.

He was silent, but the surrounding hordes were deafening. In truth, only half of them seemed to be producing most of the noise. The rest were huddled in small groups, nervously talking with intermittent looks in our direction. The nearest guard took me by the arm and led me toward the base of the wooden perch. Because we had stopped the cart immediately upon entering the circular enclosure, our path had to meander dangerously close to the crowd. Their boundary was maintained by a series of rudimentary dividers. As we drew near, I tried to drown out the shouting and catch a snippet of their conversations. Two young men near the boundary flashed me a quick glance then turned back to one another. I was just close enough to make out a few words.

"I've never seen him; is that him?" one man asked the other.

"No, that's not him," the other responded. "I saw him in Galilee, and that's not him. You'll know when you see him. He . . ."

They kept talking, but our path quickly led me out of earshot. The roaring noise and general chaos precluded me from focusing much on their words, and I instead began scanning the crowd for Abigail. All the while, I had started trying to predict the potential extent of my punishment. I cringed, remembering my record on such predictions. After stealing the watch, I had been condemned for far longer than I anticipated. Then again, when caught by the shepherd, I was shocked by the severity of my judgment. Now I found myself whispering silently to Jesus for mercy. As we finally approached the man's perch, I saw no sign of Abigail and received no reply from Jesus. The guard pushed me hard to the ground at the base of the mass. They held the other prisoner in the wing, as I was to go first. And so, lacking the assistance of man or God, I turned my head upward to face the lifted man.

"Prisoner. You have been accused of probable theft and of aiding the evasion of taxes. Your accusers will be given the opportunity to speak before any defense is mounted." He beckoned to one station of the surrounding crowd, and the man who had caught me in the Valley stepped forth.

"Governor Pontius," he began. The name brought into stark reality the historical gravity of my predicament. "We happened upon this man in an area known to house a great number of debtors. He was carrying a sack with enough goods to feed them for a week and yet could offer no explanation or payment of taxes. It was obvious he was a thief sent out by the wretches to aid in their crimes."

Pontius did not respond immediately. Although he sat high above on the condescending architecture, he did not radiate immediate decision. In fact, as the silence wore on, I was unsure whether he would ever cast a judgment. He peered down from the distance and looked intently into my eyes.

"And prisoner, what is your account of this? Did you know these people were debtors to the state, and how do you account for such a load?"

I considered a great number of lies but somehow felt it best to offer a simple response without excuse. Perhaps my encounters with Jesus had imparted some morality. Or perhaps I had simply lost my nerve with every stone cast. Regardless, I opted to stare into his blue eyes and deliver the truth.

"Those people, regardless of their debt to the state, were starving. I didn't know much other than that. And as for the food, I have no explanation."

He waited another long moment before carefully adding four slow words to our exchange, "*Did you steal it?*" Each word was crisp and cutting, obviously spoken by someone busy enough to detest banter.

I matched his clarity in my response. "No."

At this, he sat back and broke our eye contact for the first time. I was so close to the heightened seat that I could see only his shoes when he leaned back and had no expressions with which to judge his thoughts. While I waited, I considered my fate. Stealing some food. Even now, in the brutal times of old, it couldn't be the worst offense known. However, the creases of my palms filled with sweat as I remembered the guards mentioning being made an example. As the thought festered in the silence, I practically started to shake until Pontius finally spoke again. This time he spoke in a grander tone, obviously reserved for public address.

"This man is unknown to me. His lack of title or even name leaves no evidence of character. However, when I stare into his eyes, I am not convinced of the malice accused. Therefore, I turn to you, the knowing public. Is there a group among you who can vouch for this man? Are there persons here who can tell us of his past and shed light on his soul?"

His booming voice had instantly silenced the crowd, and they all continued to stare intently at him even after he concluded. His effort to discern my nature from the onlookers was, in fact, noble, but as the silence lingered, I started to imagine the voice I might hear: Abigail. Perhaps her skin, reddened but still not brown, would draw no attention since covered. But what if they demanded to know her background? I started to furiously scan the crowd, looking for any sign of her. It was a much easier exercise than before as every face was oriented toward me and all were starkly still. Just as I concluded there was no cause for concern, that Abigail had wisely decided not to attend, I saw her. The billowing black garment was following her thin frame as she climbed atop some riffraff. It looked like she was preparing to make an announcement.

With no other choice, I turned back to face Pontius and delivered my own loud, clear pronouncement.

"None of these dogs will know me, for my mother was not a bitch. I have no remorse for you or any state. To your god or any. You cannot fathom my crimes, as no one can fathom those of Rome. So judge my fate as you should Rome itself!"

The insults worked, and the crowd erupted into rage-filled chaos. This arena, and crowd-induced adrenaline therein, seemed to be a favorite form of entertainment for the people. I was certain I had doomed my fate to the strictest of judgments, but Abigail's voice was drowned out and her righteous self-endangerment extinguished. Even through the heaving crowd, I could see her standing high amongst the throngs. Her eyes were streaming with tears as she stood, still prepared to make her defense of me. Our eyes met, and I now pronounced silently just three words, "I love you." I continued to drown out the noise and take in her defeated nod until Pontius finally responded.

"I'm afraid you've left me little choice," he said quietly to me before again addressing the crowd. "He is to be propped up, secured to the intersection, and left to the setting sun!"

The crowd roared in approval. I swiveled to and fro, trying to glean more about the announcement. Before I could appeal to Pontius and ask more about his cryptic words, the guards grabbed me and forcibly dragged me away from his perch.

"Where are you taking me!? Please, where are you taking me!?" I shouted at the strong men.

Likely enraged by my comments, they only pulled more violently and offered no further explanation. They dragged me through the crowd, which took the opportunity to contribute glancing blows as we passed. The noise coupled with the impacts left me little choice but to curl my limbs toward my core and hope the trip was short. Luckily, the crowd grew less and less fervent in their anger as we moved to the periphery. Perhaps they had been unable to hear my manufactured insults, or perhaps it was the natural order of such crowds for the most bloodthirsty to force their way inward. Regardless of their motives, I welcomed the reprieve and considered our movement. We had turned a corner after exiting the arena and now approached a nearby dusty façade. On the right side of the face, there was a thick wooden member that had been sloppily exposed during construction. The front-most guard pinned me against the rugged member and started to pass a heavy rope around my chest until I couldn't move from the position. The troops stepped back and examined their work. I, too, looked down to visualize my condition. In truth, the knots seemed sloppy, but I could sense that their quality was also meant to account for my frail appearance. They nodded to one another in agreement that even their lazy effort was enough to secure a weakened wretch such as me and lumbered back toward the edge of the crowd.

As they entered the periphery of the mass, I heard a dull roar coming from its center: my fellow prisoner. I could only imagine his rebellious reaction to the proceedings, and the bloodthirsty populous again hurled their primal cry for judgment. Moments later, they were dragging him through the mass toward me. I could easily judge his position based upon the evolving resonance of rage. Eventually, they emerged from the violence. Unlike me, he had straightened every member of his stringy body in suicidal rebellion. The onlookers had obviously ripped through both his tunics and skin, as his entire chest was blood-soaked from the procession. The sight was alarming, but I couldn't help but admire the force of his energy. It was as if every part of man that screams into the night was bottled into the thrashing creature before me. Even as he exited, they kicked and scratched at him, and he offered a resilient insult with every blow. As he passed me, he flashed me a sick, bloody grin as if to say this was his purpose realized. Not sharing his violent sensibility, I could only offer a half-hearted nod in return. He, too, was secured to the post and, together, we draped ourselves against the dusty face to heave in exhaustion. Once the action of my chest found traction again, I started to scan the building tops for any sign of Abigail. I had scarcely examined the first group of architecture when we heard it: an uproar unlike any we had evoked.

This time, the cries were not so easily categorized. Some members of the crowd screamed in manic elation while others started to writhe in anger. Even the most distant members were now shoving to get closer, and the sinuous boundary started to constrict inward. As if sensing the freshly voided space, more people ran by our position and joined the pulsing mass. Quickly, the effect of these additions outweighed that of the initial constriction, and we were overtaken by the radiating edge. A sagging, disheveled man was shoved directly into my chest, and I strained to understand his outcries. However, the crowd's roar was deafening, and I could only watch as spit flung from his churning lips. What could cause such a scene!? Just as I was certain the noise alone would leave us all dead, the crowd abruptly fell silent. It was as if the gravity had been suspended, and my thoughts floated in the absence of sound. I slowly turned to take a measure of the pudgy man. His considerable weight was suspended well in front of his planted feet in an apparent effort to perceive any pronouncement from the nucleus.

The extreme silence rapidly became almost as unbearable as the noise. Moments became eons as the entire mass stood suspended, me included, for some unknown cry to move again. Finally, just as the fat man started to tumble forward, some signal was given at the core. The eruption was even more violent than before. A lanky man near us started to jump high into the air while a woman threw herself to the ground and violently attacked the earth. The plump man still lay on the dirt, either passed out or, more likely, dead. It was an eruption of the human spirit unlike any I had seen, and I was now pressed forward against my bounds, trying to see whatever figure had caused the violent reactions. As if on command, I could see a vibrating bulge of people rippling as the subject apparently moved through. I strained even harder against my tethers as the distortion meandered through the mass.

The movement was about halfway through the heaving onlookers when I felt it: the air. It was a feeling I knew well, despite only having experienced it briefly. The particles all around us were vibrating. The palpable reality of being was shaking. The moist breath of the people around me was being electrified. My own charged breath escaped, and I gasped for air. Before the crowd's boundary broke open, I knew who was to emerge. Could I have formed any analysis, I would have marveled at my own stupidity. Passover. Pontius. But I couldn't think. I could only gasp as Christ emerged from the heaving frontier. The ferocity of His beating had obviously surpassed even my partner's, and yet as He emerged, His head turned immediately to face me. He did something not yet exhibited in our previous exchanges, and it felt as if I would float away in the comfort of the gesture: He smiled. I could tell the expression was not erroneous but was a moment written into time for us. For me and God. All at once, I could see the sweet arc of my life. Curled back in time, and sometimes bent in angst, but nonetheless complete.

I wept as they kicked Him from behind toward us, and He stumbled to the ground. One of the troops grabbed His oily hair and pulled

Him upright, shoving Him directly to me. Christ draped His weight across my chest, and I suddenly felt a great desire to accommodate Him. I pushed my front out firmly to provide a shelf against which to lean. He slouched atop the manmade form and mouthed words too quiet to make it to the Bible.

"Thank you, Amir. Thank you." I could feel Him heaving against me. His breaths were so labored only I could hear Him. "I'm sorry, Amir. I'm so sorry. I needed you. This," His eyes rolled toward the ever-screaming men surrounding, "isn't man. I needed you. To see your face when you really saw me for the first time. To feel my mission so far derived. My love so circulated, one soul to another, all the way to you. Then brought back to me. I'm sorry, Amir."

He remained slumped against me, but I could feel Him weeping against my tunic. His tears seemed to possess an uncanny weight as if each one contained ten. They rolled through my bloodstained tunic and deposited even more weight against me. His words were so primal I didn't need to think. I simply stood. God leaning for a moment upon me. Not for lack of strength, but for lack of love. I pivoted and looked at the screaming faces, then back to the shriveled figure of God. Then, like a commander at war, I shoved my chest even further out to ensure His comfort.

Our connection didn't last long, as one of the troops emerged with the instrument of our demise in hand. With his back to us, he pulled the dense timbers toward us. Two lengths intersected and nailed to the other. The cross. First, one guard dragging the heavy wooden joint. Then another. And another. Three crosses now faced us. The angular tip of each dragged against the dusty earth and cleared a trail to us. One smooth clearing of life to me. One smooth clearing to my fellow thief. And one to God.

Christ leaned deeply forward upon me and whispered with finality, "It's time," before rocking away from me to face the troops. Christ was now in the front of our group, and they wasted no time ripping Him away. They were strong and fed well by the emperor's storehouses. Their hardened sinews had no trouble as they violently tore

His gown away. Then one man pushed at His head and forced Him to pivot at the waist. Another shoved at the rear of the nearest cross until it slid atop His back. Even from my vantage point, I could see the roughhewn timbers slicing through His skin. With every heave from the guard, the wood caught until the next effort would snap the splinter off deep beneath the surface. Christ cried out in pain and reached forward for my hand. He squeezed it in a distinctly human moment. It reminded me of Mum when she was scared, constricting her grip if only to verify my presence. I squeezed His hand hard and leaned low to stare into His eyes.

One of the guards sensed the moment of support and delivered a swift kick to my ribs. Normally, the shock would have been absorbed into a fall, but I was still bound and received the entirety of the force. My attacker then released my ropes and dragged me to the next cross. Again, they ripped at my tunic and left me exposed. A forceful hand shoved my head downward, and I immediately felt the first sting of the wood's friction. Just as I had seen, the coarse grain dug deep into my back with the guard's first push. Snap. His next effort cleanly deposited the massive splinter deep in my back. Now it was I who cried out. Christ stood bent beside me as push after push finally left us in a mirror image of agony. The troops immediately moved to our third companion. Even he couldn't withstand the skin-ripping process without crying out in pain. Judging from the weight of the timbers, they weren't fully dried. Instead, they were so heavy to practically force our bodies against the ground below. However, it wasn't the wood's weight I noticed as we waited for direction; it was the grain. As the painful lacerations turned to a general numbing, I looked back and forth at the cross's limbs and took in the detailed fractals of its flow. The pattern was rough but distinct, and another image rushed forth as I took in the pattern: Sterling, his feeble back crooked, examining the petrified splinter of wood preserving my blood. The petrified chunk preserving my encounter with Abby. And the petrified chunk preserving my encounter with Christ. Everything I loved: it was all soaking into the wood which now rested upon my back.

After the crosses were in place, no other direction was initially given. I wasn't eager to continue but couldn't help but wonder what we were waiting on. Finally, another guard emerged from the crowd and approached Christ. He produced a flowing purple garment from beneath his arm and loosely draped it across Christ's bloodied shoulders. Another stepped forward delicately holding an infamous relic: the crown of thorns. It was a deep shade of black, and its outcroppings pronounced pain to the world. Each thorn was about an inch long, and even the guard was careful to hold the arrangement in the right locations. However, as he placed the ring onto Christ's head, he didn't afford Him the same delicate touch. He smashed any of the spikes that were available into the crown of His head. Each tapering point was strong and easily able to withstand the force. Several tips disappeared deep into His scalp.

As His cries sprang forth, the guard turned to the crowd and relished a sarcastic announcement, "Behold, the King of the Jews!" The people exploded in a mixture of laughing and crying. Some people struggled against their neighbors as opposing views clashed.

"Move!" the guards shouted with a swift kick, just in case there was any confusion.

Perhaps because of our foreknowledge of the inevitable, Christ and I lifted our weary legs to begin the infamous journey. My fellow thief, lacking our understanding of the historical account, began again to hurl insults at his attackers. He rolled his torso right and shrugged off his cross. It fell to the ground with a resounding thud and left dust swirling in its wake. He sprang up with as much vitality as he could muster and started to heave blows at the troops. I turned my head back as much as possible without dropping my own load to watch him, but the nearest troop snapped at my movement, "Keep moving!"

I tolerated my hateful master and kept lifting one leg after the other to match the speed of Jesus. It was one of the only portions of Christ's life that I had not studied in detail with Abby. After all, even had Christ not existed, this was never supposed to be my duty. Our steps were slow, and at every turn, new onlookers joined the procession. Some were irate strangers seeming to enjoy our demise. Others were familiar faces distraught at our condition. I recognized Mark and Luke amongst the onlookers. Their faces were streaked with tears, and they flailed, trying to reach Christ. He, in return, issued them small loving nods but continued the meandering path put forth by the guards. I looked directly past them and searched desperately for my own advocate: Abigail. I knew she had to be there somewhere. I wasn't concerned with someone questioning her identity, as the proceedings had now dissolved to primal chaos. Face after face emerged, but there was no sign of her piercing brown eyes. I prayed silently, a reflex at this point as the presumed recipient was just in front of me, that she would emerge one last time. However, my proximity to Christ apparently didn't ensure a quicker response, and I was forced to keep moving.

As our procession continued, some of the crowd seemed to grow impatient with the pace. Unable to wait to satisfy their bloodlust, they began interjecting their own small blows. Even considering my hyperbolic insults of earlier, they all focused on Christ. The energy He radiated seemed to slow my racing heart, but they were conversely affected. Or perhaps they didn't feel Him at all. Regardless, they took turns delivering flurries of impatient blows to His exposed ribs. Still, Christ stumbled forward. I screamed from behind, trying anything to stop their onslaught, but no one could hear me. Without an alternative, and each seemingly stepping into the footprints laid by time, we continued down the narrow corridors.

The sun was at our right as we walked. It was low and still weak enough to be viewed freely as its rays fought through the atmosphere of the horizon. Our shadows streaked to the left below us. The combination of human limbs and timbers left the composition muddled. A black mass of pain that was not a shadow of original nature but rather one carefully created by man. Not wanting to face the pain of Abigail's absence, I focused upon the darkened companion as if staring into an obscured mirror. Just when I thought my legs had given up, my darkened brother would surprise me as he continued. Christ's shadow was even more distorted than my own after His never-ending beatings. His legs never straightened, and His head was slumped to His chest.

As our shadows continued to evolve with the rising sun, our pace finally slowed. We had exited the dusty architecture of the city and climbed a gradual hill to the north. The crowd, which had initially enveloped us, was now strung out behind. Perhaps saving energy for a final blood-drenched climax, they had quieted and were now only heard laughing and providing their own glib commentary. More guards stood atop the apex of the hill. As we drew closer, I could see sweat dripping from their brows in a testament to exertion. At their feet, the evidence of their effort: three deep, circular voids. The earth, which had been chipped away, stood in a heap next to each hole. The voids were the negative space to be occupied by our crosses, the method by which we were to hang.

Tears began to flow down my face as I realized my own proximity to death. I recalled the faces of everyone that mattered. Mum. Hasim. Levi. Abby. However, as the depth of my remorse grew with every face, I heard a voice interject. At first, it was unclear whether it was a mirage or a real announcement, but as the cries continued, I located the source: Abigail.

"Amir! Amir!" she cried out from the onlookers. She was three rows back and obviously couldn't get past these most ferocious spectators. "Amir! Use the drone! Use something! Please!"

She screamed the appeal with no regard for the futuristic language. Her hair was mangled, and her face was so shrunken from crying that I scarcely recognized her. She was crying so hard between words that her diaphragm seized to demand air. I trained my eyes upon her. I took in every detail. Despite her desperate condition, I wanted to stow away every feature for the journey ahead. In fact, as I studied her dark strands of hair that had entranced me since our first meeting, I realized she was my only concern. Mum and Hasim were taken care of; Sterling was at least good for this provision. But Abigail. She was about to lose the only companion she had in this brutal new existence. As I considered her uncertain fate, I was suddenly not so complacent with my own. However, as the seed of doubt grew, I heard Christ's paternal voice cut through the mental fog.

"Amir. I've got her. She has been a daughter of mine for many years and has never left my mind. I promise you are not abandoning her. In fact, you are saving her, for as my sacrifice preserves God's love for man, yours preserves your love for Abby. Please, Amir. I promise as you reopen your eyes, she will be before you again, for my kingdom is beyond the rule of time. As a baby is born unto man, you will not recall ever having entered, and we all will already stand before you. Each in kind will be born again, and yet none will experience another moment without the others. Mum. Hasim. And Abigail, Amir. Abigail . . . will be with you forever."

My eyes were streaming tears as I withdrew, satisfied with the assurance. Abigail was still screaming out between breaths.

"Do . . . something! Amir . . . Amir . . . Please! Please don't leave me! Call the drone! Call something! Please!"

With Christ's words still extinguishing my smoldering worry, I finally managed to bellow a response.

"I love you, Abby . . . So I have to be here. Don't you see? Your father's relic: the splinter with my blood. It wasn't a mistake; it was just a different cross. I'm not the messiah . . . I'm the thief."

As my final words announced the reality, she immediately halted her movement. It was as if her progress had been impeded by some invisible boundary. The crowd continued to ebb forward in a flurry of writhing arms and legs. However, as if paused, Abby remained stationary. She was finally realizing the loop of entangled events just as I was. This whole time we had been so careful to perform as we believed we once had. In truth, it was impossible to act any differently than our wills would compel. Our observations of Christ. Our discovery of the Valley. Our love. Getting caught. It was all part of the inevitable actions of souls bound to will. I kept my gaze pinned to Abigail as a burly guard approached me. My cross was still hoisted across my hunched shoulders. Perhaps through my focus upon Abigail, or maybe via a divine gift, I had long forgotten the heavy load.

"Raise your arms, thief!" he yelled, with a gesture of outstretched arms.

I didn't resist. Every painful action now felt like a duty. The duty of a brother, or a son, or a husband. I was not the first to die for their family, and in an odd twist of maturity, the precipice of death was the first time I didn't feel self-pity at my lot in life. I raised my arms to carefully match the wooden members atop them. I could feel the rough grain against the back of my arms, from the dull sensation behind my biceps to the lucid detail communicated behind my hands. I started to breathe deeply if only to slow time before the pain I knew was coming, but before the ritual made a difference, I heard the screams start to my left.

Christ, now positioned between the other thief and me, was crying out in agony. After having aligned His own arms with the cross's limbs, a guard was hunched to face His outstretched arms and swinging a simple hammer. The instrument, little more than a chunk of flattened iron constrained to a stout branch, arced through the scene with audible air movement only to be stopped by the head of a bloody steel pin driven through Christ's forearm. The iron extrusion was already almost completely immersed in His arm. Only His belabored cries seemed to expel the energy imparted as He managed to hold still through the blows. His eyes flashed between squeezed close and wildly open. In the moments of the latter, I stared directly at them and offered my own in return. It was in this state of locked condolence that I first felt the cold iron upon my own wrist. I scarcely had time to prepare, for, at the same pace my head swiveled to take in the scene, my guard's arm swung through the air. All at once, the dull sensation of the iron pin resting upon my skin exploded into an overwhelming message of pain. Every nerve in my arm must have run through the point. The agony surged from the point of impact to my brain, which in turn recoiled and sent the message to my agape mouth. My own cries reverberating back to my ears made for yet another alarming input, but it was another sound that was the most painful. Emerging in close tow to my own, Abigail's recognizable shrieks rang out. As the guard's arm drew back again and again in quick succession, there was a pendulum of pain. The initial impacts brought me the explosion of momentary physical sensation, while the moments between left me subject to the rise of Abigail's shouts. All these inputs then joined the cries from Christ and the second thief to form a pulsing wave of hurt.

After what felt like a marathon of blows, my guard moved to my other hand. As he picked up his spike and mallet, I truly looked at his handiwork for the first time. The spike was driven exactly where my hand met my forearm. Its tapered body was still protruding at least an inch from my skin, but considering its overall length, it was embedded deep into the hard wood below. It wasn't quite centered upon the width of my slender wrist, perhaps having meandered to miss my bone. However, it had obviously not missed whatever arterial vessel was passing in the region, for blood was now pulsing from the surrounding wound and creating a small puddle below. The wood below my arm on the limb of the cross was soaked in the deep red. The image again brought back to mind Sterling's relic. I looked below to see if the chunk had already been sheared away, but nothing but my blood collected below.

Just before the guard knelt to begin his grotesque procedure, and tasting blood now curdling in my mouth, I managed to call out to Abigail. She was still stationed deep within the crowd, and I could barely see her face as I called out.

"Abby! Abby!"

Her head snapped upright at the words.

"Abby, you have to collect the splinter. Your father's relic! You have to pick it up and make sure it gets passed on to him. I'm sorry, Abby . . . I'm so sorry. It's the only way."

She stared back for a moment between sobs before offering a small nod. She started churning her way to the front of the onlookers. Her small frame made the movement surprisingly hard. She ducked beneath the waving arms of one tall man before careening around another. Finally, she emerged as the closest to me. Just as she assumed her position, she looked deliberately at me and nodded again. The subtle gesture was clear. She knew what to do and why it had to be done.

The peace she brought didn't last long as the troops started hammering again. Christ's guard was again the first to begin, and I looked over as He reinitiated our orchestral shouts. It felt as if He knew whenever I was able to offer any meager condolence and immediately turned to face me. My guard then began swinging, and we stood hunched together and absorbed the blows. Watching the actions reflected in Him instead of focusing upon my own beating somehow relieved the pain. I found myself more concerned with His fate than mine. Blood was now seeping from so many wounds that it seemed impossible He had any left to offer. Streaks of the red traversed His face from the crown above. His wrists expelled the fluid just as mine did, and after the beating He had received along the way, His entire body was broken. The arc of the swinging mallet dominated his visual space, but I became fixated on another movement, much smaller and scarcely noticeable. His hand, the one closest to me, was slightly fluttering. One finger slightly arched, then another followed. It looked as if He was grasping for something. What all at once heightened the sight was the addition of a sensation within my own damaged fingers. As His digits silently grasped in the blood-soaked air, I could feel them. Our hands were five feet apart and immobilized by steel pins. Nonetheless, in seamless timing with His movements, I could feel every motion. After a few moments, it was as if there was no distance between the members. His hand was squarely deposited in my own. Considering the identity of my company, I was certain it wasn't an illusion. I, in turn, struggled to lightly curl my own fingers around the ghostly brother. Finally, after so many of our deafening cries, we were silent. Bound for the first time since the experience began, my hand resting upon God's, and God's just as much upon mine.

Our hands were now securely pinned to the wooden grain below, and the guards immediately uncoiled the ropes. The fibrous bounds would have relieved too much of our weight, intended to sag upon the gaping wounds once the crosses were lifted. With the ropes removed, the guards delivered swift kicks from behind to spurn us forward toward each cross's spot in the earth. I lurched forward under the weight, only to catch my foot against the ground and fall flat. The clumsy accident was a direct result of my now dimming control. With my hands pinned to the wood, it was impossible to lift myself from the dirt below. Seeing my pathetic condition, one of the guards surged forward and violently pivoted me upward by grabbing the cross's end above my head. The movement pulled me upward only by my pierced arms and sent pain shooting again through my synapses. I tried to again brace my feet against the ground but only fell again. At this point, the guard determined I was too weak to make it to my cross's hole ten feet away. Instead, he again took hold of the foremost end and began dragging me against the ground the remaining distance. My disabled hands occasionally caught rocks in the dusty ground and pinched what little flesh remained against the heavy timber. Finally, as my blood became so mixed with dust to render only a mass of brown paste, we reached my spot. The aft of my cross fell squarely into the preordained hole, just left of Christ's, and the guard began to hoist the mass vertically.

With every movement, more of my weight was transferred to the sloppy wounds surrounding the iron spikes. The holes had been so mangled at this point that they were much larger than the protruding pins themselves. Instead, the flesh formed a rugged, sagging boundary around the hangers. Looking up at the dire condition, I thought surely the flesh would give way and leave me heaped on the ground below. However, as the guards worked to fill in the deep hole surrounding the timber extending below me, they didn't worry about my condition. They had obviously performed the violent ceremony before and knew the limits of flesh as no one ought. I peered over at Christ.

Perhaps by divine intervention, or perhaps by superior character, He had managed to stay on His feet. He willingly deposited His own cross in the resting place, and the guards began hoisting Him up beside me. Perhaps by the depth of His hole, He was elevated slightly higher into the clear sky than me. As we were again aligned in space, I could feel His distanced hand invisibly nested into mine. I could feel His grip noticeably weakening, even through the unexplainable medium. His eyes, which typically pierced with mysterious depth, were fading with every blow.

At this point, perhaps finally feeling the escaping energy around them, the crowd had quieted. In the absence of the chaotic noise, another belligerent voice rang out. It was our third companion. The only one not allowed to know the role he was to play.

As he spoke, I realized that our words were following a similar script, one I'd read in the biblical account of this very event.

"Are you not the Christ? Save yourself and us!"

At this, the crowd roared in agreement. Some seemed to legitimately desire such a show, while others took the demand as a simple insult.

I knew the accounts of these moments, and perhaps without duress would have appreciated the gravity of my own role, but the pain ensured every word was spontaneous as I managed to bellow at the angry animal, "Do you not even fear God, since you are under the same sentence of condemnation? And we are indeed suffering justly, for we are receiving what we deserve for our deeds, but this man has done nothing wrong."

Again, the crowd roared, this time in rage at my defense of the Lord between us. Unable to face the bloodthirsty faces, I turned back to Christ. Quietly, I whispered to God even as he was trapped before me, "Jesus, remember me when You come into Your kingdom."

His head had fallen limp now, and He struggled to face me one final time. Managing to hold His eyes up for a moment, He whispered, "Truly I say to you, today you shall be with me in paradise."

Now, as He let his head fall limp again, the guards walked forward, bearing more of the rusted spikes. They roughly gathered our flailing legs and held them against the vertical shaft of the crosses. With one foot held over the other, they began again to pound the pins through the overlapping flesh and bones. Perhaps my nerves were already overwhelmed from the nonstop pain, but I could scarcely feel the blows. The disconnect was unnerving but a welcome reprieve. I could see the delicate bones of each foot snapping and emerging through the skin. Blood spilled violently from the grotesque wounds. The silenced nerves, perhaps afforded by God above, allowed me to focus on calming the now quivering hand of Christ. I gently imagined squeezing His hand. I didn't know how the divinely orchestrated contact worked, but I did my best to calm His tremors. It was in this embrace that I heard the resounding impact for which I had waited.

With a deafening thud, one of the guards had missed the pin and struck the blood-soaked wood beneath. I dropped my chin to my chest just in time to see the deep red grain splinter from my cross's length. The small chunk hurled through the air, rotating and tilting from the trajectory of the initial blow. Due to the guard's intense strike, it had tumbled almost to the boundary of the crowd. I stared intently at the small mass. The guards were done below, and I could feel blood flowing relentlessly down to the ground. Still, I stared at the chunk. It was a perfect match for the outline I had seen Sterling caressing. It was everything I loved. Being scarcely more than a few fibrous strands, it was as if each of my loves was condensed to a strand. Mum. Hasim. Abby. Woven and intertwined. Soaked in my blood and heaved at the feet of time. It sat slightly thrust into the dirt below, yearning for resolution as my eyes struggled to stay open. Fading to black, starving for spent blood, I could just make out the white of alabaster fingers gripping the splinter. The last vision of that great gospel that Sterling had brought to me.

ABOUT THE AUTHOR

Atticus Mullon is a nonstop creator. Using his degree in architecture, he applies himself to a number of inspired projects, from buildings to sculptures. In these endeavors and in his writing, he strives to expose new ways to consider and challenge accepted truths. Applying this approach to his own faith led him to write this debut work, *The Sterling Gospel*. Atticus lives with his beautiful wife and kids in Stillwater, Oklahoma.

What does an author stand to gain by asking for reader feedback? A lot. In fact, it's so important in the publishing world that they've coined a catchy name for it: "social proof." And without social proof, an author may as well be invisible in this age of digital media sharing.

So if you've enjoyed *The Sterling Gospel*, please consider giving it some visibility by reviewing it on the sales platform of your choice. Your honest opinion could help potential readers decide whether or not they would enjoy this book, too.

plot is so improbable + ridiculous that even suspension of disbelief isn't a valid or credible way to aid in agreeing w/ the remotest possibility that the premise makes any sense at all.

Why is it necessary to manufacture hope that has already been manufactured? It's not a space time continuum issue because the teachings of Jesus have, do and will continue to exist as hope regardless of any action or inaction. The entire schema is unnecessary + illogical.
  Will history change? No. Does hope need repair? No. Does Jesus need replacing? No. What is the point?

Huge plot hole - not fixable!

Made in the USA
Columbia, SC
24 January 2022

Received
1-31-22

54462966R00152